dissent
RENEGADES

By R.J. Furness

dissent

Cover & Map Illustrations
by Dawn Beever

To Jessica & Rebecca

Best Wishes

This is a work of fiction. Names, characters, organisations, places, events and incidents, are either products of the author's imagination or are used fictitiously. Any resemblance to actual persons, living or dead, or actual events is purely coincidental.

Text copyright © 2017
By R.J. Furness
All rights reserved

No part of this book may be reproduced, or stored in a retrieval system, or transmitted in any form or by any means, electronic, mechanical, photocopying, recording, or otherwise, without the express written permission of the publisher.

join the club

To thank you for buying this book, I'd like to invite you to join my Readers Club. Once you are a member, you can get BIG discounts on ALL my future book releases.

Joining the Readers Club is completely FREE! It won't ever cost you a penny.

You can join the club by visiting my website…

www.rjfurness.com

And, feel free to get in touch on social media too. I'd LOVE to hear from you!

Twitter: @rjfurness
Facebook: furnesswrites

other books in the 'dissent' saga

Morrigan: a dissent story

For my beautiful wife, Emma, and our children…
Without your love and support, this book wouldn't have ever been written.

CONTENTS

prologue 1

chapter one 13

chapter two 27

chapter three 34

chapter four 44

chapter five 54

chapter six 60

chapter seven 75

chapter eight 89

chapter nine 102

chapter ten 108

chapter eleven 122

chapter twelve 133

chapter thirteen 147

chapter fourteen 155

chapter fifteen 171

chapter sixteen 179

chapter seventeen 192

chapter eighteen 201

chapter nineteen 216

chapter twenty 224

chapter twenty-one 239

chapter twenty-two 245

chapter twenty-three 259

chapter twenty-four 269

chapter twenty-five 278

chapter twenty-six 288

chapter twenty-seven 297

The Great Freeze changed everything...

Before that time, our species colonised almost every part of our world. Yet centuries have passed since the onset of an ice-age which wiped out most human life. The phenomenon forced the few people that survived into a primitive existence. Living in small groups or alone, they fought to endure stark conditions. The climate was cold and cruel.

Then, two hundred years ago, alongside a species known as the elrupe, people began to form new colonies...

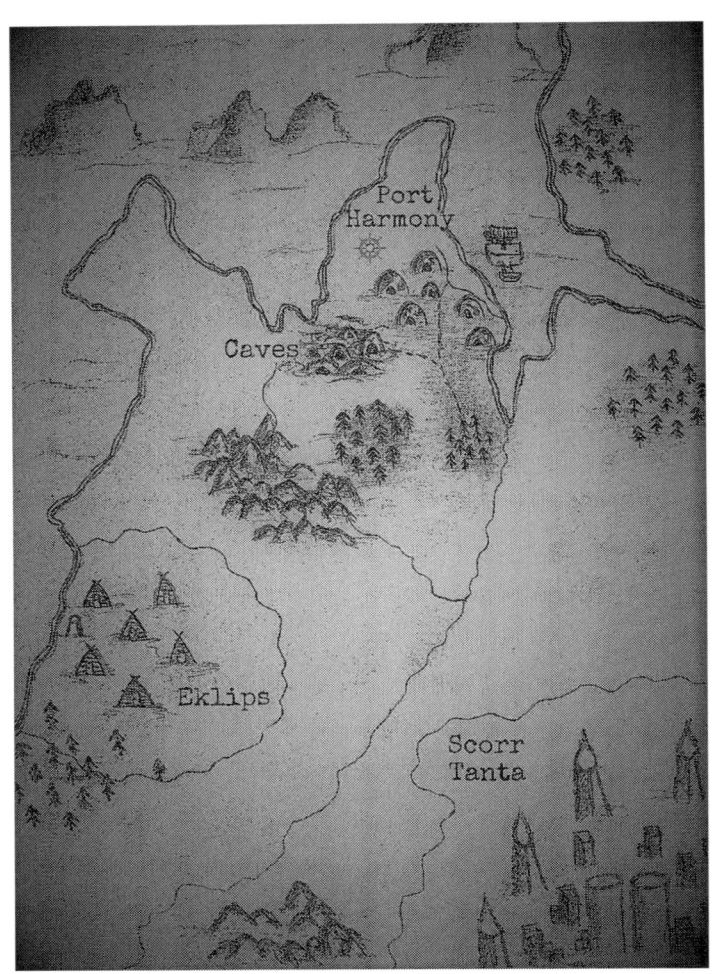

prologue

Night Terrors

Ice shelves broke the surface of the ocean, shimmering in the moonlight off the shore of Port Harmony. When darkness came, the busy harbour town would always fall silent. To escape the cold, people would move indoors; and this night was no different from any other. The cobblestone streets had emptied steadily until everywhere lay still. Everywhere, except on the wharf, where an animal trotted along the harbour wall. In the creature's saddle, a solitary rider examined a large supply store. The heavy snowfall made it hard to distinguish the buildings bordering the wharf.

Opposite, a warden known as Ermine pulled open a heavy timber gate twice his height, unaware that he was under surveillance. As a squadron leader, he was there to assess the progress of his crew. It was a job he had done for many years, which was evident by the tired way he handled the gates. He was certain someone kept making them heavier.

Within the supply store, an enormous Land Transport dominated the vast open space. The scarlet, torpedo-shaped vehicle looked immaculate and towered above Ermine. Scattered around it, his squad were busy preparing heavy crates of seafood; six wardens in total. They were getting ready for their thirteen-mile journey inland, to Scorr Tanta. Each member of the squad wore a fleecy, dark-grey cloak, made from thick animal skins for insulation. These garments flowed to the floor and covered the wardens' crisp, white tunics. It was the standard uniform for a warden, and the same as Ermine's; although he also wore a purple band on his arm, to signify his rank.

A seventh warden—the pilot—inspected his vehicle. He was paying close attention to the caterpillar tracks, encasing the two large sets of wheels at the front. These were crucial for the transport to travel across the thick ice and snow. It was essential to check for any damage that may hinder their journey. Scorr Tanta wasn't that far, but Port Harmony was situated on a steep hillside leading to the ocean. The frozen terrain wasn't the pilot's only challenge. His machine would have to travel through the meandering streets, up the hills and away from the coast. Those sharp gradients always proved treacherous.

The pilot looked confident as he stepped away. Absorbed in his work, he didn't notice Ermine approaching.

'Magnificent, isn't she?' Ermine announced his arrival at the top of his voice. His nostrils filled with an overpowering stench of fish. Eating seafood was one thing, but Ermine hated the smell and already wondered when he would be able to get clean. The transfer of supplies to Scorr Tanta was not the best part of his job. But luckily, he wasn't the one who had to go out to sea and catch it.

'Yes sir…sorry…didn't see you arrive,' the pilot replied. He swung around to greet his superior and almost stumbled on his cape.

'Renegade proof?'

Grinning, the pilot patted his dirty palm against the solid rubber tracks. 'Won't get in our way this time! Nothing is going to interfere with this…'

'It would be wise…to not underestimate these Renegades.' Ermine's eyes wandered across the tapering frame of the impressive vehicle. 'This thing may offer more protection than moving the crates with orgo. But we shouldn't be over-confident...not until we've reached Scorr Tanta.'

Nodding, the pilot acknowledged the warning. 'Yes, sir. Of course, sir.' He then turned his attention to the small rudder wheel at the rear of the transport.

Conscious of his schedule, Ermine studied the room. He counted more than a dozen containers, each marked with the Scorr Tanta insignia. The dominant, bright green *S*-shape, overlaying the greyish-*T*, looked glorious. Goosebumps ran all the way up Ermine's arms every time he set eyes on the metallic emblem. Each of the marks reflected the hazy light, cast from timber pendants in the ceiling. The wardens, however, were struggling to haul the containers, despite the tough metal runners fixed beneath. Time was precious, and they needed to work faster.

'We need to be ready to leave…soon!' Ermine called out to his squad. 'The sooner, the better. Time to get those crates loaded. Rada isn't known for her patience. There is also a Bicentenary to prepare for. Scorr Tanta is depending on us.'

Ermine acknowledged that he feared Rada. As both ruler of Scorr Tanta and head of "The Union", she was formidable. Her lack of tolerance for anyone who disappointed her was well-known. It had been fifteen years since Rada's ascension; a time which had created divisions in Scorr Tanta and resulted in people leaving. Those that departed built Port Harmony, whilst The Union itself was created once a peace evolved between the two colonies. That was the time when Rada moved Ermine's squad from Scorr Tanta to Port Harmony. Their role was to ensure that those in Port Harmony followed Scorr Tanta law. Not to mention, that they had to supervise shipments moving between the two colonies.

Ermine missed their home city, and Port Harmony was not his favourite place to be. Even so, he always embraced any orders from Rada. Nobody argued with her; especially not Ermine.

One of the wardens looked up. 'I was thinking sir,' she said, gasping for breath whilst going about her work. 'Two hundred years since people got together to build our city. Two hundred! Who would have thought that Scorr Tanta was that old? And it's four years since The Union agreement too, isn't it sir? Incredible! To think…how far we have come. Before that…before Scorr Tanta…our ancestors barely survived. Well…if you believe all that. I mean…it's fascinating. Now, look at us…three colonies working together. Us…the people here in Port Harmony…those folks in Eklips up the shore. Sometimes, I wonder if there's more…you know people and—'

'What's your name warden?' Ermine said sharply, marching toward his subordinate. She appeared young for a warden, and much too inexperienced. That, and she talked a great deal too. Wardens were not recruited for their ability to think for themselves—or to talk quite that much.

'Er…Dee Nine…sir.'

'Well…Dee Nine!' Ermine spoke in the sternest tone he could master. 'It isn't our job to be thinking. It is our job to be moving these crates to Scorr Tanta.'

With her spindly fingers fiddling with her plaited hair, Dee Nine's face crumpled. 'Yes, sir…sorry sir…I was just thinking—'

'Well don't! You are Dee Nine…and your job is more important than your thoughts. Your job…is to make sure this lot gets to Scorr Tanta for the Bicentenary. That is if you're happy to do your job? Would you prefer to discuss your career with the commander?'

Dee Nine bowed her head and carried on with her work. 'No sir. Happy to do my job, sir,' she muttered, understanding her place.

Nonetheless, as an infant, Ermine had also heard stories about their human ancestors. Those that had been pushed to the brink of extinction during The Great Freeze. Tales about the creation of Ermine's home city, Scorr Tanta, often got shared with children too. But, they were just stories. Ermine gave little consideration to how much truth they held.

'Now,' he shouted, 'unless anyone else has some…thoughts they would like to share…let's get—'

His orders cut short when the shelter gates flung open, and something charged inside. Stopping in its tracks, the beast observed its surroundings. Its bulky body was taller than any of the squad members. Snow clinging to the animal's thick, black fur was dripping onto the floor creating a small puddle. With a distinctive shape, a short stumpy excuse for a tail and a long slender neck, the creature was easily identified. An orgo!

More than any other animal, orgo coped well with the cold. A dense mass of wool kept their plump frames well insulated. Their two powerful legs toward the rear of their frame formed the source of their agility. This meant that they could outrun any man-made vehicle with ease. Having such unrivalled capabilities, most orgo were domesticated by the people living in Port Harmony. Even some of the wardens employed by Scorr Tanta owned them. Orgo were undeniably useful.

Tapping its razor-sharp claws against the solid floor, the beast watched the wardens with interest. Tiny eyes set deep in its head, flickered. Then, the creature shook to loosen the snow that invaded its fleece. With caution, it began moving further inside the building.

'Sir…' Dee Nine said, staying as still as her colleagues. 'Did…did someone forget to tell them…that we don't use orgo to move supplies anymore?'

Ermine stared at the animal, refusing to take his eyes away for even a second. 'Lances…now!' he said, in a soft but commanding tone, trying not to unsettle it. This orgo wasn't one of theirs, and Ermine was certain that it wasn't alone either.

In a ridiculous attempt to go unnoticed, the pilot started clambering up his vehicle. He had barely taken a step before the orgo snorted and turned to face him. Panic took hold, and he clutched at handrails, heading toward the cockpit. Few feared the orgo; they were generally docile creatures unless they felt threatened. The pilot, it seemed, felt differently.

The rest of the crew edged away from the transporter, closer to their weapons. With each step they took, the orgo moved closer toward them, lowering its head and stretching forward with curiosity. In turn, each warden removed their lance from the rack on the wall, preparing to defend themselves.

'Hold position,' ordered Ermine, when the orgo took a step away. For a few seconds, he tried to predict its next move. He refused to let the orgo out of his sight. But then, unexpectedly, its neck swung around, and it hurried back through the gates.

'What was that all about?' Dee Nine asked as the orgo vanished into the night.

Ermine screwed his face and shivered. For the first time, it seemed cold inside the building.

'Wait...' He wanted his squad to remain on alert. They would be stupid to assume this was a random intrusion.

'We need...to get finished...now,' the pilot said, spluttering over his words. He had managed to clamber into his seat.

'No! Wait—'

Interrupted, Ermine stood in horror as three more black orgo exploded into the building. Each animal was saddled and accompanied by their owners. Ermine recognised the crimson cloaks and bizarre animal skulls, which concealed the intruders' faces.

'Renegades!' mumbled Dee Nine, stating the obvious.

'Scorr Tanta...our home!' Ermine called proudly. His call instructed the squad to defend themselves, and their shipment. He had not expected this. The Renegades always ambushed them on their journey. They had never attacked the shelter before. With their new Land Transport, Ermine expected that the Renegades wouldn't be a problem. How wrong he was.

Acting on their orders, the wardens immediately charged toward the orgo. Their lances were poised for attack. The orgo responded and dodged their enemies with ease, as they galloped inside the building. Two of the Renegades busied their foes, whilst the other dismounted and drew an axe from his saddle. Tossed and thrown around in the direction of the Land Transport, the weapon wasted no time cutting deep into the tracks that covered the wheels. The Renegades were efficient and well prepared; as always.

'Stop!' said Ermine. 'In the name of Rada!' But it was pointless. His words meant nothing to these outlaws.

The Renegade ignored him and continued severing the vehicle's tracks with unrelenting aggression. Whilst he worked, the other bandits lurched at the warden squad on their orgo. Each warden thrust their lances at the animals in front of them, but they were all unsuccessful in their attacks. Although they outnumbered the Renegades, the squadron still appeared outmatched. The orgo stretched out their necks and began butting their aggressors. They were systematically protecting the bulk of their bodies—and their riders—from injury. Each orgo avoided every lunge of a lance. Persistent, the wardens continued with their uncoordinated attacks.

Ermine ran toward the Renegade vandalising their new vehicle. 'Drop your weapon. Stop what you're doing!' Instantly, another of the bandits knocked him from his feet.

His attempts to stop them was futile. The Renegades weren't the sort to surrender, and wardens couldn't match their skill. Holding their ground, the Renegades pressed on and distracted the squad. After only a few minutes, the tracks on the vehicle began to fall away. The armed Renegade had rendered it useless and joined his accomplices.

In a flash, the outlaws changed formation and cantered out of the shelter; mocking the squad. Orgo were too fast for the wardens, but the Renegades didn't make any attempt to race away with haste either. Ermine wondered why the outlaws had left the supplies behind.

'After them!'

With the wardens trailing behind, the Renegades trotted away from the supply building. In some way, they appeared triumphant. Stunned by their arrogance, Ermine was still confused. *Why hadn't they taken any of the crates?* he thought. His ambition to detain the Renegades took over. Ermine wanted to be the hero, and he wanted to stop these criminals when nobody else had been able to. Joining the other wardens, he pursued their enemy.

***

Everyone moved across the slushy wharf, whilst the lookout remained hidden in the shadows. He had been there throughout the entire raid, and since before Ermine's arrival. Knowing exactly what to do, he raced across the wharf toward the supply shelter at the exact right moment. Once at the entrance to the building, the Renegade dismounted and prepared to work alone—the way he liked it. When he entered the shelter, he immediately caught sight of the pilot that the rest of the wardens had left behind. The man cowered in his cockpit. His head could just be seen through the glass cover, but he didn't concern the Renegade. The pilot wouldn't challenge him—it would be stupid to try.

The thief worked fast, binding the abandoned crates together, shoving each into place and creating a chain. It was easy to work with no interruptions. Within no time, the Renegade completed his makeshift contraption and fastened it to his orgo's saddle, using two pieces of spare rope. The beast was the engine, and the Renegade became the driver, of a long "sort-of" train of supply containers. He made his job look simple, twitching on his reins and cantering out of the shelter. With incredible strength, the orgo pulled the load behind them. In minutes their task was complete, and the Renegade laughed to himself whilst he dismounted by the shelter gateway. The thought of the pilot, quivering in his cockpit like a child, amused him.

After removing a corroded can from the saddle of his orgo, the Renegade stomped up to the huge timber gates. From inside his container, he lifted a brush and began writing. He wanted to leave a mark and send a message to those who wished to stop them. On the gates, in large lettering, he wrote — RENEGADES. Then, returning to his saddle, the solitary Renegade punched the air to celebrate. He galloped across the wharf undetected; his mission a success. The wardens were oblivious that their supplies had been taken.

They were easily fooled.

chapter one

Daybreak in Port Harmony

Ellie loved riding the orgo. She had often dreamt about it since being a small child. Now that her father wasn't around to voice his opinions, she finally could. Twenty years had been a long time to wait.

With ice-cold air biting at her nose, Ellie raced through Port Harmony's maze of frozen streets. She sat comfortably in the saddle of her employer's orgo. Winter was ending, but that didn't make it particularly warm. Ellie couldn't remember a time when she didn't feel like she lived in a bubble formed from pure ice. The snow had stopped falling, but the breeze tugged on her knotty mass of once yellowish hair. It was still thick with muck from her work. Ellie's heart pounded with the thrill as she continued to build momentum on the back of Sage. Stone, dome-shaped buildings surrounded them. The intricate designs etched into the surface of each structure, had blended into a grey blur.

Kicking down hard, Ellie urged the animal she commanded to give more. Her huge smile revealed the shallow dimples usually hidden within her pale cheeks. She was convinced that it was impossible for anyone to reach the speeds that she could on Sage. For a few minutes, Ellie felt like a champion in a world far removed from her reality. A reality where she was an apprentice orgo-keeper, on her way to the market, wearing loose brown overalls that stunk of dung.

'That's it, boy,' Ellie said, as loud as she could. 'Faster. C'mon Sage…faster.'

Sage stretched forward when Ellie thrashed her legs. She couldn't believe how fast he picked up speed; the excitement wanted to burst from inside her. Despite hearing ice and slush crunching between his fearsome toes, she had faith in Sage's experience. He could cope well with the difficult terrain. The reins burned into Ellie's fingers when Sage extended his neck, charging toward a bend in the street. He knew where he was heading. They had made plenty of trips to the market together.

Within seconds, Ellie noted a strong smell of cooked fish and the noise of market chatter growing louder. They were close, and Ellie pulled back on Sage's reins, slowing him to a canter. Taking a deep breath, she dusted down her overalls one last time and tied back her hair.

'Okay, boy...you know what to do. It's round there...give me everything you've got!'

Clumps of dirt flew from Sage's claws as they sped forward, but Ellie felt her saddle jolt. Something was wrong. A clasp had worked loose, and Ellie screamed; she hadn't fastened it properly before leaving. Wondering how she had been so careless, Ellie tried to slow Sage down.

'Whoa boy...whoa,' she cried. But her commands came too late and wouldn't make a difference.

As they swung around the corner at the entry to the street-market, the saddle slipped further. Ellie was tossed from the back of Sage onto the cobbled street behind. A dull, hollow grunt was forced from inside her, as her entire body thumped against the solid ground. Dazed, Ellie lay still. Sage turned back to examine her and nudged his snout into Ellie's side to provoke a response.

'I'm okay...' Ellie grumbled as she sat upright. 'I think.'

She could not believe how ridiculous she felt, or how stupid she looked. Glancing down into the market, Ellie's face tingled with shame. Everyone was staring at her. Everyone. The busy market appeared to have frozen in time; with every single person gawking in her direction.

The street was the same as any other in Port Harmony. Low level, plump dwellings lined either side of the road up the incline. Large openings in the front walls of each of the buildings served as entrances. Yet, where some of those cavities contained doors, others were covered with simple sheets of fabric. The carved gritty surfaces of each building acted as decoration, with designs specific to the families living there. Ellie admired the patterns every time she wandered Port Harmony's streets. She thought they were all stunning, in their own individual ways.

Staggering to her feet, Ellie clutched Sage's reins and started to lead him into the market. The freedom she had embraced moments before, had been replaced with humiliation. After what felt like hours—but was probably more like a few seconds—people in the market began to move again. Suddenly, it was as though they hadn't seen anything. Nobody even seemed to register Ellie's accidental dismount. Everyone was carrying on with their own business.

Hobbling toward a wooden post, close to the stall she needed, Ellie tethered Sage. 'Be back soon,' she said, petting her steed and sinking her fingers into his light tan wool. 'Don't be goin' anywhere!' Which she knew he wouldn't; he looked exhausted.

Sage's snout nuzzled into her armpit; it tickled. Releasing an echoing snort, he was showing Ellie that he was happy. Ellie giggled, and rubbed Sage behind his head, in the way he appeared to like. Moments like this one were why she had grown so fond of the orgo.

Finally, she stroked down her orgo's neck. 'Okay boy, work to do. We need to get back before Cedric wonders where we are.'

Ellie lifted her head to shake off her embarrassment, then trudged amongst the stalls laid out at the front of all the houses. The market was frantic, with dozens of cluttered counters lining each side of the dirty street. People were bumping into one another, desperate for a bargain. It was possible to buy almost anything at the market. Assorted items were strewn across every table, or even hanging from timber posts between. The aroma from squid, shrimps and various fish, blended into something tempting. Ellie's mouth watered with the fragrance.

Gazing around as she manoeuvred her way through the crowds, Ellie avoided eye contact with anyone. Discreetly positioned next to some of the stalls, wardens patrolled. They were watching for anyone to make a mistake. The wardens called it keeping Port Harmony safe, but to Ellie, they looked like they were hunting. Armed with lances and standing bolt upright in their grey and white uniforms, the wardens seemed to be waiting for something. In any case, situated as they were, they could monitor the whole market with ease.

When she caught a whiff of ground orchid leaves, it didn't take Ellie long to find the stall she wanted. 'Hey,' she called out, uncertain of the response she might get. Ellie approached a tall man with scruffy dark hair, but a well-kept beard. It was Evan, and Ellie was always eager to see him, although she tried not to show her enthusiasm too much.

Evan was a few years older than her, and always appeared distinguished for a market trader. He wore a thick, pale grey tunic and cloak. This was unlike most people in Port Harmony, who generally dressed in brown. A scarf made from animal fur was hung around his neck for warmth. Evan peered around from behind a slanted metal table as Ellie drew near. He gave the impression he was anxious. Beautiful, but anxious all the same.

'Riding with no saddle...' Evan responded once Ellie arrived at his stall. 'That's new! Bareback orgo riding...it's the future. Ask anyone...other than those who can ride I reckon.'

Ellie had to listen carefully to hear Evan over the noise of the market, but then wished she hadn't. She had hoped he hadn't seen her when she had been thrown from Sage. It wasn't her most elegant moment. Of anyone in the world, Evan was the last person she wanted to witness her mistake. Choosing to ignore him, Ellie glanced around at a nearby group of children. They were playing a game known as "Land the Pebble". A group of opportunistic puffins flapped around near them.

'You shouldn't be here Ellie,' Evan went on. 'Not after last time.'

'Bosses orgo are hungry, precious.' Ellie softened her voice, resting her hands on the table. 'Where else can I go?'

'Anywhere but here I reckon.'

Evan's stall was well known as the only place in Port Harmony to get decent orgo food. But Ellie knew that he would be worried her presence may cause trouble. It had the last time she had visited. Now she thought about it, her behaviour then hadn't been that attractive either.

'Like where? Besides…you like me coming here.' Ellie said, offering a smile. Evan's stall was cold, and she snatched her hands away before her fingertips went numb.

Evan grinned and turned away. Ellie was sure he was trying to hide it.

'Do I?' he said, chuckling. 'After last time, I thought you might have kept your head down. There's enough trouble in The Union…without people fighting amongst themselves here.'

Ellie raised her voice a little. 'Who's fighting Evan? Can't a girl look around the market anymore?'

'Well…don't say I didn't warn you.'

'Warn me?' Ellie turned, noticing someone familiar browsing around one of the other stalls. Although she was a bit shorter that Ellie, the girl always seemed a similar age—early twenties at most. Faint freckles decorated her fair skin, and her coppery hair commanded attention. It was Evan's sister, Haylee. Ellie's muscles all tensed at once.

Evan kept his head down, fidgeting with metal buckets of animal food on his stall. 'Wherever my sister goes...'

Haylee staggered toward a blacksmith's table on the street corner. Her thick black tunic was tied at the waist with a grey belt, and a smoke coloured cloak hung from her shoulders. It ran all the way down to her boots. Appearing to take little notice of her surroundings, Haylee knew that she only needed to walk through the market to get what she wanted. She nodded with gratitude, as the man in front of her scurried over, and placed a drink on the table. Most people in Port Harmony respected Haylee. In some way, her quiet charisma was domineering. She didn't say much, but when she did, everyone listened.

'I need to tell you something,' Ellie said, deciding to have some fun. She was determined to win Evan's affection.

He moved closer to the counter where Ellie was, then grumbled as she grabbed his hand, tugging him towards her. 'You're asking for trouble.'

Ellie refused to release Evan, and stared toward Haylee, waiting for a reaction. On the contrary, Haylee seemed oblivious, and completely unaware of Ellie's presence. Much the same as anyone else in town, Ellie idolised Haylee; even though she felt intimidated by her. Sometimes, when Ellie finished her chores at Cedric's, she would wander down to the wharf. There, she was able to watch Haylee and her friends racing their orgo. She had heard many stories about 'The Dispute' too; a dangerous sport held in Eklips territory. Haylee and her friends were all renowned warriors, who fought battles on whomphorn—amongst other animals—to earn their living. Well, so Ellie had heard. She had only ever dreamt about attending The Dispute one day; it sounded exciting. Ellie often imagined what it would be like to be a warrior like Haylee. For whatever reason, it had placed Haylee's gang in high regard. Well, around Port Harmony it had.

Evan yanked his hand away. 'Enough!' he said, in a sharper tone. 'What do you need? Quickly.'

Smiling, Ellie was sure that Evan felt the same way as she did. He would never admit it though, because of the potential consequences. Ellie was an outsider as far as Haylee and her friends were concerned, and Evan was her brother. It didn't matter if he liked her—it mattered if Haylee did.

'You know what I want,' she answered. 'Orgo feed.'

Evan's eyes widened, and he took a step backwards. 'You need to go Ellie…Now!'

Ellie swung round, alarmed by the sudden change in Evan. A pod of three white orgo were skidding to a halt. Although why they were referred to as *white* orgo, Ellie had never been sure. Their snowy coats were prominently dappled in black splodges.

The riders of the animals dismounted; binding their reins to wooden posts. Ellie wasn't certain, but it looked like they were in a rush. Their orgo snorted aloud, before dunking their heads into troughs of feed placed around one of the stalls. As the group entered the market, Ellie's heart hammered inside her chest. A man and two women, all dressed like Haylee, were walking toward her. She knew them all too well from the last time she had visited Evan. Concealing the anxiety that consumed her was hard.

Realising she needed to look somewhere else, Ellie glanced back at Evan. Preoccupied, he continued to reorganise his counter. Ellie shivered as one of the women stopped beside her. It was Morrigan, and she always looked the more youthful of the group. She was definitely a couple of years younger than Ellie was. Hair flowed over her shoulders like shadows, and she had dewy skin. Morrigan's cheek was also inked with the silhouette of an orchid moth, although Ellie had no idea what it meant. None of Haylee's other friends had any similar markings.

Ellie often thought that she detected an inexplicable suffering in Morrigan's eyes; a sort of hidden torment. Yet, despite her demeanour, and the beautiful fragrance that floated around her, there was something about Morrigan that also felt threatening. For a second, Ellie regretted not listening to Evan and her arms began to prickle.

'Thought we told you not to come here?' Morrigan said. She was staring toward nothing of any interest to anyone else.

Ellie didn't answer but flinched when she spotted the oldest of the gang. This one placed her bruised hands on the stall next to Evan's, where gugubat patties sizzled over flames. Ditto didn't say very much and was somehow scary because of that.

Tucking her snarled brown hair behind her ears, Ditto grinned strangely at Evan. 'Hi.'

Evan seemed unsure how to reply.

'Well lady?' said Tik, the last of the group. This one was not far from Evan's age. He decided to position himself even closer to Ellie, scratching his stubbly chin and making an effort to look menacing. 'My friend asked you a question.'

To look at, Tik was by far the vainest member of the group. His large build and short-shaven head made Ellie cringe. Not to mention that he had arms that wanted to burst from beneath his tunic. Also, he was the only member of their group who didn't wear their unique animal skin cape. People suggested that it was because Tik didn't believe the garment showed off his physique. They were probably right, but he must have been cold in a solitary tunic.

A balkutar clung to Tik's shoulder. Ellie had only seen one a couple of times before. They were small, fluffy, ape-like animals and pale grey in colour. She assumed this particular one was Tik's pet. Standing tall, it was maybe a foot long in total. Its bizarrely long arms stretched the length of its body and legs combined. In contrast, much shorter limbs led to its huge feet that looked more like hands. Each one held three identical small toes, and a larger one twice the size of the others. In the wild, balkutar lived in the hillside pine trees, and their feet were designed to help them grip branches. With its tiny ears twitching, Tik's pet glared at Ellie through enormous bulging eyes. It looked as though it was waiting for her to speak.

'Doesn't look like she says much,' said Tik. Ellie assumed he was talking to the odd little animal bouncing against the top of his arm. 'Does it Toze?'

Ellie knew Tik wanted her to hear, but she chose to ignore him. The easy option was to apologise for returning to the stall when they had clearly told her not to. She remembered her last trip when she was caught flirting with Evan. Ellie hadn't realised that Ditto had similar feelings towards him. Having made a lucky escape that time, she had often thought that it would be wisest to find other ways to get feed for Cedric's orgo. But then, she liked Evan and was desperate to get acquainted with Haylee's group. They intrigued her.

Ditto turned toward Ellie and scowled. She looked furious that Ellie had come back, but at the same time, like she was trying to manage her temper. Evan was much more of a peacemaker, and Ditto must have known that. Likewise, the wardens wouldn't tolerate any disruption.

'Okay,' said Morrigan, still refusing to look at Ellie. 'Let me try this another way…You need to leave!'

Ellie stood firm and swallowed her panic. 'A barrel of orgo feed please Evan.' Her voice felt a little shaky and she was certain someone had put a large pebble in her throat. Maybe more than one.

As Evan went to fetch the barrel for Ellie, Ditto interrupted. 'No!'

'My barrel please Evan,' Ellie said, trying again.

Ditto stared at Ellie.

'Not today Dit...not today.' Tik patted his friend's shoulder as she became jittery.

Ditto's screechy voice was able to pierce eardrums. 'Leave!'

Ellie gulped. 'What's your problem, precious? I'm here for Cedric.'

'You're here for Evan, and Ditto doesn't like it,' said Morrigan. 'This has nothing to do with your new boss.'

'Can we all calm down?' Evan interrupted. 'I will get her barrel, and she can leave.' He turned to face Ditto. 'Agreed?'

Ditto's deep breaths were easy to see. Ellie assumed it was to impress Evan with her composure. Normally, Ellie didn't like conflict, and most of the time chose to resolve it. On this occasion, she was finding a strange enjoyment in provoking Ditto. So, she chose to push her luck a little further. After all, annoying Ditto wasn't hard, and Ellie was becoming good at it.

'You know what,' Ellie said. 'Before I go back to work, I'm going for a drink. Will you join me, Evan? We could have—'

Ditto flew toward Ellie like a predator. She seized her prey by the hair and dragged her to the orgo that her friends had tethered moments before. Scanning the street, Ellie waited for the wardens to help her. Not one of them reacted.

chapter two

Scorr Tanta

As warden commander, Nolan took pride in her appearance, and her uniform was much more ornate than that of her subordinates. White trimming on her grey tunic and a green band hugging her arm declared her significance. Her silky black hair was tied back perfectly, whilst unblemished skin completed her impressive look. At the age of thirty-one, she had earned her position, after spending her whole adult life in service. Standing in a gleaming white passage, inside one of Scorr Tanta's Central Buildings, Nolan was formidable. Two sentries were positioned alongside her as protection, in their simple ivory robes. Yet Nolan could well protect herself if necessary, even if she was older than most of her staff.

She turned when she caught sight of a warden sprinting toward her.

'Ma'am...Ma'am,' he called down the corridor, sliding across the smooth floor as he approached. 'Ma'am...I have news...from Dee Squad!'

'Speak!' Nolan was stern when she addressed the tiny warden now standing before her. She had been waiting for a report from her team in Port Harmony. Although her subordinate seemed terrified, and that put her on edge.

The warden stopped as if taking time to think about what he needed to say. 'Dee Squad report...another attack!'

'Renegades?' Nolan's fists tightened. She knew she had given them everything they needed. The successful transfer of supplies should have been easy. Bewildered by the incompetence of her wardens, the rage smouldered inside her.

'Yes...umm...er...yes...Renegades. They—'

Interrupting, Nolan took a step closer, tired of the warden's feeble stuttering. 'They stole more supplies. From the illustrious Dee Squad!'

'Ma'am...they...' the warden fumbled with his words, bowing his head. 'They raided the shelter this time.'

Nolan felt her heart racing. What would she tell Rada? As ruler of Scorr Tanta, Rada did not tolerate failure. With the warden trembling like a coward in front of her, Nolan stretched out her arm and propped up his chin.

'Get to the point!' she said, staring at him. At least he would witness her fury, even if he was only the messenger. 'What did we lose?'

The warden tried in vain to avoid her gaze. 'All…um…all of it!'

Releasing him, Nolan stepped away. She had lost patience with her division in Port Harmony; something had to change. Their lack of success was disgusting. Worse than that, was the fact that she was responsible for them. Rada had warned Nolan, that further failure would be met with consequences.

'Ma'am…we will do better.' The warden's voice drowned in fear.

'Recall them!' Enough was enough; Nolan would find a better team for Port Harmony.

The warden frowned. He didn't appear to agree with her orders.

'That won't be necessary,' a faint voice called out.

Without hesitation, Nolan straightened her posture and turned around. That voice was the only thing she feared, and now, more than ever before, terror filled her body. Her chest squeezed the air from her lungs.

'My Lady…' Nolan addressed her superior appropriately. 'Apologies…I thought you were in the palace preparing.'

Marching toward them, Rada clutched a solid stone staff; embossed with the Scorr Tanta insignia. An emerald cloak dragged behind her, and a grey, featureless mask concealed her face. She was dressed for her weekly address to the people of Scorr Tanta. They gathered to hear from Rada every week and had done throughout her fifteen-year reign. Yet she never permitted civilians to see her face. Despite being alone, Rada's very presence immediately ripped away Nolan's authority.

'Your Dee Squad will remain in place,' Rada said, to clarify her order. 'New plans are in motion to uncover these Renegades. Removing your squadron will only serve to raise their suspicions.'

Nolan noticed the warden moving aside to ensure he didn't get caught in the exchange. He was probably trying to make sense of the conflicting orders. The hatred she felt toward him was overbearing. How could her wardens have done this to her?

'Plans?' Nolan hadn't been made aware of any plans, yet she was well informed most of the time. Rada was excluding her, and that was not a good indication of her fate.

Rada thrust her staff forward, demanding compliance. 'Plans...that are none of your concern. All will become apparent soon enough!'

'But...My Lady,' Nolan said, aware that her insolence may not be well received. 'There is already a plan. My people—'

'Your people,' yelled Rada, 'are pathetic fools, who have missed every opportunity to stop these outlaws! I have implemented a new plan. One which will end this for good. For now, your people will remain in place. They can…at least…manage to do that. They can…can't they?'

'Yes, My Lady.'

Nolan felt her influence slipping. She couldn't justify, or even excuse the failings of her wardens. Receiving punishment on their behalf was becoming much more likely.

'You have your instructions,' she said to the warden, lacking in conviction. 'Do nothing.'

Taking his opportunity to leave, the warden gently nodded. He scurried away without saying anything further.

Nolan faced Rada, feeling smaller than she had ever felt before. 'Is there anything else My Lady?'

'Yes. Rumours have started to spread about these Renegades. They have caused enough trouble, and if I'm right in my suspicions, they may continue to cause disruption. People will want someone to blame.'

'Yes, My Lady.'

Rada was merciless, and Nolan had seen many people suffer for failing her. After standing by her ruler's side, heartlessly watching the demise of others, she now wondered if she would be Rada's next target. It was inevitable.

Edging nearer, it was Rada's intention to further intimidate Nolan. 'The wardens are under your command, and as such, their failings...are your failings. The people will decide your fate. I have every confidence they will choose to banish you from Scorr Tanta. In fact, I will make sure of it.'

Nolan knelt in submission and could feel her body trembling. 'Please, My Lady...show mercy.' Begging for her life was Nolan's only option. After such devotion to Rada, she could only hope for pity. Her loyalty must count for something, and she would do anything to avoid being sent to Eklips territory.

'Your whining shows weakness...and weakness has been your undoing,' Rada continued. 'Kayden's willingness to turn our outcasts into slaves, and accept them in Eklips, benefits us all. There is no place in The Union for incompetence or insubordination. People guilty of such things have the same destiny as common criminals. They will live the rest of their lives without privilege. For now, the people are waiting, with the celebration of our Bicentenary at the front of their minds. We will soon discover what they know and what will become of you.'

Nolan recognised how weak she looked, condemned to a fate she had never imagined. *How could it have come to this?* she thought. Only moments earlier, she had held her head high as the confident warden commander. Stripped of her power, status and everything she had worked hard for, Nolan realised that it all meant nothing. She understood how fragile she was — how fragile anyone was. Rada could crush her at any time. Nolan could only hope that the rumours were over-stated. That way, Rada may have time to regain confidence in her.

'My Lady,' Nolan said. Her stomach rolled inside her and her thoughts became muddled. 'The celebrations will go ahead without distraction. I'm sure of it.'

Rada's cloak filled the passageway as she turned away. 'I'm sure they will. Now…our people are waiting to hear from their leader.' Moving with haste, Rada left Nolan far behind, still on her knees.

chapter three

Trouble at The Market

'Haylee,' Evan cried, attempting to get help. But Haylee didn't seem to notice the skirmish unfolding a few feet away from her. Either that, or she was trying to avoid provoking the wardens.

Ellie screamed, falling to the ground when Ditto released her. 'Get off me!'

Ditto wasn't done and wasted no time lifting Ellie to her feet with one hand — swiping with a fist from the other. 'Go!'

Ellie fell backwards in pain, as Ditto's fist thrust deep into her belly. She was back on the stony floor but quickly bounced back. Ellie would not be beaten and ran toward her attacker. Her fear had somehow turned into anger, and she leapt onto Ditto's back, punching with all the energy she had. After her not-so-graceful entrance earlier, Ellie's determination to earn respect was overpowering. But whose respect she wanted, she was not so sure of.

Tik and Morrigan could be seen running in the direction of the fight, as their orgo became unsettled close by. Distracted by the animals and working hard to calm them, they couldn't intervene. Ellie and their friend pummelled each other, while Tik and Morrigan gripped the reins of their orgo.

Ditto span around several times, before being able to toss Ellie from her back. She then raced back toward her opponent with her hands clenched. Before Ellie found her feet, Ditto took advantage, and with one kick she knocked her back to the ground. Leaping on top of Ellie, Ditto pinned her down, striking her fiercely.

Morrigan joined Evan's plea for help. 'Haylee!' Her gentle tone wasn't very noticeable, and it was pointless.

Haylee remained silent; seemingly unaware of the commotion. She carried on sipping her drink and chatting with the blacksmith. They were only a few feet away, yet it was like they were in another world, unaware of anything around them.

Ellie managed to free her arms and began to block Ditto's punches. With each blow, the pain got worse; like she was being battered with a solid mallet. Somehow, with a quick thrust of her body, Ellie managed to throw Ditto off and staggered back to her feet. Injured, but not ready to surrender, she clenched Ditto's thick, dirty brown hair and pulled hard. Ditto screamed in pain, but Ellie was enraged and continued her assault. Whilst she had the advantage, she hauled her opponent toward the pod of distressed orgo. They were pounding the ground with their large toes and scraping at the frozen dirt below them. Cruel, Ellie threw Ditto amongst the group of animals and stepped away. Without stopping to consider her behaviour, Ellie was blinded by her temper.

Morrigan watched with a look of horror, whilst Ditto was being thumped from one orgo to the other. She pulled hard on the reins of her animal, but there was nothing she could do to help her friend.

'Haylee!' she repeated.

Ditto's cape was torn from her whilst she struggled to break free from the orgo pod. Screaming, she tumbled about like a rag doll, until she met the ground. Claws from the orgo dug into her flesh, as the distressed animals reared and stamped in protest. Then, crawling between the animals, Ditto somehow managed to pull free. She ran squealing at Ellie. Wrapping her arms around Ellie's waist, she wrestled her to the ground and onto her front. With her opponent now unable to turn toward her, she sat on Ellie's back and beat her.

Defenceless, Ellie hoped Evan wasn't watching, although she knew he must be. His opinion was more important than her own for some reason. Her fingers scraped in the slush beneath her, but she couldn't budge. Ditto had her fixed to the floor. Peering through the hair covering her face, she spotted Haylee pacing in their direction. Her stride was full of conviction, and she held a barrel in her arms.

Passing the pod of orgo, Haylee smiled at Morrigan. After stopping momentarily, she kicked at one of the wooden tether posts lodged in the ground. It didn't take long for the lump of timber to pop free. Placing the barrel on the floor and arming herself with the wooden post, Haylee reached forward, clutching Ditto's tunic. Wrenching her friend away from Ellie; she forced Ditto backward.

'Back off!'

Ditto didn't move and stood to pant, then pointed toward Ellie. 'She started it!' she said, whimpering like a young child.

Haylee looked disgusted. 'Ditto…You're embarrassing me!'

Obediently, Ditto turned back toward Evan's stall and tried to make her appearance more presentable.

Ellie pulled at her sodden overalls; soaked from the slushy ground. Disgusted, she hadn't finished with Ditto and ran at her screaming. *My last chance to win respect*, she thought.

Haylee thrust with the post and knocked Ellie from her feet. Then, with a second merciless strike, she tore Ellie's overalls across the waist, grazing her belly. As the unquestionable leader of her group, Haylee didn't seem familiar with defiance. She established her influence well. Taking a handful of the tattered material, that Ellie was wearing, Haylee dragged her through the dirt.

'Take the barrel and leave...now!' Haylee lifted Ellie and forced her into the side of an orgo. Her fingers locked onto Ellie's neck; pinning her in place and steadily choking her. Ellie wriggled and fought when Haylee tossed the post to one side. Nonetheless, Haylee continued to hold her battered prey, raising her free hand to point at Ellie's face.

Clutching at her attacker's fingers, Ellie tried to remove the hand that squeezed at her throat. Her breathless body weakened, and she knew surrender was her only option. It was the sensible choice considering how ashamed she felt. Ellie raised her hands in defeat. Yet something else caught Haylee's attention and she didn't seem to notice Ellie's gesture.

'Ditto,' Haylee said, sounding edgy. 'Time to go! Get the others. Eyes...on...me!'

Ellie gasped and fell to her knees when Haylee released her. Catching a glimpse of another pod of orgo approaching, the reason for Haylee's alarm became evident. The six animals looked threatening. These were black orgo too; the wildest and hardest to tame of all the breeds.

Haylee's group took little time to untether their own animals. Then, finding their saddles, they galloped away. Within seconds they had gone, as the pod of black orgo trotted into the market with their owners. They were heading for Evan's stall. Ellie meanwhile, was still slumped on the ground nearby.

'Who are they?' she asked, facing Evan. She couldn't help but wonder why the wardens still hadn't reacted. Regardless of all the disturbance, the squad remained at their posts.

Evan stared at the figures riding in his direction. 'Kayden,' he moaned. 'You should go. You should have gone a while ago.'

Uncertain whether standing was a possibility, Ellie contemplated the sort of impression she had made with Evan. Yet, the fearsome folk that were closing in on them were much more of a concern. Ellie didn't know much about the people living in Eklips, the mysterious third colony within The Union. She had never been there. As far as she had heard, it was a dimly lit coastal territory, situated around eight miles away from Port Harmony. It was said, that the people there either lived their lives as slaves or slave owners. Apart from a privileged few, most from Eklips obeyed their leader out of fear alone. Kayden had a reputation for being a brutal dictator, who turned The Union's criminals into slaves.

When the group moved closer, it was easy to identify which one was Kayden. Dressed differently to the others; his heavy black cloak, somehow made him even more terrifying. He looked much older than Evan, with hair that was shaved short. A frail slave was tucked behind his saddle.

'I'm here for Ditto,' Kayden said, stopping his orgo right in front of Evan's stall.

Rather than looking at Kayden, Evan stayed silent. He was studying the private army that flanked the man addressing him. They were assault rangers. Ellie had been told about them too, and their reputation wasn't pleasant. Neither in fact, was their long slimy hair or dreary faces. On the other hand, the crimson uniforms they wore were stunning.

Evan glanced up at Kayden. 'Not sure you're welcome here.'

Ellie couldn't take her eyes away from Kayden's slave. She seemed slightly younger than Ellie was, and her dark hair looked like it had been hacked short with a blunt blade. Her eyes were dulled, and sparse, flesh-coloured rags were all that covered her. Ellie could see that the slave's skin had even tinted blue from the cold. Looking like she hadn't eaten in days, but was beaten instead, Kayden's prize was in poor health. The welts across every visible part of her body horrified Ellie even more. She had no idea how badly the people of Eklips treated slaves and felt lucky to be in Port Harmony. At least she had a barn to sleep in and warm clothes. The orgo droppings were somehow appealing for the first time.

Kayden had waited long enough for Evan to answer him. 'Ditto…where is she?'

Whatever it was that Ditto had done, it was reason enough for Kayden to come looking for her. It was well known that he rarely left the security of Eklips.

Evan smiled and replied, 'You won't find her here!' His gesture was brave, to say the least.

Kayden looked furious but had little leverage with Evan. Where a stranger from another colony was concerned, the people of Port Harmony would most definitely protect their own. Locals filled the market, and Kayden obviously didn't want to take his chances. His reputation wouldn't matter to them. Ordering his assault rangers to stand down, he caught Ellie gazing at his slave.

'What is your interest in Pandra?' he asked. His voice made Ellie queasy.

Ellie stood and snubbed Kayden when she hobbled over to collect her barrel. Even though she had a deep concern for Pandra; as Kayden's slave, there was nothing that Ellie could do for her. Ellie glanced over at Evan, but his head dropped. *Perhaps Evan was right*, she thought. *Perhaps she shouldn't go near them again*. She should certainly learn to stop interfering where she wasn't welcome; for now, anyway. That strategy wasn't doing her any favours. Without any further hesitation, Ellie took hold of the barrel and dragged it toward Sage. He had started to create a deep, rumbling growl, and was glaring at the folk from Eklips.

'It's okay Sage,' whispered Ellie. 'We're goin' home now.' Taking another look around the market, Ellie thought it was strange that the wardens still hadn't reacted. They didn't seem interested in Kayden's presence and hadn't bothered when she had clashed with Ditto either.

Kayden roared. 'Can no-one in this town answer questions? I want Ditto...who will tell me where she is?'

'I've told you,' said Evan. 'You won't find her here!'

'Very well. I will find her myself. Tell that sister of yours to watch her step too. If she is hiding that friend of hers, I will soon find out.'

Whilst Kayden and his people turned and trotted back through the market, Ellie became concerned for Ditto's wellbeing. She was almost as anxious as she was for poor Pandra; which was bizarre. Minutes before, Ellie had been fighting in the streets with Ditto, and she hadn't liked her one bit. Not hatred as such, but a very big dislike. Yet encountering Kayden, she had an uncontrollable urge to protect the very person that had hurt and embarrassed her. Then again, Ellie had done a good enough job of hurting and embarrassing herself. Perhaps she wasn't that unlike Ditto.

After roping the barrel to Sage's saddle, Ellie decided that it would be better if she minded her own business. At least for a little while anyway.

Mounting Sage, Ellie left the market behind her on her way back to the barn. No matter how hard she tried, vivid images of Pandra intruded on her thoughts.

chapter four

The Trade

Ditto's gripes were all Morrigan heard as they cantered toward the wharf. Her friend wouldn't have expected her clash with the apprentice to go so badly. Still, Morrigan found it entertaining to watch Ditto grumble whilst rubbing her sores.

Tightly-packed buildings bordered each side of their route; each of them as round as the last. They were typical of the structures found in Port Harmony. Around them, many of the locals stopped whatever they were doing. They gawped in awe of the orgo-riders. Travelling side by side, their group commanded attention. With matching steeds and similar outfits, they were quite the spectacle as they passed each of the residences. Morrigan was proud to be a part of it.

'Eyes on me!' Haylee's orgo quickened to a trot.

Morrigan complied, followed by Ditto then Tik. Their formation was always well coordinated; Haylee made sure of it.

'Where we goin' anyway?' asked Tik, whilst they all shadowed Haylee. He was generally a little slow to catch on.

Haylee let out a noisy sigh. 'Do you have to ask?'

Tik chose not to pursue his curiosity; he never challenged Haylee. Toze meanwhile, bobbed around behind his master, enjoying the ride. The ape was quite happy frolicking in the orgo's fleece. At times, he even tried to blend with the black patches that decorated her white fur.

Morrigan overheard Haylee talking to Ditto.

'Told you that he would come after you,' she said, referring to Kayden. 'We have enough going on without inviting more trouble.'

Ditto chose to not reply. That was her usual manner.

'We were all at that Dispute Hay,' Tik intervened. 'Ditto's fight there was a fix. She shouldn't have lost, so she owes him nothing. Kayden coming after Ditto…it isn't her fault.'

'But still, it always seems to be Ditto bringing trouble.'

Morrigan flinched. 'Haylee…if it weren't for Ditto, where would we be? You've said that yourself.'

Ditto offered Morrigan a grin to say thank you. She never spoke much, unless using physical force, but then she never really needed to. Despite Haylee dishing out the orders, Ditto was critical to their bond. Morrigan often got the urge to offer her a hug but knew she would come off worse if she did. Ditto showed little sign of accepting gestures of affection.

Haylee turned to face Ditto. 'They're right Dit. I'm sorry. It's not your fault...I shouldn't be so hard on you.'

'I never question anything you ask of me. Ever!'

Haylee must have been shocked to receive actual words from Ditto, but she didn't get chance to respond. Ahead, a noise like someone was yelling, was easy to hear. Haylee held her hand high and everyone steadied their orgo. As they halted, the sound erupted again. This time, it was even more sickening.

'This way,' Haylee called, and she altered course toward a nearby building.

Morrigan followed but didn't want to. 'Don't like it, Hay. Just leave it.'

Neither Tik nor Ditto spoke up. Like always, they were all shadowing Haylee with little resistance. Morrigan knew any more protests were useless. None of them would listen.

Haylee directed their attention to a larger building, becoming more cautious as she approached. 'There!'

The cry came again and Tik jolted behind Haylee. 'Yep...it is definitely coming from there!'

With pronounced gestures, that looked like she was taking flight, Haylee directed Tik into position first. After that, she guided Ditto. Lastly, Morrigan saw her signal and nervously joined the others. Haylee had huddled them all around the entrance to the building, and they waited for her next instruction.

Another noise prompted Ditto to speak. 'Someone needs our help.'

'Wait!' Haylee bent forward to get a better view. The moment she did, a figure stumbled out of the doorway. He was easy to recognise. It was rare to see a warden on their own.

'Halt!' he ordered, arming his lance immediately.

Haylee stretched her arm out to the side to make sure nobody reacted in haste. 'Is there a problem?' she asked.

'I will speak with him,' the warden said, pointing at Tik. 'Only him. Not you.'

Tall and muscular, the warden was quite domineering and refused to address Haylee. Inside the building behind him, Morrigan could hear what she assumed was the rest of his group. They were clattering about and showed little interest in joining their colleague. Like Ditto, Morrigan held her position.

Tik dismounted. 'Why me? Why won't you speak to my friend?' he asked. 'You will treat her with the respect she deserves.'

Twitching, the warden pointed his lance at Haylee. 'I will treat her how I wish. You all need to move along. Away from here. Now!'

'You will drop your lance,' Tik said. He stepped forward to protect Haylee's honour. 'Then...you can tell me what's goin' on in there. We're not goin' anywhere until you do.'

'As a warden, I don't take orders from you. You have no business poking around here.'

'We're not causing any trouble,' said Tik. 'Where is it that you expect us to be? We're good citizens, just wanting to help someone who seems to be in distress. I assume there isn't a problem with that, is there?''

The warden glanced between Haylee, Ditto, and Morrigan. 'Be good citizens and leave!'

Surfacing from their hiding place inside the building, three more wardens joined the first. Oddly, they were all men, and the group was quite a distance from any regular posts. Unlike the first officer, these wardens didn't ready their weapons. Instead, they stared in a way which made Morrigan uneasy.

'Leave them be,' one of the new wardens advised. 'They're not worth the hassle.'

Haylee dismounted. 'No! I'd like to hear what he has to say for himself. And I'd like to know what you're doing in there.'

Stepping toward the first warden, Haylee held her hand high. She was giving the order for Morrigan and Ditto to stay put. Morrigan couldn't bear watching. Wardens made her itch—severely. She hated them, and it was taking a great deal of restraint to remain in her saddle. Haylee didn't want any more conflict than necessary, and Morrigan understood that. Yet, at the same time, Haylee was approaching a hostile warden with a charged lance. *How well could this go?* Morrigan thought.

'Stop! Don't come near me!' Without remorse, the warden lunged at Haylee and struck her with his lance.

Morrigan winced, watching her friend collapse when the energy from the lance struck. The weapon grounded Haylee with a single blow. In that instant, all four of their orgo started stamping the ground. A dust born from ice drifted from their fierce claws. The snorts meanwhile, must have been heard all over Port Harmony. In the commotion, Tik swung forward, snatching the lance from the assailant.

'We will take it from here,' said one of the three less aggressive wardens, walking toward his associate. 'Please accept our apologies for our colleague's approach. Feel free to be on your way.'

Tik looked fierce, holding the lance and taking the upper hand. 'I want an explanation. What are you doin' in there? Why won't *he* talk to my friends? And why did he just attack one of us?'

A group of people appeared from the building where the wardens had been. Each of them was restrained; arms tied behind their backs.

'That's why,' said Morrigan.

'You're taking slaves!' Tik roared, aiming the weapon at the first warden. 'What? Wait! Did you think I'd be okay with that in some way? Why? Because I'm a man?'

Stepping back, the warden held up his arms in surrender. 'No…no…I—'

'They're not just taking slaves,' said Haylee, standing as though she hadn't been attacked. 'They're taking them illegally.'

With a loud clang, the lance hit the cobbles when Tik tossed it back at the warden. Morrigan wasn't sure why he had when the trooper could potentially attack them again. How Tik had not struck him—killed him even—baffled her. She watched, whilst Tik and the warden locked in a sort of standoff. However, not much time passed before the warden thought better than to aggravate them any further. He began stepping away.

'So, what now?' one of the other wardens questioned. By now, a group of seven innocent men were beside him.

'You release them,' Morrigan said. Until then, she hadn't realised how fast she was breathing. Staying put wasn't easy, but it was what Haylee wanted.

Haylee took her place in her saddle. 'Trading with Kayden. That's why he's come to Port Harmony. Not sure how Rada would feel about that…*boys*.'

A false laughter emerged from the first warden. 'You think we're scared of your threats?'

'She's right,' said another member of the patrol. 'We can't risk Rada finding out.'

Together, the three wardens charged their lances and advanced. Their colleague meanwhile, remained unarmed. As they closed in on Haylee, Tik mounted his orgo; ready for a fight. Then, whilst the patrol held their focus, Ditto charged at them. Morrigan knew that it was time to keep the upper hand.

'Yah!' She kicked down and galloped to the aggressors. The wardens instinctively scattered as Morrigan hurtled toward them.

With every lance now targeting Morrigan's orgo, Ditto pressed on. One by one, she booted their weapons away as she passed. None of the lances fell at first, but then Haylee and Tik joined the assault.

'Wardens,' Tik laughed when his steed knocked one of the men from his feet. 'You've got to love how dumb they are.'

Morrigan tore at her reins, manoeuvring amongst the group chaotically. The wardens hadn't a clue where to aim, and she noticed one lose his weapon. With little effort, their group had already reduced the patrol to a single armed man.

Haylee intervened as the first warden ran to retrieve his armament. 'Don't think so,' she teased when her orgo stamped onto his lance.

'Enough!' screeched the last of them still holding a lance. 'Wardens...retreat.'

That was all the encouragement they needed, and the group disbanded. In the meantime, Tik found fun in rearing his orgo at them whilst they fled. As they departed, Morrigan noticed an uncharacteristic smile growing on Haylee. Ditto, meanwhile, leapt from her orgo and removed a knife from her saddle. The prisoners left behind by the wardens were in shock, and as Ditto approached them, none of them spoke. Even so, Ditto cut them free effortlessly. Their expressions seemed to offer a simplistic gratitude.

'Go,' said Haylee to the frightened group. 'You're free to go now. Quickly. Get back to your homes.'

All the captives fled, darting between buildings and into town. At the same time, Morrigan gazed about checking for any more wardens. Content that they had liberated the bunch of innocent civilians, she trotted over to her friends. Haylee however, looked nervous again for some reason.

'Eyes on me!' she shouted, pointing at the sky whilst the strangers disappeared.

The shadows flitting across the street suggested Kayden wasn't far away. Gliders were above them. He was probably on his way to collect the illegal slaves. In a flash Ditto saddled, and with speed, they all trailed Haylee away from the scene.

chapter five

Discontent in Scorr Tanta

With her servants retreating, Rada walked through the gates of the palace, into the centre of Scorr Tanta. Behind her, two cylindrical towers gleamed. They were symbols of her undeniable power. Outside the palace, a crowd had gathered around the stage. Their cheers became louder when Rada emerged and paced toward them; sentries at her side for security.

Rada considered the rumours of the Renegades and knew that there would be questions. Not only was she having to find ways to bring these outlaws to justice, but she might also need to answer for the failings of her wardens. It had been reported that many people in Scorr Tanta were beginning to feel unsettled. Some were even questioning Rada's leadership in secrecy. She was barely an adult when she had become ruler, but never in her rein had Rada been so challenged to defend her authority.

She took the stage, and the roar from the crowd was deafening. Rada held her staff high above her head. Fiercely embracing the adoration, she ensured that nobody could take her influence away. Concealed by her mask, the way she always was, Rada felt superior. She believed that her features may symbolise fragility.

'Scorr Tanta…our home!' Rada cried.

From the polished granite court in the heart of the city, the crowd began chanting. 'Our home…our home…our home,' they repeated, over and again.

This chant was the same every week, and voices echoed around the buildings encircling them. Everyone acknowledged their gratitude. Those living in Scorr Tanta were encouraged to cherish how lucky they were, to have a secure city in which to live. Unlike their predecessors, they no longer had to fight so hard for survival. There was much to celebrate.

Rada grinned slyly beneath her mask as she surveyed her people. She gazed around the city and breathed in their adoration, as though it filled her with strength. From the stage, Rada could admire much of Scorr Tanta. Colourful, majestic buildings dominated the skyline. Beyond them, immense towers were positioned around the outskirts of the city, projecting heat to overpower the cold. Within the borders of the great city, it was a much warmer place to live.

People rarely even noticed the frozen landscape that surrounded them. When snow fell, it dissipated before it even found ground level. Those in Scorr Tanta lived in an artificial climate, much different to that in Port Harmony or Eklips. Since Rada had risen to power, those loyal to her and that valued her ideals, had remained there. They enjoyed a much wealthier lifestyle than those living in other colonies.

Bringing the heavy, stone staff back down to her side, Rada commanded the crowd to fall silent. Obediently, they waited for her to begin. But instead of hearing their ruler's voice first, someone spoke out from amongst them.

'Who are these Renegades, My Lady? Do you know where they are coming from? People say they're stealing from us!'

Her mask hid disgust, and Rada knew that she couldn't stall with her reply. Their faith in her depended on it. A small part of her had hoped she could spare Nolan. The warden commander had been devoted for as long as she could remember. In some way, Rada even pitied her. Then again, Rada also enjoyed demonstrating her influence. If this time it meant that Nolan would suffer — so be it!

Rada addressed her crowd, whilst they listened in silence. 'Our way of living...is indeed being challenged! These so-called Renegades are stealing our supplies. Attacking our transports. They are traitors of The Union.

Threatening the bond that exists between this place and Port Harmony. They must not be allowed to go on...and must be destroyed! Which is exactly what we will do.'

The crowd continued their quiet, and Rada waited to see if anyone else would dare to speak. After a short pause, she continued.

'As you go about your lives in Scorr Tanta...know that our forces will not stop until justice has been served. We will extinguish the Renegades. We will not allow this. I...will not allow dissent. I will bring them before you once we are triumphant. Dead...or alive!' Rada pointed her staff toward the crowd to illustrate her dominance. 'Wardens will now be increased on the streets of Port Harmony, and we will continue to watch Eklips. We will find them. Separate units will ensure that the next transport the bandits attack...will be their last!'

Rada's noticed her voice was consumed with the anger she felt toward the Renegades and the individual who dared to question her. She wasn't familiar with being challenged.

Once more, the crowd cheered aloud and began chanting. 'Our home...our home...our home,' they went on.

From amongst the people, a solitary man stepped forward, nearing the edge of Rada's platform. He was possibly the one who had spoken out. Someday, he would pay for his stupidity. The people hushed whilst he spoke.

'I think I speak for all of us, My Lady. We need to know how this has happened. How does anyone manage to steal from us? Why haven't you informed us before now? And…shouldn't our wardens have taken down these people already?'

Glancing down to face the man who questioned her, Rada contemplated her reply. She refused to exhibit her fury but would pound him with her staff, if given the chance. The sight of him left a foul taste in her mouth, but now wasn't the time to let anger cloud her judgement. Rada needed to reassure her people.

'I agree,' she said, 'that our wardens should have done better. I have already identified the person responsible. You must all decide her fate when the time is right. But…telling you before we had captured these criminals…jeopardised our chances of success.'

Unsatisfied, the man carried on. 'But…you haven't been successful!'

Gasps of dismay engulfed the crowd, as they responded to the man probing their leader. Nobody had ever questioned Rada before. Moving closer to the edge of the stage, Rada looked across the people of Scorr Tanta with confidence. She refused to be challenged and sucked in her resentment.

'We must protect The Union and preserve our agreement. This ensures our mutual survival,' she roared loudly. 'For that reason alone, we do not tolerate traitors. The goals of these Renegades will soon be undone. Be certain of that! Next week…we *will* celebrate our Bicentenary. Those who defy us…will have been dealt with. They will pay a heavy price. Scorr Tanta is…our home!'

The chants from the crowd resumed. Slowly, the man stepped back amongst them, seeming more confident in Rada's resolve. Rada hated him for challenging her and didn't care how bold he was. To her, he was impertinent and outspoken, and she would remember his face. For now, however, it was her warden commander who must answer for her crimes.

Relentless, the noise continued. Whilst the crowd displayed their adoration, Rada stepped back to leave the stage. She turned deliberately to one of her sentries.

'Bring Nolan to me…now!'

chapter six

Cedric's Place

Junkyard studied the clay cubes on the gameboard in front of him. Appalled by the stale odour that filled the barn, he wondered how Cedric spent so much time there. For Port Harmony, it was a warm place to be, with pine burners dotted about here and there. But that was about the only appealing feature of Cedric's building. In Junkyard's opinion, the barn was a big stone structure lacking in character. Not to mention that it was filled with an unthinkable amount of rundown orgo pens, that had seen better days. What confused Junkyard more, was that the tiny doorway didn't have an actual door. It was just a simple hole in the wall.

'Cedric,' Junkyard said, placing his hairless head in his hands.

'Yes, old friend?' replied Cedric.

'You…are terrible at this game!'

'Ellie's been trying to teach me. But I'm still no wiser. She wins every time.'

Junkyard smiled. The way the cubes were arranged on the playing board made the next move obvious to him. He wondered how many times he could beat Cedric before his friend decided to never play again. No bigger than pebbles, there were six red playing cubes and another six in green. In each set, the separate cubes were individually marked on their top surfaces. The images were silhouettes of different animals.

Shifting his narwhal piece, Junkyard kept his eyes fixed on every one of his green blocks. 'So, how is that new apprentice of yours?'

Cedric seemed thoughtful as he took hold of his gugubat cube, ready to take his turn. 'As well as can be expected.'

'Expected?'

'Seems to make far too many trips to the market,' Cedric said. Rubbing his balding head, he made his move.

'Oh…I see!'

Cedric grunted for no reason. He did that a lot. 'I don't want her falling into trouble.'

'Haylee, you mean?' Junkyard knew exactly what Cedric meant. Yet, he was more focused on winning their game. His decoy — one of Cedric's red cubes that he had chosen before their game started — was in a perfect position.

'Any of them!' Cedric wrinkled his wrinkles as far as they would wrinkle. 'Ellie seems to have found a fondness for Evan too.'

Junkyard shrugged. 'Well…who can blame her? Really though…what's the worst that can happen?'

'We will see.' Cedric didn't seem like he wanted to make light of things.

'Deception!' shouted Junkyard, as he made his final move. After bouncing from his stool, he began an awkward dance to celebrate. Clumsily spinning around in the open space of the barn, his long arms waved by his side. Junkyard didn't care how he looked. He still enjoyed the winning; even if it was inevitable. Triumphant, he strutted his lanky frame in his filthy grey overalls.

'Yes, yes. You win…again! I never see it coming!'

'Nope…when it's right under your nose too!'

Whilst he watched Junkyard bounce around the barn, Cedric grinned. It wasn't often that he showed such emotion, but perhaps he could excuse his own uselessness this time. Even if only to watch his friend look so ridiculous.

'No one could ever question how humble you are,' Cedric said, before a sudden look of fright glued to his face.

Junkyard stopped; troubled by Cedric's expression. 'What is it?'

'Gliders!'

Cedric clutched his walking stick and appeared to fight with his stool until his feet found the floor. Nonetheless, wearing his bronze tunic and matching cloak, he still looked dignified. Limping toward the doorway, he went to investigate.

Junkyard understood his concern and followed. 'Kayden?'

'Who else?'

If gliders were in the sky, you could be sure Kayden was nearby. They trailed him like orgo pups with their mothers. When he peered outside, Junkyard caught glimpses of them. Horrible beasts. Lengthy whip-like tails swept behind their tiny bodies, all supported by huge leathery wings. They threw shadows over the snow beneath them. Animals were generally not his thing, but Junkyard could easily say he loathed the gliders.

Cedric sighed. 'If Kayden is here…we both know who is likely the cause.'

With his eyebrows shifting upward, Junkyard bobbed his head. 'You don't know that for sure,' he said, wanting to show calm. 'I have to go back to work. My incredible creations aren't goin' to create themselves, now are they? Try to not let it bother you…it isn't your concern anymore.'

Ellie passed through the entrance as Junkyard finished speaking. She was guiding Sage and a food barrel rolled behind them. It was hard not to notice the rip in her grubby clothing. Junkyard remembered Cedric's remarks from earlier.

'What's the worst that can happen?' Cedric repeated when he set eyes on his apprentice. Frowning, he walked lamely back into the barn.

Junkyard laughed louder than he should, plodding onto the street. 'It will all be fine…I'm sure of it.' Although he wasn't that sure and understood Cedric's worries.

***

The distinctive snorting sounds of the other orgo welcomed Sage's return. They all trotted to the fencing at the edge of their pens, as if waiting for news from the outside world. Each with different coloured fleeces, they created a striking array. Sage was housed alongside the tan orgo, whilst the enclosures for the greys and whites were further away. Cedric liked to keep them organised by fleece colour; it represented their temperament. Any prospective buyers could locate the orgo they wanted with ease.

'How was the market?' Cedric was avoiding the obvious questions, whilst dithering around the pens.

Ellie thought he looked grumpy, but she might have imagined it. She tried to disguise the split in her overalls as if Cedric hadn't seen. He must have, but hiding the gape seemed like a clever idea at the time.

'Great sir…thanks,' was all she could think to offer as a reply.

An unexpected grin appeared on Cedric's clean-shaven face. 'Still sir?' he sniggered. 'Cedric will do.'

Ellie stroked Sage whilst returning the smile. It wasn't often she saw Cedric make any type of happy-face. The gesture felt soothing after her ordeal in the market. It was also better than the interrogation or telling off, that she had assumed. Removing Sage's saddle and bridle, Ellie was conscious that chores needed to be done. They weren't about to do themselves. Nor was Cedric about to do them, that was what he employed her for.

'Have you checked on Ash yet?' Cedric asked, intruding on Ellie's wandering thoughts. 'That egg must be about ready to hatch.'

'Will do.' Ellie knew the time to go to work was overdue, so petted Sage one last time. She didn't know anything as soft as an orgo fleece.

Leaving the pen, she caught a glimpse of her makeshift bed in the corner of the barn — an old table with its legs sawed down. Ellie panicked and rushed over to it. She hadn't realised that she'd left all her belongings scattered around earlier. Cedric didn't approve of disorganisation. At the same time, she didn't want him to see her things lying about either; they were private. Whilst fixing the sheets, Ellie shoved a bulky, leather chest underneath the timber frame, with a single kick of her boot. She then covered the object with more rags to hide it from sight. The thought of giving Cedric the opportunity to ask her questions was unpleasant.

Cedric was already at Ash's pen, and his twisted finger pointed in the direction of her nest. 'Looks like you're just in time.'

Still flustered, Ellie glanced around in a daze. 'Erm...well...I...,' she choked, not entirely sure what she wanted to say.

In the centre of her enclosure was Ash — a large female grey orgo. A little unsteady on her feet, she was staring at a mound of dirt in the corner. Within her nest, lay the solitary egg she had been keeping warm for the last few months. The egg was twitching, about to hatch, and a dull scratching sound emerged from inside.

'It's time...' Cedric said. There was hardly a jump for joy, but he seemed somewhat elated. That lecture Ellie had expected, had become less likely.

Ellie gasped when she realised what was happening. 'It's hatching!' She had never seen an orgo pup before, and now she would get the chance to watch one hatch. There was no chance of Ellie containing her enthusiasm.

'It is...' Cedric agreed.

'I was beginning...to think...I'd never get to see this!' Ellie hurried over to Ash's pen. She watched in amazement, as chunks of the egg's shell began to split. If Cedric hadn't pointed it out, she may have missed this moment. In an instant, the thoughts of the market, Evan and even of Pandra, had dissolved. The feelings she had, whatever they were, had replaced all her worries; at least for a little while.

Cedric snorted like an orgo, saying, 'It won't take long girl…soon have another mouth to feed.'

'What do we do?' Ellie did an excellent job of ignoring the fact that Cedric had referred to her as girl. She found the word patronising, but she was too busy with her excitement to care. 'Can we help it?'

Cedric leant against the splintered wooden fence that ran along the front of the pen. He wasn't very good at standing for too long and struggled for each breath that he took. That was no different from how he always was.

'We wait…and watch,' he advised. 'Only help if we need to. But hopefully, we won't need to.'

Long minutes seemed to last hours, whilst Ellie stood with Cedric at the edge of the enclosure. Together with Ash, they waited with reluctant patience. In the meantime, the pup found ways to fight free from the egg which contained its body. Ellie had waited months for this moment, and in a few minutes, her tenacity would be rewarded.

Fragments of shell crumbled away. Ellie could make out the pink, fleshy lump inside, as it came into sight. 'No wool?' she asked, a little perplexed.

Cedric chuckled. 'Nope...less hair than me when they're born. Thing is...it will grow...not like m—'

A piercing crack interrupted him, and the egg fell apart freeing the pup. The little pink ball rolled into the grime. At first, it just flopped around and kicked away fragments of the shell. Trying to stand, the orgo pup looked comical as it fell around in the nest. Snorting softly to clear its tiny nostrils, the new-born blinked several times. It was attempting to focus on its surroundings.

With a bounce, Ellie threw her arms around her employer. Carried away with all the excitement, she wasn't that bothered whether he reciprocated. She swaddled Cedric in her arms, and it felt like he tensed from discomfort. Regardless, Ellie carried on squeezing him. After everything he had done for her, she looked up to him as a sort of surrogate father figure; a mentor even. She was never sure if the feelings were mutual, but what was certain, was how much she loved her new life. Ellie wanted to show that appreciation. Either way, to avoid over-stepping, she put Cedric down after only holding him briefly.

'Funny little thing,' she said, gazing at the pup.

Cedric straightened his tunic that Ellie had crumpled. 'Will look better in a few days. Doesn't take long for the fur to grow.'

'I hope so. It's...a lot uglier than I thought. Like...super ugly!'

'You'll hurt his feelings.' Cedric sounded serious.

Ellie ignored him and carried on, 'And I thought you said it would be bald? What's with the scarf? Wait...*His*...feelings?'

The pup had a ring of pure, chalky fur around the base of its neck, which had caught Ellie's attention. She was surprised at how ridiculous a mini orgo looked. Actually, she had expected something much different. Ellie loved the orgo and had always thought of them as a thing of beauty: one of nature's incredible gifts. Not this thing though, it wasn't in any way beautiful—well not yet.

'Yes...*his* feelings,' Cedric said, sounding delighted. 'The pup has a mane. It's a boy.'

'Because of the scarf?' Ellie looked at Cedric through curiosity. She had never seen an orgo with a mane before. Giggling with amusement, Ellie turned to watch the pup's long neck stretch out from a ring of fur.

'Manes are rare,' explained Cedric. 'Not seen one in a while. But...where there's a mane...you can be sure it's a boy. Few males have manes...but those with manes are certainly male.'

'It's a pink blob. With a fluffy white scarf…and its neck just stuck on top.'

Ash moved in to inspect her pup. She seemed a little disturbed by its appearance too. After nuzzling the strange creature, she returned to her place on the nest. Guided by his instincts, but not seeming to know how to use them, the new-born thrashed around Ash. He was finding his way into his mother's thick wool for warmth.

Despite the pup's unusual appearance, Ellie smiled at him. 'Hey, precious,' she whispered, before turning to face Ash. 'I know you can't answer me…but…he needs a name, don't you think?'

Ash sniffed, staring at Ellie as though she agreed with her. She appeared to be fascinated by the idea of naming her pup.

'Well…' Ellie was thinking aloud. 'It looks like its collar has been eaten by an enormous ball of snow. I'm thinking…er…well…something to do with that! What about Snow? Better still…Snowflake? Or Thaw even? Seems appropriate after all. That white stuff drippin' round his neck.'

'Not sure if Snowflake suits him,' Cedric said. He glanced at the new arrival, finally tucking into his mother's fleecy coat. 'Well, it's your first new arrival…so it's right that you name him. We will go with Thaw.'

Ellie turned to face her employer, feeling proud. 'Yes, sir.'

'Cedric,' said Cedric. He definitely didn't like to be called sir and jostled his walking stick in the direction of the doorway. 'Trust you will be okay for the rest of the day? I have things I need to get on with.'

Cedric's need to leave intrigued Ellie; especially when he was in such a hurry. 'What about Thaw?'

'Ash knows what to do,' he muttered. 'No need for me to stay. Unless you wish to discuss that tear in your uniform of course. Hope you plan to make sure your injuries don't get infected. Don't have time for you to get sick.'

'No sir.' For a second, Ellie hoped that a chance snowstorm might whisk her away. She thought she had escaped the prospect of explaining herself.

'What happened at the market anyway?' Cedric asked, being more direct this time.

Pausing to think, Ellie wasn't sure how to explain herself. 'Well…Ditto. Ditto…she kinda happened.'

'You were at Evan's stall?'

Ellie felt her face twisting. 'Where else am I supposed to get the food?'

'You like him,' Cedric said, facing away. Even he seemed to feel awkward asking that question.

'Whether I do or don't,' Ellie snapped, 'isn't the point. His stall is the only place to go for orgo food. You've said it yourself.'

Cedric grunted. 'Good place to pick a fight too it seems.'

'She was asking for it!'

'Haylee's group of friends are trouble,' Cedric said, turning back to connect with Ellie. 'I've told you this before. You'd be wise not to associate with them. Look at you.'

Determined to shake her own discomfort, Ellie felt like she was drowning and needed air. 'But Evan is a good man,' she offered, hoping that her employer may see her point of view. 'And with respect...Haylee is incredible. I know you don't like her, but have you seen how well they all ride on their orgo? Haylee especially. I mean...it's something else. And everyone in town loves her. And—'

'Love her? It's not love, Ellie. They just don't want to get on the wrong side of her. People tend to come off worse if they do. Trouble follows Haylee and she is best avoided.'

'You don't understand,' Ellie said, not sure if she wanted Cedric to hear. 'I'd give anything to be like Haylee. Fearless and strong. She's amazing.'

Cedric headed for the exit. 'Would you?'

Ellie thought it was time to change the conversation. 'Watch out for those big flying things out there. Where'd they come from anyway? Have you ever seen them before?'

'More questions...always...so many questions.' But Cedric didn't answer any of them. He just grimaced when he glanced back at her.

Trying to offer a reassuring smile, Ellie watched Cedric stumble toward the exit. 'Okay…well, everything will be fine here. Trust me.' She wasn't convinced he would trust her, judging from the state she had arrived in. But maybe saying it would help.

Without uttering another word, Cedric left the barn. There appeared to be no real reason for his departure.

Whilst the hours passed, Ellie went about her work attempting to impress her employer. Mucking out the orgo wasn't glamorous, but she found a sense of satisfaction in caring for such magnificent animals. Ellie had spent time building relationships with each of them, and they seemed to appreciate her efforts. With plenty of food to fill their bellies, and clean dirt to roam around in; how could they not? Besides, Ellie needed to make sure that Cedric saw her as an asset too.

The barn was quiet, and Ellie made final checks on all the orgo. A few of the animals were resting, whilst others came to their gates for a quick fuss off their keeper. Ellie left Ash's pen for last. Approaching, she admired the new-born once again. Thaw was tucked underneath his mother and Ellie beamed. Maybe the pup wasn't so ugly after all.

With each of the enclosures cared for, Ellie made her way toward a battered, old cistern in the corner of the barn. Pipes ran from the unit, across the ceiling and down into each pen; supplying water to empty troughs. Then, as Ellie opened the valve to release the water, something outside caught her attention. She recognised the pod of orgo and edged closer to the barn entrance, to get a better view.

Kayden and his rangers were there, and they were studying each of the buildings. Presumably, they were still searching for Ditto. Ellie couldn't see a single other person nearby. Not even Junkyard, whose workshop was opposite the barn surrounded by chunks of scrap metal. Inquisitive, Ellie returned to the cistern and closed off the water supply. She knew it wasn't her place, but Ellie had never been able to control her curiosity. She wanted to investigate.

For only a second Ellie had mixed feelings, but only because of what Cedric might say. 'Okay, boy, let's go take a look,' she said, heading for Sage's pen. Cedric's opinion was not going to dampen Ellie's overwhelming need to explore.

Sage didn't seem very eager to be going out again when she unlatched the gate.

chapter seven

The Wharf

Tik untied his orgo and jumped into his saddle with his usual look of confidence. Behind him, a fair few fishing boats were still moored; their sails swelling in the sea breeze. Anyone would have to admit that Tik was an impressive sight, parading on his snowy orgo near the harbour wall. With his arrogance, it was no surprise to anyone that his steed was the most well-groomed orgo in Port Harmony. Her white fleece was spotless and the black mottling perfect. It was obvious by his face that Tik was up to something.

'Rematch?' Tik smirked at Morrigan. He was most definitely addicted to the adrenaline rush of racing orgo. In fact, Tik probably didn't even race to win; to him, it was more about showing off. On the wharf, he could parade all he wanted unless shipments were arriving. Wardens were only stationed there at nightfall when supplies tended to be unloaded.

'You want to at least try to beat me this time?' Morrigan said, mocking her friend. 'Let's do it…if you can face another humiliation.'

Riding toward his friend, determination spread across Tik's face. Even if he couldn't beat Morrigan, he would be sure to try. The orgo that he rode took care with her footing. She was making sure that she didn't squash any of the hungry puffins that had gathered in the wharf. The colony of birds made their home around the harbour and tended to growl in human company. His orgo's caution around them was frustrating an eager Tik.

'Let's do it!' he said, as his balkutar, Toze, jumped into a safer position in front of his saddle.

Morrigan took her place next to Tik, ready to beat him. 'Well, the bigger they are…C'mon boy, they want showin' up again.' Petting her orgo, she smirked at Haylee.

Haylee watched from the saddle of Fuse — her own orgo — and enjoyed Morrigan's teasing of Tik. 'You never learn. Ever.'

'We will see,' Tik said, looking like nothing ever bothered him. 'What do you think Toze?'

Toze offered a piercing squeal as his reply, looking excited about the race.

Haylee laughed and realised how strange that felt. 'I will bet Fuse that you can't beat Morri,' she said, moving into position.

'It's a deal! Will be a pleasure taking your orgo off you.' Tik almost looked like he was trying to concentrate. He tipped his head from one side to the other, which looked peculiar. Like Morrigan, he then focused on Haylee, ready for the race.

With one hand, Haylee pointed at her friends. When she tugged on Fuse's reins, he grunted aloud to signal the start of the race. In a veil of ice, Tik and Morrigan sped away from the harbour. Haylee always enjoyed watching her friends do what they did best. Races around the wharf felt like home and she loved being close to the ocean. There was nothing more soothing than the fragrance of the breeze that gushed around her. Similarly, the rustling Port Harmony flags on the harbour wall filled Haylee with pride. Free from the restrictions of their lives, Haylee and her friends could enjoy themselves. Even if it was only for a little while.

'Woooooo!' cried Ditto, in an unenthusiastic sort of way. She never showed much passion for anything unless it involved real conflict—or fists.

Neck and neck, to begin with, Morrigan and Tik galloped across the wharf and towards the narrower streets. Fiercely defending her reputation, Morrigan was deliberate. Tik meanwhile, chose to wave as they moved out of sight, just in case anyone was watching.

People's adoration fed his ego much more than winning any race.

Haylee turned to Ditto when she trotted alongside her. 'So, while they're busy...let's talk. Any ideas what we do about Kayden?'

Ditto shrugged.

The fact that she didn't seem to care worried Haylee. Things would be much better without pointless attention right now. Their lives were difficult enough, and Kayden hounding them was not ideal. What bothered Haylee more, was that Ditto seemed to have become so talented at upsetting people.

'You need to care more Dit. I've said I don't blame you for Kayden. But your lack of interest is frightening. As well as your lack of discipline. It puts us all in danger.'

'Don't know what you're so bothered about!' Ditto's face remained still, but her tone was rude.

Steadying Fuse, Haylee was frustrated and her whole body felt rigid. 'Cedric's apprentice...you drew attention to us. Again! Right in the middle of a busy market. We were lucky the wardens were feeling lazy.'

Ditto grunted.

'That one...was on you,' Haylee went on. 'Your lack of self-control doesn't show much honour.'

Ditto stayed silent. Her expression didn't give much away either. Haylee couldn't tell if she didn't care or didn't want to admit the mistakes she had made. Maybe Ditto didn't even think they were mistakes.

Before she could give it further consideration, Tik and Morrigan came back into view. Morrigan first, as expected, followed by Tik who was still waving—because he could. Morrigan raced from between two huge shelters with competence. In no time, she was back on the wharf. With the snow having turned to slush, her orgo's feet slid on the ground, but Morrigan pushed him hard. She wouldn't be beaten—not by Tik.

Haylee watched, a little horrified, as Morrigan's steed slipped just a few feet from the finish mark. His leg buckled beneath him and he lost his footing. Skidding on the ice, he threw Morrigan from her saddle. As he crumpled under his own weight, he grunted and stumbled on top of her.

Morrigan was silent and appeared unconscious on the ground.

Without hesitation, Haylee dismounted and ran to help her friend. She grasped the orgo's reins and yanked them hard, to encourage him to stand up. Her efforts were of no use; Morrigan was trapped beneath him. Haylee tugged on the reins again, but the orgo still didn't respond.

'Morri!' Ditto squeaked, as though something had finally caused her to express emotion.

A dim voice slurred from under the fallen orgo. 'I'm okay. Just get him off me!'

Haylee tightened her hold on the reins. 'Yah!'

The animal twitched, then rose to his unsteady feet. By responding to Haylee's command, he allowed Morrigan to slide out from under him.

'Serves me right,' she groaned.

Haylee looked serious. 'Could have been worse. You need to be more careful. Don't push him too hard…know what ground you're on.'

The shadows cast around them caught Haylee's attention; making her uneasy. Coaching Morrigan had to wait. Gliders soared in the sky above, causing the sense of safety in the wharf to dissolve. Then, a noise in the distance made her look up. *Kayden,* she thought, when she heard the familiar snorts of orgo.

'Morri…can you ride?' Haylee called out. A shudder ran through her.

Morrigan shifted her head from side to side, examining the wharf. 'Of course! But…it's Kayden…isn't it? I'm staying.'

Wanting to protect her friends, Haylee disagreed. 'You all need to leave.'

'Fine by me,' Tik said, with Toze springing up and down in front of him. 'What about you though Hay?'

Haylee shook her head, then faced Ditto. 'I will be fine. But you all need to leave. Especially you Dit!'

Leaping back into her saddle, Morrigan said, 'I don't know about anyone else…but I'm ready for a fight.'

Haylee was persistent. 'I know you are…but not here…not now.'

'But—'

'Go! Now!' Haylee was beginning to feel annoyed that her friends hadn't left already.

The oncoming threat even concerned the puffins. In a flash of bright coloured beaks, they took to the sky together.

'Okay,' whinged Tik. 'We need to do as she says.'

Morrigan looked at Ditto for support, but with Kayden almost upon them, she couldn't carry on debating. Instead, she pulled on her reins, signalling their move. Together with Ditto and Tik, Morrigan sped away from the harbour. They disappeared into the winding streets in good time.

Alone, Haylee noticed an anxiousness building inside her. Without her friends, she was prepared to face up to Kayden alone. That way it would make less of a disturbance. But even so, she was still questioning her decision. Her priority was protecting Ditto, and she wasn't scared of Kayden. Although, she was outnumbered on this occasion. Fixing her cloak to conceal her face, Haylee led Fuse away from the harbour. She had a ridiculous hope that Kayden wouldn't recognise her.

Now on the wharf, Kayden stared in Haylee's direction and didn't speak at first. Slowly, they passed by each other, whilst the rangers rode behind their leader. Then, suddenly, Kayden halted his orgo.

'Haylee. How good to see you!' he said, looking smug.

Nauseous, Haylee turned to face him. She felt even worse when she saw the state of the slave that Kayden had brought with him. The girl looked sick; propped against her owner's back half conscious. Haylee couldn't understand how anyone would want to treat her that way.

'Well…can't really say the same!' Haylee released Fuse's reins as she spoke and turned to run the other way. All five assault rangers were already grouped on their orgo behind her, and Haylee had nowhere to run. The hateful, scraggly troop had her surrounded. She couldn't help thinking, that somehow, they had known how to find her all along. This was an ambush. If the slave behind Kayden was anything to go by, Haylee had no interest in being taken captive — or worse.

'What do you want? You plan on taking me as a slave too?' she said, wondering how she had been so easily outwitted. 'I'm on to you.

Saw the wardens you were paying off…to sell you innocent civilians. You're disgusting.'

Kayden looked thoughtful, which didn't suit him. 'Shut up Haylee. Ditto…I'm here for Ditto.' He dismounted and walked toward Haylee with a look of aggression, leaving his slave slumped over the back of his orgo.

'Out of luck.' Haylee offered a false smile, whilst trying to plot how she might save herself and Kayden's slave. 'Ditto's not here.'

'Maybe not…but she owes me for losing her last Dispute,' Kayden said, gesturing at his rangers. 'Find her!'

With undeniable compliance, two rangers pulled away on Kayden's orders. They left the wharf to renew their search.

No matter how much she analysed her predicament, Haylee still couldn't work out how to get away. 'Your ranger cheated. Ditto won't be paying anything!'

Kayden shook his head. 'Very well…have it your way.'

Before Haylee had a chance to react, sparks flashed around the remaining assault rangers' saddles. Nin! They were firing nin, and there was no way to block the nasty little beasts from hitting Fuse. All Haylee could do was watch, as dozens of insects slammed into the side of her orgo. Fuse's legs gave way as he succumbed to their poisonous fangs. He collapsed almost instantly. Nin killed their prey with next to no effort, then consumed it over the course of days.

Haylee felt like she had swallowed a scream but refused to show it. Spots of blood emerged from tiny wounds beneath Fuse's fur whilst she watched him die. She had owned him since around the time The Union was founded. They had an incredible bond. Seeing him murdered was impossible, but Haylee had her own life to consider too.

Kayden gripped his slave's tattered clothing and slid her off his steed. 'Perhaps now...you will think differently?'

The rangers nudged their orgo forward when Haylee fell to a kneeling position. She wondered how she had underestimated Kayden. For the first time in her life, Haylee was defenceless, and there was nobody around to help her. She had to escape, or she would die trying.

'Well...this is new!' said Kayden, looming over Haylee. 'The undefeatable Haylee...on her knees! Defeated.'

'Yep. Right before I kill you!' Haylee had no idea how she might.

Taking hold of their weapons, the assault rangers prepared to defend their leader. Sharp metal spikes covered the top of their maces. It was certain that they were designed to cause severe damage, to whatever they struck. Kayden's life had been threatened and the rangers were well armed to protect him.

'New toys?' said Haylee. 'Shall we play?' Leaping up between the rangers, she was ready to go down fighting. But Haylee reeled and fell forward, when a ranger behind her, swiped his weapon in response to her taunts.

'What did you say?' Kayden was desperate for Haylee to continue and would be enjoying her suffering.

Digging her hands into the sludge, Haylee span round. In a single move, she tossed clumps of dirt at the man who had attacked her. 'I wouldn't try that again if I were you!'

The ranger wiped the muck from his face and shrugged at his colleague on the other side of Haylee. Once more, they lunged with their maces, this time targeting Haylee's legs. With glazed expressions, they struck. Haylee's skin ripped against the spikes.

'What was that?' Kayden ridiculed. 'Didn't catch it.' He looked conceited, just standing whilst his troops did the hard work.

Her wounds were superficial, but without protection, Haylee felt as though her legs shattered. She plunged to the ground. Alone, she was no match for the rangers, and her injuries throbbed from the attack. Until that moment, she had never thought her death would be at the hands of Kayden. All three rangers moved closer on their orgo, waiting for Haylee to get up. They raised their maces, ready for attack.

Unexpectedly, Haylee saw the rangers shift their attention away from her. Something was bothering them. Haylee tried to stand, but the sting in her legs was unbearable. Moving the reddish hair from over her eyes, she saw something approaching fast in the distance.

Kayden looked up, shoving his slave in front of him as a shield. It was plain to see that she was barely able to stay upright. 'Looks like someone else wants to join the party.'

The rangers changed their formation, whilst someone galloped toward them on another orgo. Not a black orgo like theirs either, this one was more of a light brown. It was the girl from the market — Cedric's apprentice — and she was charging toward Kayden's army fearlessly. Haylee couldn't remember the girl's name, but she was sure she knew it. As the stranger rode between them, the rangers seemed disorientated. Without a strategy, they were stunned. Their orgo shook their dark fur wildly, stepping back from the threat.

'What are you doing?' Kayden's voice was piercing, as he barked orders at the rangers. 'Don't just look at them. Kill them!'

'C'mon!' shouted the apprentice, beckoning at Haylee. She had arrived from nowhere and it looked like she wanted to help. Her orgo — Cedric's orgo probably — growled at Kayden and his people.

Unable to organise her movements, Haylee crawled unsteadily between the assault rangers. They were busy doing absolutely nothing and this was her only chance of getting away alive. With her agony subsiding, she reached out her hand toward the orgo in front of her. At that exact point, as if coming back to life all of a sudden, the rangers all swiped at once. Haylee dodged them skillfully, whilst the apprentice's orgo reared and stamped hard to resist attack. She noticed that the apprentice looked saddened, gazing over Fuse's body a stone's throw away.

'Eyes on me!' Haylee wailed with everything she had. Finding her opportunity, she sprang forward and clenched the hand that waited for her.

It must have taken all the girl's strength to drag Haylee up her orgo. Wasting little time in snapping on her reins, the unexpected rescuer encouraged her orgo to hurry. Haylee tucked herself behind the saddle. By the time the rangers thought to fire their nin weapons again, their enemies were too far away.

Relieved, Haylee checked to see if Kayden would follow them, only to discover that he was beating his slave like she was worthless. In some way, he had convinced himself that the slave should suffer for Haylee's escape. Normally, Haylee was capable of controlling her feelings when things were not her concern. Yet she couldn't shake the overwhelming urge she had to rescue the slave. Knowing that she couldn't, made her angry in a way which she wasn't familiar with.

chapter eight

No Place Like Home

'You okay?'

Ellie knew it was a stupid question but was desperate to start a conversation. She continued to urge Sage up a particularly steep alleyway and inspected the rolling hills in the distance. Dense clusters of pine trees made their home in the landscape beyond Port Harmony. Ellie wondered if they may be safe in the woods for a while.

Haylee shifted into position and sat upright behind her rescuer. 'I almost had them!'

'Yep…I could see that!'

'You didn't see…anything!'

Ellie smiled; her companion had a reputation to protect. 'So…Where to now?'

'Keep goin'. Anywhere but here!'

Sage slowed to a trot; he was shattered from their ordeal but carried on up the incline. Snow had started to fall, and he had to take care with his footing.

'It's okay,' Ellie said. 'You take it easy for now boy!'

Haylee was quiet for a few moments, only offering occasional murmurs that sounded like a reaction to her injuries. They must have caused her some pain, and there were some obvious spots of blood across her boots. Still, the thick blobs of snowfall would soon wash it away.

'Sage hasn't got much more in him,' said Ellie. 'It's been a tough sort of day for him. Not as tough as yours though. I'm sorry, I saw your orgo.'

Haylee seemed to calm. 'It's okay. Take me home. To be honest…you were the last person I ever expected to turn up.'

'Well…just goes to show. You never know who your friends are,' Ellie said, wiping flakes of snow from her face. 'But home. Wh…what…about Kayden? Surely it's not safe?'

Haylee pointed her finger, showing Ellie the direction she needed to take. 'This way. No wardens this way. Kayden…he came to the harbour! He knew to find us there. Doubt he knows where I live. Few do. But it does look like he knew to find us on the wharf.'

'What does he want? What did Ditto do that's worth this? I heard him talking about her at the market earlier. And what on earth are those things?' Ellie gestured toward the objects circling in the sky above them.

'Wow, blue eyes!' Haylee teased. 'Don't you ask a lot of questions.'

'That's what they tell me,' said Ellie, wondering how Haylee had even noticed the colour of her eyes. 'Anyway…What are they?'

'Gliders! They come from Eklips…seem to follow Kayden around as some sort of protection. Like flies round orgo sh—'

'Got it! And Ditto…what did she do?'

'It's about honour. But back there…on the wharf. I think it was because the rangers don't like the sound of my mouth—'

'The what?'

'Or…maybe it's what comes out of it,' sniggered Haylee, seeming to be in good humour considering what she had endured. Maybe she wasn't that scary after all.

Ellie didn't yet see the funny side. 'She seems to have caused you a lot of trouble…Ditto, I mean.'

'Well…' said Haylee, pausing to grunt with pain. 'She's a friend. Sometimes…when you feel like you're in a fistfight with a whomphorn…and you're all alone. You turn around to realise you have a whole army of people to catch you if you fall. These are the people that matter. They…are your friends.'

A silence followed, whilst Ellie processed what she had heard. Haylee was undoubtedly faithful to her friends; Ellie had witnessed her almost sacrificing her own life for Ditto. She didn't know what could have happened if she hadn't arrived to help. In all likelihood, the situation with Kayden wouldn't have ended well. Having friends, like Haylee's group had in each other, was something Ellie had never experienced. Not that she remembered.

With her thoughts drifting, images of Pandra bothered Ellie. 'His slave though...I. Well...I can tell why people don't commit many crimes.'

'It's strange. Don't often see women. Kayden's slaves are usually men. Seems like he is making some sort of point bringing that one here. Whenever I've seen him want to show force...it has always been with a male slave.'

'She looked awful.'

'Awful wasn't the word in my head,' Haylee said, laughing again. 'Oh...her injuries. He doesn't treat the men like that. Kayden doesn't have any respect for women. He hates them. He despises the fact that Rada is head of The Union too. I know that. But even though that might explain why she looks the way she does...it doesn't explain why he chose to bring that particular slave here. Why her?'

'Pandra?'

'What?'

'Her name is Pandra,' Ellie said. 'I heard him at the market. Kayden...he was at Evan's stall.'

'Was he? So...anyway. How come you're crazy enough to get involved? Is being an apprentice not exciting enough for you? What's your name anyway, blue eyes?'

'Now who's asking a lot of questions? It's Ellie. How did you know I was an apprentice?'

Pointing down a narrow slope Haylee said, 'You're Cedric's new apprentice.'

The haze around them distracted Ellie. With the weather worsening, it was difficult to make out the street ahead. Navigating took a lot of concentration. But still, she was intrigued by her exchange with Haylee.

'You know Cedric?' she asked.

Haylee giggled fleetingly. 'I live over there. And yes…we have a history.' She directed Ellie further into the darkened passage but didn't offer the answer Ellie was hoping for.

As usual, Ellie couldn't control her interest. 'How do you know him?'

'Here is fine.' Haylee dodged Ellie's question for the second time. 'Listen…you're alright…thanks, Blue.'

Ellie smiled, pulling back on the reins as Haylee jumped from Sage. Her legs didn't seem that bad after all. Either that or Haylee was very good at hiding her pain.

'Any time,' Ellie said. 'Wasn't expecting to save any lives today.'

With eyebrows raised, Haylee pulled an awkward expression. The thought of being saved by an apprentice clearly didn't fill her with enthusiasm. For warmth, Haylee wrapped her arms around her body. She hobbled toward a larger building than most, offering a half-hearted wave.

'You know this doesn't make us friends, right?' she said, moving into the dark.

Ellie countered, smirking. 'Not even close.'

'Not possible Blue!'

'Nope!' Ellie realised where she was as their exchange ended. The tighter streets like the one she was on, ran behind bigger buildings like Cedric's barn. She immediately understood how to get home. The barn wasn't that far, but she would need to take care. Snow had created a thick white covering all around them, and it was still falling hard.

With a twitch on Sage's reins, Ellie cantered back down the passage. 'C'mon fella, let's get you home.'

Taking little time to reach the main streets of the town, Ellie encouraged Sage to increase his pace. She was tired, and it had been a day that she couldn't find words to describe. All she knew, was that the thought of her rickety bed was tempting. Returning to the barn as quickly as possible was all she wanted.

Dazed, Ellie reflected on how her day had transformed. Hours before, the morning had seemed like any other for an orgo-keeper. Yet since then, things had changed. She hadn't intended for any of the day's events to happen either—they just had. For quite some time, Ellie had tried to get Haylee's attention, not to mention Evan's. This day had been beyond her expectations, and she wondered if Haylee would talk to her again.

Ellie saw the barn in the distance, but something stirred inside her. There was an ugly feeling as the building came into view. Something wasn't right, but Ellie couldn't work out what. With Sage beginning to snort loudly, she trusted her intuition and approached with caution.

'Steady boy,' she whispered, trying to calm Sage.

Two black orgo burst from inside the barn as Ellie got closer; assault rangers in their saddles. 'Yah!' screamed Ellie as she galloped toward them instinctively.

Before she could catch up, the rangers were gone, but pursuing them wasn't Ellie's priority. With Sage slowing as they neared the opening to their home, Ellie dismounted and rushed inside. Then, an uncontrollable sadness hit her when she entered. Lumps of wood and debris were strewn across the floor and orgo were rearing in their enclosures. Some of the animals—six altogether—lay on the ground lifeless; their pens destroyed.

'No,' Ellie cried. 'No!'

Undoubtedly, the animals had been killed the same way Haylee's had earlier. They must have been. There were specks of blood in their fleeces, and they had obviously died quickly.

But why here? Why attack the barn? Ellie thought. *What did they want?*

'Cedric!' she said, with tears rolling onto her cheeks at the sight of slaughtered orgo. Wasting no time, she began searching for her employer, wondering if Cedric was the reason for the rangers attacking them. Yet she didn't understand why he might be. Ellie searched the barn thoroughly, tossing the remains of the timber pens aside. Cedric was nowhere to be seen, and she hoped that was a good thing.

'Kayden!' Junkyard's voice was familiar, and he was standing at the opening behind her.

Ellie span round, dropping the logs she held. 'How did you know?'

'Saw the rangers!' Junkyard sounded dismayed. His head lowered, as though he was paying respect to the fallen orgo. By reputation, Junkyard was no animal lover, but even he would be horrified at this sight. Moving past the brown corpse of an orgo, Ellie wept. Her sorrow was impossible to contain any longer. She didn't even know what was upsetting her more; the fact that Cedric was missing, or the murder of some of her beloved animals.

Junkyard stepped inside the barn, his expression full of compassion. 'They were too fast El. By the time I saw them, they were already leaving. Then I saw you.'

'Cedric?' Ellie asked, grabbing hold of Junkyard and sinking her face into his dirty overalls. She couldn't remember when she had ever felt so powerless.

Junkyard squeezed. 'It's okay…he wasn't here.'

A deep breath caught Ellie by surprise. The relief helped her find some clarity. Releasing her grip on Junkyard, Ellie looked toward Ash's pen. Clumsily striding across the wreckage, she could tell that Ash had been a target. Splintered wood was strewn where the enclosure once stood. Ellie set eyes on a grey carcass in the dirt as she peered across, and she fumbled with haste. Her head felt as though it would burst.

'Thaw,' she called when she saw the pup nuzzling its mother, desperate for a reaction. 'It's alright boy.'

Ellie scooped up the baby orgo and stuffed him in the top of her overalls for warmth. Crouching beside his mother, she reached out and brushed her hand over Ash's wool. Ellie felt destroyed. *How could anyone do this to such innocent creatures?* she thought. She stayed with Ash for a few minutes, hoping that the pup may still live in her honour. Thaw trembled against her skin, but he was still warm and that gave him a good chance of survival.

'Can you help it?' Junkyard asked when Ellie emerged from Ash's pen.

Drenched in her own tears, Ellie fought to speak. 'They better hope I can!'

'That's a fresh look for you. Not sure if I like it.' Junkyard held out his arm and grinned in a forced way. His tactless comments were oddly soothing. Junkyard was known for his unexpected humour at inappropriate moments. Yet somehow, his words were a comfort. Besides, Ellie knew how comical she must look; still wearing torn overalls. Not to mention the tears on her face that merged with the grime from Junkyard's outfit.

'Here…old man,' she said, wiping her face on her sleeve. 'Make yourself useful and look after him.' Ellie pulled Thaw from her clothes, holding him in Junkyard's direction.

Junkyard, on the other hand, looked stunned. 'What am I supposed to do with that?'

'Put him in the brooder,' Cedric said, entering the barn behind his friend. 'He will be fine in there.'

Ellie felt angry with how calm Cedric appeared. 'Where were you?'

Her comments were greeted with silence, as Cedric refused to answer. It was strange to watch him, as he struggled inside his barn, and began clutching at pieces of timber. He was tidying up. No questions or blame — tidying.

Furious at his response, Ellie rushed to the corner of the room. Made from roughly cut log pieces, the brooder was a small enclosed area with burners positioned either side. It was there for emergencies — when orgo couldn't care for their own pups—and it provided much-needed warmth. Ellie had never used it before. Carefully placing Thaw inside, she closed the hinged lid to secure him. Orgo didn't take long to start regulating their own body temperature. Thaw was fine in the brooder for a little while. After all, in the wild orgo had to care for themselves at just a few days old.

'We need to inform the wardens,' Junkyard suggested.

'No!' Cedric argued. 'There is no need. No point.'

Junkyard scratched his cheek. 'We can't let him just—'

'Leave it alone,' Cedric barged in.

As their conversation ended, Ellie thoughts sharpened, and she turned toward her bed. The area didn't look like it had been disturbed. Instead, the assault rangers had sent whatever their message was by slaying orgo. Nevertheless, she needed to protect her stuff. Ellie pulled the chest filled with her possessions from underneath the rickety frame. She unclipped the buckles efficiently. Reaching inside, Ellie then removed a single lump of rock that fit inside her palm.

'Why did they attack us?' she grilled, sliding the item into one of the pockets of her overalls. Ellie was sure Cedric must know something, or he would seem more shocked.

Cedric continued without words. Slowly, he struggled to pick up objects. Junkyard joined him in the effort to clean up the mess.

Ellie clutched one of her shabby blankets and clambered back to Ash, groaning along the way. Covering the orgo was all she could do as a mark of respect. Again, she paused whilst she made sure the cloth covered Ash, bowing her head. The urge to act was eating away at her. Stepping over the remains of the pen, Ellie headed for the exit.

Sage was still waiting obediently outside; his fleece glistening with white patches. This had become Ellie's fight too now, and she wasn't about to let Kayden's people get away with what they had done. Whatever he wanted with Ditto may not be her concern, but this definitely was. She unhooked her saddle which was already buried in snow. Then, she tossed it aside and climbed onto Sage's back. Maybe she was better riding bareback anyway, like Evan had suggested. Either way, she needed to move fast now. As her fingers took hold of the fur around the base of Sage's neck, Ellie considered her next move sensibly. She was determined to not let her sentiment get in the way of her judgement, but it probably would.

'Where do you think you're off to?' Junkyard wasn't really that interested in her answer whilst he was sweeping together a mound of wood.

Refusing to reply, Ellie looked over at Cedric. He looked like he was in a world of his own and was making no effort to stop her. Her feet dug into Sage's side, and they galloped away from the barn.

chapter nine

Rada's Decree

'My lady,' Nolan said, entering the Throne Room. 'You sent for me?'

Rada slammed shut a panel within the arm of her shadow-like throne. The warden commander appeared composed, marching with an air of confidence. It was impossible to tell, that Rada had told Nolan she would face a public trial, for her failure to apprehend the Renegades. A judgement that would not end well for her.

With a sentry posted either side of her and still masked, Rada glared at Nolan. 'Indeed. You have been reassigned.'

Nolan's feet appeared to glide across the grey tiled floor, and she was choosing to inspect the elaborate carvings that adorned the walls. The etchings that depicted Scorr Tanta's architecture were the only real decoration. That was, apart from the ornate chandeliers hanging from the ceiling. Globular in shape, their dark wiry structure contained several dangling candles.

Altogether, six of them vividly spread light through the room.

'Reassigned?' Nolan asked, still gazing around.

Grinning, Rada noticed Nolan sigh through relief. 'The Renegades can be found in Eklips. Kayden is responsible. I'm certain of it now.'

'And what do you need from me?'

'You will go there,' continued Rada. 'If my sources are correct…Kayden isn't there at this time. Go to Eklips, find them, and destroy anyone who stands in your way. Let it burn, so Kayden had nothing to go back to.'

Her orders had concerned Nolan and the fear could be seen in her face. 'Yes, My Lady, and what if your sources are wrong?'

Tired of her spineless warden commander, Rada lifted in her seat. 'They're not wrong! Now leave, before I change my mind. This is your only chance to save your pathetic life. You need to work quickly and get to Eklips before Kayden returns.'

'Yes, My Lady.' Nolan span and hurried away, passing one of her wardens, who entered the room as she made her exit.

'Aah,' said Rada. 'You have come.'

The warden was a new recruit and bounced into the room with enthusiasm. 'My Lady, I was told to report to you.'

'You have been told about your mission to Eklips?' Rada spoke softly to the warden. He was so young, but she was certain he would not think of failing her.

The warden nodded.

Making sure her instructions were clear, Rada stepped down from her throne toward him. 'You are aware, that if we do not locate these Renegades, it is your responsibility to ensure success? To make sure there are no consequences of an unprovoked invasion. You have been told of these orders?'

'But...My Lady. I have to say...respectfully...I am not completely comfortable with the orders I have. Should we not be certain of the Renegades' whereabouts before we invade Eklips?'

Rada removed her mask, exposing her auburn hair that coiled around her neck. Curls gently sprang against the top of her cloak. With a reassuring smile that spread from her blood red lips into blushed cheeks, she considered her response. The warden would find the orders she referred to difficult to follow, and she had to be sure that he wouldn't falter. If revealing her true self guaranteed success, then showing her face would be worthwhile. This was a time where her humanity was essential.

'Let me be clear,' she said, stroking the warden's cheek. 'I am certain that the Renegades can be found in Eklips. But there is always a chance of mistakes, and if this mission fails, you are to follow your own separate orders.'

The warden appeared to be analysing the scar on Rada's neck. 'These orders come from you, My Lady?'

'They do. Of course.'

Rada attempted to position her head in a way that made her feel less exposed. The warden's prying eyes glared at the wound from her past, dredging up a pain she preferred to not remember.

'If the Renegades aren't in Eklips, there will be friction,' she went on. 'A conflict we would be wise to avoid. Kayden won't take kindly to an attack on his territory. I need to ensure things don't get worse.' Rada was choosing her words wisely. She needed the man before her to engage in her plan.

The warden looked puzzled but froze whilst Rada's fingers explored his face. 'I assume the warden commander is not aware of the contingency?'

Rada groaned. 'No, and nor will she ever need to know if she apprehends the outlaws. Which she will...that is what our sources have told us. But sources are sometimes not as accurate as I would like. I can't trust everyone. Not the way I am trusting you.'

'Sources?'

'There is much you don't know, but you know what you must...to make sure we are successful. Like you said…you are my contingency.'

The look on his face made it clear that the warden still didn't feel at ease, with what Rada was expecting of him. 'I see,' he said, nodding in agreement anyway.

Rada's hand slipped onto the warden's arm and clenched with force. 'Go to Eklips. If this information is right…follow the same instructions that your commander has just received. Burn it. Destroy it all. There must be nothing left for Kayden.'

The warden finally took his eyes away from Rada's scar when her hand started crushing his arm. He mustn't have expected such strength from her.

'And if the information is wrong?' he queried.

Rada laughed purposefully. 'Then you apologise, of course. And follow the contingency as you call it.'

'Yes, My Lady. But what will become of her? The commander.'

'Not your concern,' Rada said, releasing the warden. 'She knew what she was getting herself into. It was her responsibility to get me the Renegades. You…if you follow my orders to my satisfaction…will progress through the ranks quicker than you could ever imagine. This stays between us…am I clear? It stays that way. Or you will see the same fate as your commander.'

The warden bowed his head, muttering, 'Perfectly clear, My Lady. I understand.'

'Do everything you can to find these Renegades,' Rada ordered, as her cloak swept behind her and she returned to her throne. 'Whichever way…as long as you do what is asked…things look good for you.'

'Is that all, My Lady?' The warden had already started moving away.

Relaxing back into her seat, Rada felt confident in her ability to manipulate the youthful warden. 'Yes…that will be all.'

chapter ten

In Search of a Solution

Ellie's knuckles throbbed from banging on the door so hard. Leaving no time for anyone to emerge, she thumped again constantly until it creaked open.

'Didn't expect to see you here!' Evan squinted through the entrance to focus. She was the last person he would have expected.

Barging passed him, Ellie stormed into the house where she had left Haylee earlier. She was desperate and didn't care how rude she seemed. Once inside, a large simple room confronted her. They were all there — Morrigan, Tik, and Ditto — all except Haylee.

Sprawled on rolled up fleeces dotted around the floor, the group sat bolt upright when they saw Ellie enter their candlelit home. They were also surprised to see her. Ditto already looked edgy, and Ellie noticed she had a new cloak on. Haylee however, was nowhere to be seen. Beyond the others, through a small opening, Ellie could just make out a darker, more secluded chamber. She wondered if that was where she might find their leader.

'Haylee…' Ellie said, glancing at Evan. 'Your sister, where is she?'

Whilst he secured the main door, Evan looked alarmed. 'She's out back. Are you okay?'

Unsure whether rushing into the rear area was her best move, Ellie didn't reply and stood her ground. Haylee's people hadn't been her biggest fans so far.

Morrigan grumbled. 'How did you know to find us here?'

'She brought me home,' a familiar voice said. 'After helping me get away from Kayden.'

Wrapped in a single sheet, Haylee emerged from the separate room at the rear of the house, stopping Ellie in her tracks. In her hand, she held her tunic that dripped over the bare floor. She must have been bathing after her ordeal with Kayden; her hair was soaking. The wounds on Haylee's legs were obvious, but they had stopped bleeding. They didn't appear to be giving Haylee any real trouble.

'The orgo,' Ellie spluttered, still short of breath. 'Cedric's…they attacked Cedric's. Kayden's people. They killed orgo.'

'Cedric's?' Haylee gasped. 'Why Cedric's?'

'That's what I want to know.'

Morrigan walked between them and gawped at Haylee. 'Why did you bring her here? Her?

Here? What…we tell everyone where we live now?'

Haylee thrust her finger in Ellie's direction. 'Blue helped me,' she said, defending her actions. 'After everything that happened in the market, she came. She did. She didn't have to. She is probably the single reason I'm alive. I trust her. You would do well to show her some respect.'

Morrigan turned away, shrugging. 'You told us to leave!'

'Yeah, you did Hay!' Tik added.

Ellie gazed at Haylee's friends. She hated that their opinion of her was still so important. But in many ways, it was crucial if Ellie wanted to connect with Haylee. As her eyes wandered in Tik's direction, Ellie noticed the fleece closest to him wriggling. Intrigued, she studied it for a moment.

'I need you,' she insisted. 'Or you need me…or…or…we need each other. We must stop him. He needs to leave Port Harmony. Like now. And we need to make him leave.'

'No-one will be doing anything,' Evan said.

Haylee scowled. 'What do you suggest big brother?'

'We keep ourselves to ourselves. Lay low here for a while. He's unlikely to find us here and will return to Eklips soon enough.'

Picking up another scrap of material from the floor, Haylee started rubbing her hair. 'That's it then…we hide? We can't do that forever…we've got work to do. Tonight.'

Evan looked serious when he placed himself between Haylee and the others. Ellie became conscious of how calm she felt whenever she looked at him. It was as though everything would somehow be okay, even though nothing was. Still inspecting the fleece where Tik was sitting, she saw Toze's head pop from beneath. At least there was an explanation for the fabric's mysterious movements. Springing away from his owner, the little bundle of fluff bounded toward her.

'None of that matters Hay,' Evan said, sounding determined. 'Not if it gets any of you killed.'

Ellie stiffened when Toze leapt onto her. 'None of what matters?' she questioned, feeling like she was missing chunks of the conversation. Tik's ape pet gripped to the material around her middle, and Ellie cringed.

Silence followed. It was an uncomfortable quiet that made Ellie feel uneasy. Nobody could answer her question. Well, nobody wanted to. She looked at Evan, hoping he would talk next, but it was obvious he wasn't about to. Toze's fuzzy finger started to poke at her belly where Haylee had torn her overalls earlier. His stubby nails scratching at her flesh felt even more disturbing than the unexplained lull in the conversation.

Ditto broke the awkwardness and took to her feet. 'It's me he wants. We can give him me. Problem solved.'

'We're not giving him anything,' said Haylee, looking slightly amused by the idea. 'And we're not hiding either.'

Evan's expression was brimming with disgust, and he marched out of the room toward the back of the house. 'Then you all deserve whatever is coming.'

Haylee didn't seem concerned by her brother's outburst. She continued to dry her hair whilst Ditto paced up and down the room. Tik and Morrigan meanwhile, looked like they had engaged in some sort of telepathic conversation of their own. Their eyes were locked onto each other, and subtle shifts in their faces were plain to see.

'You all…live here…together?' Ellie quizzed. She was trying to cut through the unbearable struggle to find common ground.

'Yep,' laughed Tik. 'One big unhappy family, living very unhappily together. Unhappily ever after.'

'Shut up,' Morrigan screeched aloud.

'Alright listen,' Haylee said, her tone commanding respect. 'Morri. You and Dit go to Cedric's with Blue. Give them some help. If they have already attacked there, they won't be back anytime soon. Meanwhile, Tik…we got work to do.'

'Who's Blue?' Tik looked confused.

Morrigan obviously wasn't happy with the instructions. 'But—'

'You have a better plan?' Haylee cut her short, heading into the back room.

'Er…not now. No! But I say we face him…show him he is not welcome in this place.'

'You see,' Ellie said, trying to ignore the—now very annoying—balkutar prodding her cheek. 'Even Precious agrees with me. We should make a stand and send him packin'.'

Morrigan's eyes widened. 'Did she just agree with me? Wait…did she call me Precious?'

'She did.' Tik spoke with laughter amongst his words. 'Not something I'd have ever called you.'

'That barn…Cedric…it's where we get our orgo,' bellowed Haylee from the distance. 'We need to offer our help.' She seemed concerned for the wellbeing of Cedric and his animals; even if it was for selfish reasons.

'Hay…I get it!' said Morrigan. 'But I still say it's time to fight. I need a good excuse to kill him. Now I have one?'

Not knowing where to look, Ellie vaguely saw Haylee dropping the sheet that covered her and pick up what looked like a clean set of clothes. Ellie wasn't certain, but the injuries she glimpsed across Haylee's back, looked almost as bad as the ones on Kayden's slave. She wondered if they were wounds sustained in The

Dispute, or if something else was to blame. Either way, they must have caused Haylee agony at some point or another.

'I agree with her. Can we not get them to leave? Besides, someone needs to get Pandra away from him too.' Ellie spoke in a nasal tone. Tik's pet had decided her nose was of interest, waggling it around between his fingers.

Re-entering the main room, Haylee sniffed. 'We might die trying Blue. They're armed, and if nothing else...our orgo wouldn't survive. Look what happened to Fuse...and the animals at your place. We do need to do something about Pandra though.'

'Whoa wait! Who's Pandra?' quizzed Tik, both hands rubbing his face. 'I'm lost.'

'The slave that Kayden has dragged with him,' Haylee filled in. 'Blue, everything in good time. Believe me...we will save Pandra. For now, you need to go with Morri. Check on Cedric.'

'Ellie,' Evan called out, from wherever he was. 'You shouldn't get involved. Go back to your life.'

'Isn't that what I'm sayin'?' snapped Haylee.

'But I am involved,' Ellie said. She lowered her voice when she realised Evan was closer than she had thought. 'We can work together.'

'This isn't your fight,' Evan insisted.

Tik raised his hand. 'Sorry...really sorry. Still lost. So...Pandra is Kayden's slave...I get that one now. But who is this?' he asked, swinging his finger in Ellie's direction. 'Thought she was called Blue…and now it's Ellie?'

'It's Ellie,' Ellie said, trying to add clarity.

Haylee threw Ellie a smile that looked full of warmth. 'I say Blue suits you better.'

'If you get involved…you're as crazy as they are,' Evan said, moving even closer to Ellie and glaring at her. 'This isn't your fight.'

Not certain if Evan was trying to protect her, or whether this was another form of rejection, Ellie felt frustrated. 'It is my fight. His people came to my home…destroyed some of the animals. And why? For no reason…that's why? He needs to go.'

'No reason,' Morrigan said, in a sort of grunting fashion.

Another odd silence followed. Ellie was growing tired of the tiny primate mauling her face through his unbearable curiosity. Whilst he stretched the skin on her forehead, Ellie lifted her hand and flicked Toze discreetly with her finger. He didn't seem to flinch. Checking that nobody was watching, Ellie struck him a little harder. Startled, Toze squeaked loudly and bounced off her, rushing back to Tik.

'What's up little guy?' Tik spoke to the animal with an affection Ellie couldn't quite understand.

Turning her thoughts back to her dilemma, Ellie couldn't help but wonder what was holding Haylee back. Surely, she wanted Kayden out of Port Harmony, after what his people had done already. Ellie understood how dangerous he was but was certain that gave Haylee even more reason to want to fight back.

In no time, Ellie's contemplation was disturbed. Behind the building, she heard orgo snorting and Haylee's group looked troubled. When Ellie gazed around, everyone's expressions had frozen on their faces. The sudden noise had startled them. They all listened intently, but as quickly as it had started, the sound stopped.

Morrigan marched toward where the disturbance had come from. 'I've had enough of this. After everything we have suffered…everything Kayden has done. Still…we do nothing. The orgo might talk more sense. I'll see what all their fuss was about.' With that, she disappeared into the darkness of the back room.

Ellie detected a sense of despair in Morrigan's voice. She knew she was angry at Kayden, but there was something else. Morrigan's loathing of Kayden seemed to be built on much more than had happened in that one day. Whatever it was, forced a sadness to surface.

'Suffered?' Ellie stared at Evan, hoping for an explanation. 'Am I missing something?'

'Don't!' Haylee said, directing her brother. 'Morri wouldn't want you to.'

Evan sighed. 'Her parents. They were sent into slavery...in Eklips. As far as we can tell...they're dead now.'

'Evan!' Haylee boomed, glowering at her brother.

In a few words, Evan had offered a sort of transparency to the pain Ellie had sensed in Morrigan. There was little doubt why she wanted to see Kayden undone. With her eyes itching, Ellie held in her sorrow. After seeing Pandra earlier, she wanted to hold Morrigan tightly and comfort her. To lose her parents that way was awful, and to not know for sure whether they were even alive, must be torture.

'But she goes there...with you,' Ellie said. 'Doesn't she? The Dispute. They say you all compete in The Dispute.'

Haylee forced a rumbling sound.

'Not me,' Evan reacted. 'But they do. When her parents were taken, Haylee took Morri in. Offered her a home here. Then gave her the chance to go and look for her parents, by entering that so-called sport. That way, there was a reason for her to go to Eklips.'

Ellie took time to digest what she was hearing. 'But?'

'Evan!' Haylee tried hard to stop her brother talking.

'But she never found them,' Evan went on. 'So...over time...she has come to the conclusion they have been killed.'

'How old was she?' Ellie asked. 'When they took her parents.' She was ignoring how much Haylee wanted to put an end to Evan's disclosure.

Evan looked down. 'About fourteen I think. Her parents were amongst the first sent into slavery after The Union.'

Seeing them all in a different light, Ellie was finding things hard to process. Haylee was devoted to her friends; that much she had already known. But now she was learning the lengths Haylee went to, looking after those close to her. Morrigan's anguish was much clearer too. It explained a lot about the uncertainty that Ellie had sensed from her whenever they had crossed paths. Passionate and strong, yet conflicted and fragile, Morrigan's trust would not be easy to earn. Ellie appreciated why for the first time.

Behind them was an abrupt rustling noise. 'Orgo are fine,' said Morrigan, scuttling back in Haylee's direction undetected. 'So...are we goin' to Cedric's then? Why is everyone still standing here?'

Haylee flinched. 'Exactly.' She looked stunned, probably hoping Morrigan hadn't heard Evan.

'Well…I'm with you,' said Ellie, trying to nudge along the process.

Evan threw on his cloak. 'Right! Do what you need to do. You always do. All of you. Ellie…don't say I didn't warn you.'

Ellie shivered when he stared at her. Evan's expression suggested she was being reprimanded, and she didn't like it one bit. Rather than feeling safe in his presence, she felt like she had been thrown amongst a pack of whomphorn. Even though Ellie wanted to unite with Haylee and the others, she hoped that wouldn't sacrifice any possible friendship with Evan. She offered him a smile, then turned to face Morrigan.

'Stop lecturing her Evan…Blue's one of us now, whether you like it or not.' Haylee sounded severe. 'Where are you goin' anyway?'

'Clear my head,' Evan barked.

'Thought you wanted to hide?'

Evan's eyes appeared to jump from their sockets. 'It's not me he is after. Why would I need to hide?'

'No!' said Haylee. 'It's your family and friends he is after. And, that's not enough for him. Are you forgetting he just attacked Cedric's? If you want to protect Blue so badly…help us!'

His sister's bawling was lost on Evan, and he made his way to the door. 'I'm aware he attacked Cedric's. But my family and friends seem to be asking for trouble. Ellie too…she has made up her own mind. This is not my battle. I didn't ask for it.'

'Fine! Morri…Dit…You're still going with Blue!'

'Isn't that what I said a minute ago?' Morrigan said.

'Yep,' grunted Ditto.

Together, Morrigan and Ditto disappeared into the back room. Their orgo were at the back and they were doing as they were told. Meanwhile, Evan stormed away, banging the door as he went. Ellie hadn't seen him that mad before, and her overwhelming curiosity started to take hold. She rushed after him.

'Blue…where are you going? Eyes…on…me!' Ellie heard Haylee use that phrase earlier when they were at the wharf. From watching their races, she also knew that Haylee used the phrase to command her people's attention, or if she was issuing a new instruction.

'Sage is out front.' Ellie offered, to appease her.

'Go with Morri and Dit,' said Haylee. 'You will be safe with them. Don't even think about following my brother.'

Torn, Ellie knew she needed to check on the orgo, and especially Cedric. He had been so good to her. Yet there was a bigger part of her that wanted to comfort Evan. She had no intention of following Haylee's friends when she left.

chapter eleven

Breathing Space

Evan wrapped his arms around his body as he walked down the street. The air outside was getting much colder. From behind him, he just about heard someone calling out his name.

'Evan! Stop! Wait!'

Something inside Evan seemed to force a grin on his face, and he turned to find Ellie cantering behind him on her orgo. She was riding bareback like he had suggested; even though he hadn't been at all serious when he had. There was something about Ellie's voice that was almost familiar. He had been aware of it since he met her, but for some reason, it felt more obvious when she called out to him. Not understanding what it was, frustrated Evan. Distracted by the dense mat of snow surrounding them, it was hard to gather his thoughts.

'No saddle,' he said, giggling and protecting his eyes from the weather. 'Suits you.'

Ellie stopped her orgo beside him, throwing a slight grin. 'Where are you goin'?'

'Need to clear my head.'

Ellie thrust her arm forward. 'I got that, precious. But where?'

'Anywhere.' Out of instinct, Evan took her hand, mounting the orgo and sitting behind her.

'We need to find Kayden. I need your help.' Ellie's voice was beginning to sound croaky and tired.

'And what exactly do you plan on doing when you find him?'

Ellie looked thoughtful. 'No idea. But we can't let him go around killing. It's not right.'

Whilst he pondered Ellie's determination, Evan realised that there was something about her that confused him. She always seemed naïve to the difficulties they faced living in Port Harmony. It was like she had spent a long time wearing blinkers. Now she was directly affected by Kayden, the strength oozing from Ellie was admirable. Then again, Evan wasn't sure if it was a strength or an innocent foolishness. Whatever it was, had begun to compel him to support her.

'I need time to think girl,' he said, softly. 'I'm not saying I won't help…but right now…I have no idea how.'

'That will do for now,' Ellie replied, snatching the offer. 'C'mon Sage, I know just the place.'

With almost blizzard-like conditions, Evan placed his arms around Ellie, allowing her to lead the way. Her courage made it easy to understand why Haylee had trusted her so easily. Evan just hoped Ellie's resolve didn't end up making her as reckless as his sister. With it being so difficult to see anything through the snowfall, Evan had little choice but to trust Ellie too. There did at least, seem to be a purpose to the direction she was taking.

'So,' Ellie said, whilst they meandered through Port Harmony's tighter streets. 'Kayden...he frightens you?'

'Haylee. It's Haylee that frightens me.'

Ellie stayed quiet. From the looks of things, she was monitoring the cloud of gliders flying right above them. They were unpredictable, menacing animals, who flew erratically to intimidate anyone below. Gliders were one of nature's most evil creations, and Ellie was probably trying to work out their purpose.

'Kayden is who he is,' Evan continued. 'And who he is, is dangerous. He is the leader of Eklips. A place best avoided. But Haylee...and the others...they seem to have found ways to upset people like him. Now, we have those hideous flying mammals filling Port Harmony's skies.'

'He almost killed her,' Ellie said, shifting her focus away from the gliders. 'He almost killed your sister. And he did kill orgo...Haylee's and the ones where I work. I don't understand why that doesn't make you want to stand up to him.'

'I don't expect you to. And I've already said…Let me think.'

Evan realised they were already passing the edge of town. They were heading toward the hills beyond Port Harmony. Ellie somehow knew much faster routes through the town than he did. They hadn't even passed any wardens along the way.

Impenetrable snow made it impossible to see much at all, and the orgo carrying them became sluggish as they struggled up the slopes. Pressing onward, Ellie was determined to reach wherever it was she was taking them. Her orgo, Sage, was not as enthusiastic. With each unsteady footstep, he was finding things difficult.

'We need to go the rest of the way on foot,' Ellie hollered, as Sage stopped in his tracks.

Evan straightened his cloak and tunic when he dismounted. 'The rest of the way to where?'

Tittering in a slightly childish way, Ellie jumped from Sage and stumbled into Evan. Resting her hands on his chest, she glanced up at him. Her smile was infectious. Appearing nervous, she reached up and brushed Evan's chin with her fingertips. Her eyes were entrancing, and her touch hard to resist.

Evan felt like he sank into the ice when Sage intruded by snorting obnoxiously. Turning away, Ellie also seemed reluctant when she went to comfort her orgo.

'Okay boy,' she said. 'It's okay. You rest here a while, we won't be long.'

As Ellie petted Sage, he nudged into her with his snout. The bond they had was remarkable. Ellie sniggered again, ruffling the orgo's fur. Orgo always had a good relationship with their owners — they had to — but there was something much more than that with Ellie and Sage.

'Right,' Ellie said, curtly. 'This way. Wait for us here Sage.'

Taunting Evan, Ellie ran into the snow ahead. Without hesitation Evan followed, slipping and sliding along the way. In the meantime, Ellie almost vanished into the white fog in front of him. It was demanding work moving at such speed up the hillside, but Evan had no choice if he wanted to keep up.

'C'mon, precious,' Ellie called. 'It's not far.'

Evan wondered where Ellie found her strength, as he chased behind her up the rugged path. Pines and cedar were scattered along the route she took. Their green, spiky branches drooped under the weight of the snow that hung on them. Ellie darted between the trees with ease; watching her was draining. They seemed to run for a few minutes when Evan noticed that the snowstorm was easing. It was much easier to make out their surroundings. The ground had become more even, and they were obviously near the top of the hills.

The trees appeared to rustle all at once. High overhead, the upper branches danced, as though an incredible force was shaking them all at the same time. Ellie screeched so loudly it must have disturbed people in town. Running faster, Evan sped to find out what was causing her distress.

'Get them off!' Ellie shrieked. 'Get them off me…Evan…please!'

There were dozens of balkutar dropping from the trees around Ellie, which made Evan grin. Some of them grabbed onto her, inquisitively examining the stranger in their woods. Ellie looked hilarious, spinning round, sinking further into the snow. Her arms were flapping like she wanted to take flight. One of the animals held its hands over Ellie's eyes, whilst others tugged at the arms of her overalls, probably wondering if it was her fur.

'Ellie,' Evan laughed. 'Stand still.'

'Get off. Get off!' Ellie discounted his suggestion and continued to twirl.

Trying again, Evan barely contained his amusement. 'Ellie!'

'Help! Get them…off…me.' Still, Ellie carried on, dithering about, unable to escape her dilemma. The balkutar were crawling all over her, and the more Ellie fought, the more curious they became. Forcing its way through the rip in Ellie's overalls, one of them even wriggled inside. The fur rubbing against her skin would make Ellie uncomfortable.

Evan took a deep breath. 'Ellie!'

'What?'

'Stop moving around.'

At last, Evan had Ellie's attention, and she stood still. Approaching her, Evan tried not to alarm the animals clinging to her, treading carefully in the snow. A few steps away, he stopped and waited for his opportunity. He could see the apes poking and prodding at an alarmed Ellie. She had an uncharacteristic look of fear in her eyes, even though balkutar were generally harmless.

'Please. I need you to get them off. I hate these toze's...is...toze'sis, tozey things.'

'Balkutar,' Evan said. 'They're called balkutar.'

Ellie scrunched her face, which was endearing. 'I know! Whatever they're called...I don't want them mauling me.'

A sudden cracking sound echoed around them when Evan clapped his hands together. The apes scrambled from their positions, spontaneously jumping back into the tree branches. For a minute, they continued heading as high as they could reach. Evan was uncertain why, but the balkutar were easily startled by unexpected loud noises. They would always run to safety without delay.

It was funny to watch Ellie looking so bemused by the instant departure of the apes. Brushing away any hair they had left on her overalls, she turned and began trudging back through the trees. Her distress had dissolved in an instant.

'C'mon,' she said, calling out to Evan, whilst fastening her own tangled locks back into place. 'Don't just stand there.'

'Where are you going?'

Ellie picked up speed. 'To the top. It's not far.'

As she left the wooded area, Ellie moved onto open ground and took wide steps. She was attempting to reach the peak quickly. Evan rushed behind her, but his feet were sore, and he wondered why she was so deliberate. *What is so important to her?* he thought.

'Here,' shouted Ellie, reaching her destination. 'Look!'

A few more strides allowed Evan to see what had caught Ellie's interest. Lighting the horizon, a blurred orange glow was beautiful in its simplicity. The source of the light was miles away from where they were standing. Evan immediately knew where it came from. A place he was very familiar with, but not for many pleasant reasons.

'Scorr Tanta!' Evan was breathless.

Ellie looked at him, seeming much less troubled than she had been all day. 'It's beautiful.'

It was only at that point, that Evan realised the daylight was fading. He didn't know how to react to Ellie's comments. Scorr Tanta's monstrous heating towers did indeed create a stunning image in the distance. But the very thought of the city left Evan feeling on edge.

'It's going dark,' he said. 'We need to go home.'

'Stand with me.' Ellie's voice was soft and full of warmth.

Evan was reluctant. 'For a minute. But we need to get back before it's too late.'

Together, they stood silently for a few moments. Ellie took Evan's hand, perhaps intending to find safety alongside him, or maybe wanting to share her experience. Her skin was soft, despite the work she did, and she was so warm, considering the temperature around them. For that brief time, things were peaceful. In the end, Evan pulled away without a word and Ellie followed. Darkness was looming closer.

Ellie stumbled back down the slopes behind Evan. 'We're not goin' to get back before nightfall, are we?'

'Keep going.'

The orgo that had carried them up the first part of the hill was in the distance. He had waited obediently for them, and both Ellie and Evan ran back towards him. Even though it was much easier to make out their route, the icy carpet beneath them was still thick and hard to tread. The snowstorm had left behind an altered landscape for the night. Tramping through the deep white terrain, Evan could see Ellie springing after him until they reached Sage.

Mounting the orgo, Ellie took hold. 'Okay boy. Take us home.'

'We won't make it,' Evan said, taking his seat. 'But I know somewhere.'

He pointed his finger forward, where the path that had led them up the hillside forked. An alternate route back down into Port Harmony, formed at that junction.

Ellie shrugged, but kicked down hard, directing Sage to the other path. 'I need to get back to Cedric. Check he's alright.'

'You will. You'll just have to be patient. It's getting dark…we need to find shelter. Trust me.' Evan put his arms back around Ellie's waist.

'Hope you know where you're goin', precious. I certainly don't.'

The pathway Evan had suggested was steep, and Sage instinctively took care. Each rock, or clump of ice, was like punches to Evan's legs as they journeyed down the treacherous track. But Evan had no intention of attempting to get all the way back into Port Harmony. Where he was taking them was much closer, and it offered shelter for the night.

'Over there,' he directed.

Ellie turned slightly, with a look of confusion. 'The caves?'

chapter twelve

Into Eklips

Wooden structures were all Nolan distinguished when the back panel of the transport opened, and her wardens prepared. It seemed much darker in Eklips at nightfall — and completely terrifying. She had never seen anything like it. Within Scorr Tanta, the elegant buildings were stunning, and their buffed stone surfaces dazzled the sun. Lamps lit up the city when darkness came, and it always looked inviting. But the brightness and warmth that Nolan was used to, would evidently not be found in Eklips. Here, it was bleak and colder than she had ever imagined possible. Eklips was a place found in her worst dreams.

With the ramp down, over twenty wardens thundered away from the vehicle. They were focused on their mission and determined to locate the Renegades. Nolan scrutinised her team as they left, arming their lances and preparing to attack. They would work efficiently and let nobody stand in their way.

That was how she had trained them, and she had done a magnificent job. Releasing the leather strap attached to the roof of the transport, Nolan edged forward, and then the horror really began.

Scattered timber lumps were the homes of slaves living in Eklips; Nolan had often been told about them. *Homes not fit for an animal* she thought, remembering that she had condemned many people to this life. The ground was icy sludge and nothing more. In this part of the territory, it would be impossible for anyone to live any better than their ancestors had, centuries before them. The smell of the ocean gushed around her, making her nauseous whilst she continued to step away from the vehicle. Nolan's feet sank in the mud.

Already locked in fierce conflict, Nolan's troops attacked natives with their lances. They were cruel in their approach and none of them appeared to care. Right in front of her, one of her wardens lunged forward. The metal tip of his lance contacted a man dressed in measly cloth and the charge was released. Nolan stared, disgusted, as the sparsely dressed slave jerked and fell to the floor. The man probably hated Kayden as much as anyone. He would not have chosen to live in this desolate territory. Nolan had no idea why, but the once ruthless warden commander no longer seemed to be a part of her.

Now, she had sympathy for the very people her wardens attacked—on her orders.

The warden she observed, clenched the slave's rags and pulled at him. 'Where's Kayden?'

Groaning, the slave made eye contact with his assailant, spluttering words that nobody would understand. When the warden released him, he slumped back to the ground. To Nolan's dismay, her subordinate hadn't finished. He stepped over his victim, directing his lance toward the man's chest. With his other hand, he stretched down and wrapped his fingers in the cloth that covered the slave's torso, before yanking hard and tearing it away.

'Where is Kayden?' the warden demanded again. Nolan should have been proud of her warden, but somehow, she wasn't.

With the slave still unable to muster much of a response, the warden placed the tip of his weapon on his victim's exposed chest. Nolan couldn't watch, but the man's helpless screams were sickening.

Flashes increased as the troops pressed on into Eklips. The cries from every person they assaulted were deafening. They were cutting a direct route for Nolan, confronting anyone that stood in their way, whether they resisted or not. In the distance, she identified their target— Kayden's palace. Built at the edge of the cliffs, behind the palace was the open ocean, and for this place, it was a much more inspiring building. Cylindrical in shape, it seemed to almost touch the clouds, and looked more like a tower than a residence. Some sort of temple perhaps. Nevertheless, it was Kayden's palace; Rada had described it to Nolan. Surrounded by more than twenty other, much shorter buildings; the arrangement looked like a fortress. Nolan assumed these smaller structures would be occupied by Kayden's more fortunate associates. They looked, after all, just as secure as his palace.

In that way, Eklips was much like Scorr Tanta, where those close to Rada also lived in the central buildings encircling her palace. Yet there were many differences with this place. Where Scorr Tanta was home to the privileged, and those who provided skills and resources, Eklips was not. In the city, people were well looked after—certainly, those Rada deemed to deserve it. On the other hand, those who committed crimes anywhere in The Union, especially Scorr Tanta, were banished into slavery and sent to Eklips. That was why this coastal territory was different; slaves mostly populated it. They lived in the timber huts and were owned by a handful of more fortunate residents.

'There,' Nolan said, pointing to Kayden's building. 'That's where we need to be!'

Closest to her, one warden responded, 'Yes Ma'am,' before getting over eager with his weapon. He plunged it into another slave's legs.

What is wrong with them? Nolan thought, hearing the electric charges fizz. One by one, the wardens took down anyone who happened to be close by. It didn't matter if they weren't a threat, Nolan's army seemed to take pleasure in their assault.

Beyond the carnage, Nolan could see reddish figures congregating in front of the palace. Kayden's assault rangers; some on the back of orgo, and others on foot. They were intending to protect the stronghold. Scattered around them, gliders lurked here and there. Nolan had seen them before, but only flying around outside the boundary of Scorr Tanta. These ones were grounded, foraging in the mud, presumably looking for scraps. Gliders were gruesome beasts; creepy to look at closely, with their wings dragging by their sides and tails thrashing about behind them.

Nolan paused after stumbling in the dirt. 'Wait…'

Off balance, her whole body had become incapable of functioning. Nolan staggered, and with nothing to cling on to, she fell to the ground. With her veins feeling like ice ran through them, she was completely disorientated. She gazed around, trying to discover who had attacked her and if she was about to die.

Nobody was even near, and she realised that she was somehow hurting herself.

From a few feet ahead, one of the wardens saw that his superior was in trouble. 'Ma'am...ma'am,' he cried, backtracking toward her.

Nolan couldn't speak. All of a sudden, it was like the air was sucked from within her and the ground was being tugged away. The urge to escape her plight and avoid imminent death was unbearable. She choked on the ground, whilst a grating chatter from the gliders sliced through her.

'Ma'am,' the warden said, reaching out to help his superior. 'Ma'am, what can I do?'

'Don't...' Nolan screamed. Only she would be able to overcome this — alone.

The warden realised his mistake and turned to continue with his mission, whilst Nolan breathed deeply and managed to stand. The realisation that she had never left Scorr Tanta before, was clear in her mind. Not wanting to be beaten, she marched onward behind the onslaught.

When they closed in on Kayden's stronghold, the orgo-back rangers positioned themselves. Yet behind Nolan, a faint rumbling got increasingly louder. More vehicles were approaching, and she turned to get a better look. Her own squad circled around her for protection.

Speeding in their direction were three-person sleds. Only two of them, but that was enough to ease Nolan's difficulties. She hadn't expected them and was grateful for any extra help. Armed with rock cannons, armour plates protected the sled pilots at the front. They were fast but could also cause great damage if required. Nolan raised her arm, signalling the wardens on sleds to halt. Their motors roared when they stopped deliberately behind her. With increased authority, Nolan found an inner strength as commander of Rada's wardens.

'In the name of Rada,' she cried at the rangers, 'you must stand down.'

Nolan had to listen carefully for a response from the assault rangers. They were riding toward her, and she hoped they may be reasonable.

'Why?' The ranger that replied only looked young. With a dirty face and unkempt stubble, he didn't seem like the military sort. Tufts of scraggly hair dangled across each of his shoulders.

'A search is required,' Nolan said, making sure her tone sounded commanding.

Glancing one way then the other at his associates, the young ranger was looking for a consensus. 'Why?'

Nolan took a deep breath and stepped forward, determined to take control. 'It is possible…that the ones known as the Renegades originate in this place.'

A slight smile appeared on the young ranger's face. 'Very well. Rangers…stand down!'

Suspicious, Nolan held her head whilst the rangers loosened their formation. For some reason, they weren't resisting and were almost willing to accommodate Nolan's demands. Without much question, they had complied, yet this wasn't what she had expected. Kayden's people were strong and independent, and whilst they were associated with The Union, they protected their own. They had little interest in the other two colonies.

'Your supply store…where is it?' Nolan asked.

The young ranger pointed in the direction of one of the smaller structures close to Kayden's palace. Responding efficiently, most of the wardens fell in line, stampeding toward it. Further orders weren't necessary, and Nolan stood her ground whilst her army began their search. Four remaining wardens positioned themselves at her rear, between the sleds.

'There is an agreement,' the young ranger said, brazenly, 'that your army doesn't enter our territory.'

He was right, but Nolan believed they were justified in their actions. 'That agreement…does not stand where outlaws may be concerned.'

'What makes you so confident these Renegades are here?'

Nolan contemplated her response; she had no idea why Rada was so convinced that Eklips was to blame. 'We have information— '

'What information?' the ranger interrupted, moving toward her on his orgo. He was trying to intimidate her. Kayden's culture in Eklips was evident, and the ranger seemed to be refusing to accept the influence of a female officer.

Nolan thrust her palm forwards. 'Stop! Moving any further will be met with consequences.'

The ranger ignored her and proceeded. Responding hastily, Nolan slammed her arm down by her side. A sharp sound exploded from behind her. Wardens controlling the sleds had reacted well, and lumps of rock crashed into one of the structures the rangers were protecting. In the commotion, the gliders beat their wings and took to the skies at once. For Nolan, there was a magnificence in watching the sides of the building crumble. Her unquestionable power had been well displayed. Even the gliders had scarpered for their own safety.

With his delusion of superiority removed, the ranger stopped his advance. 'You won't find what you think here.'

Eyes fixed on the shelter being searched, Nolan wondered if they may find the supplies marked as belonging to Scorr Tanta. Concerned that her ruler was wrong, Nolan didn't want to consider how Rada may react to another failure. It wasn't worth thinking about, because Nolan would surely take the blame. The search was fast, and she heard her wardens shouting from the building. Looking back at the ranger who she had engaged with, Nolan noticed sweat irritating her brow; even though she felt cold to her core.

Withdrawing from the supply store, one of the wardens hurried back. He looked flustered and Nolan's chest tightened. Without addressing her, the warden rushed passed and a slight breeze crossed her shoulder. All her senses were ready to explode. The stink of the ocean was overpowering, and the noise her people made was well-defined as they rustled through the shelter a few feet away. Next to another member of the squad, the warden whispered. Nolan could hear him unmistakably.

'It's all theirs. There is nothing that belongs to Scorr Tanta.'

Inching closer, the young ranger smiled, his arrogance intolerable. 'You found nothing. I told you. And as such, you are now trespassing.'

The wardens were muttering and rustling behind Nolan. With their voices blending together, she couldn't single out any words. She turned to face them as one warden stepped nearer.

'We have brought Kayden a gift!' He said, sounding deliberate. 'In exchange for Pandra.'

Nolan wasn't aware of the gift he referred to. *Why would Rada want Pandra back?* she thought, feeling confused. Pandra had been one of Rada's most valuable wardens. Despite that, after being found guilty of stealing from Rada's palace, she had been quietly exiled to Eklips. Pandra hadn't even been granted a public trial. With such a direct betrayal of Rada's trust, she had deserved nothing more. Yet now, for some unknown reason, Rada wanted her returned.

An unexpected crushing sensation ran through Nolan's spine and traumatised her. Petrified, she saw the other wardens turning their lances toward her. She was the gift they spoke of, and they had hit her with a low charge from their lances; now ready to continue if she resisted. Fighting them wasn't an option. Instantly, Nolan sensed hands in her hair. It felt like someone was rotating her head with incredible force, but nobody was even touching her. Nolan realised that she could barely move her fingers, as though her whole body had chosen to join the wardens in attacking her.

The young ranger laughed. 'Pandra? Kayden had a feeling she was a spy,' he said. 'I'm certain he will enjoy punishing her accordingly. There will be no exchange, but I am sure your gift will be appreciated. We have nothing to hide. As you can see...you have no business here. Kayden will expect to be compensated for such an intrusion.'

Without hesitation, one of Nolan's squad wrapped a chain around her waist, whilst another ripped the green band from her arm. They no longer recognised her rank. The wardens must have had direct orders from Rada in case their assault had gone badly. Appropriately called a Limiter, the chain was fastened snugly to Nolan's middle. Two more shackles connected to it were attached to each of her wrists. Limiters were remotely controlled and able to deliver a powerful shock to the prisoner wearing them. When necessary, the blow would be fatal. Nolan had used them on prisoners many times before. The thought of wearing one crippled her further.

With the last cuff fastened in place, the warden imprisoning Nolan placed his hand on her shoulder. 'I'm sorry Ma'am,' he muttered. 'I wish there were another way. Just following orders.'

His words washed through her. He was only a boy and was full of an unbearable sympathy for her. Whilst the restraining device was fitted, Nolan had felt little, and her emotions had dampened out of self-preservation. She had instinctively resigned to her fate, knowing there was no way to avoid it. But the humanity shown by the warden was too much and had crippled her ability to cope. As she became woozy, Nolan wasn't sure how much longer she could stay upright.

Another warden stepped forward, handing the control device to the ranger, seeming much less remorseful. 'Rada sends her apologies. There has been a misunderstanding, and she would appreciate any co-operation you could offer with returning Pandra.'

'The slave is not here...and neither is Kayden,' one of the other rangers said, from the rear of the formation. 'There will be no exchange!'

A malicious look in the young ranger's eyes was evident, and it was all Nolan registered when her vision tunnelled. Speech had become impossible and her arms limp. Convinced she was about to die, and that for some reason all her organs were fading, Nolan hoped that it would be quick. Death was the only way she could avoid slavery. Seeing the expression on the ranger, was the only proof she needed to know that slavery was her worst outcome. Kayden would certainly not show mercy to Rada's warden commander.

The cackling from the assault rangers was all Nolan heard when a powerful jolt flooded her core. Reeling in pain, she slumped in the mud releasing a prolonged, but dull, gravelly moan.

No longer able to open her eyes, she overheard the young warden talking from above her.

'I think it is time for you to leave now. Don't you?' His suggestion was directed at the wardens and received no reply.

In place of a response, Nolan detected the roar of sled engines. But the noise melted quickly, and it was obvious they had retreated. The wardens had no leverage, and as the ranger had pointed out, they had no right to be in Eklips. Kayden's people weren't responsible for the attacks; they weren't the Renegades.

Nolan was the payment for their mistake, and worst still, she wasn't about to die — she knew that now. Her fate was sealed as a slave. With her face sinking in the mud, she was alone. Her wardens had abandoned her, leaving Nolan stripped of her independence and any rights she had once enjoyed. A firm hand locked into her hair, then dragged her brutally through the mud. The ranger who held her issued further instructions.

'Inform Kayden immediately. The warden commander has been enslaved. But as he suspected, Pandra is a scout reporting to Rada.'

chapter thirteen

Pandra's Plight

'On your feet,' ordered Kayden. 'You need to stand!'

Most of the residents of Port Harmony had retreated to their homes when the darkness came. The street where Kayden waited, just beyond the wharf, was almost silent. It reminded him of Eklips, with many crumbling structures. For Kayden, there was also a sense of security at night. Besides, his well-armed rangers were there with him, still saddled in their orgo. Nobody would dare to challenge them, and with no wardens in sight, the hunt for Ditto would be much easier.

With Pandra slumped at his feet, Kayden could see his other two assault rangers returning. They galloped between the tight rows of gritty dwellings and he waited for their report. Kayden hoped they would bring news that would be of some use.

'Well?' he called out, as the rangers joined his pack. 'Have you located her?'

'No sir,' one of the men answered, with a tremble in his tone. 'But we sent your message.'

Kayden shoved Pandra away with his boot. She had never looked so pathetic and made no effort to defend herself. Pacing on the cobblestone, he was becoming desperate to find his target. Ditto needed to be located before morning. The people of Port Harmony wouldn't tolerate Kayden's presence for that long.

'This message,' he said, pulling his hefty cloak tighter for warmth. 'Was it clear?'

'Very,' returned the ranger, patting his steed triumphantly. 'Cedric is down a few orgo now.'

Smiling, Kayden turned toward his slave. 'That should get their attention.'

'What of Haylee sir?' asked one of the rangers.

'Rescued,' Kayden explained. 'By some stranger who I have never seen before. Someone very competent at riding orgo too. Haylee will get what is coming to her…in time.'

Pandra was trembling on the floor and her hands fought to keep her balanced. It was possible that Kayden had pushed things too far. A dead slave was of no use to him. He knelt beside her and lifted her head to face him. The life in her eyes was fading.

'You need to stand slave,' said Kayden. 'We need to move on.'

Pandra didn't seem able to speak but pulled away from him. With his frustration contained, Kayden took hold of her arms and dragged her to her feet. Her body was limp, and it was evident she couldn't hold her own weight. Lifting her, Kayden lay her across his orgo, knowing that he needed to treat her with a little more care.

'With respect sir,' said one of the assault rangers. 'Perhaps Pandra needs time to recover. Orchids would help.'

Kayden's finger flew in his direction. 'The slave is the perfect deterrent for Port Harmony's wardens. They will think twice about getting in our way when they see her. She was one of their own. One look at her will force them to see things our way.'

'Yes sir…but…even though she was a warden…she won't survive without help. She is still only human.'

'So be it,' growled Kayden. He didn't like being questioned.

A drawn-out groan escaped Pandra. The sound was only quiet, but it was enough to make everyone stare at her. Snorting, each of the orgo reacted too; stamping their feet and becoming restless. They always sensed when people were in distress. Pandra's fingers pulled at the wool on Kayden's orgo. She was trying to aggravate his steed, possibly making an effort to escape. Yet her muscles were so flimsy, the orgo didn't appear to notice.

Kayden approached his slave who was beginning to annoy him. 'Do I need to leave you behind?'

Looking up, Pandra's eyes pleaded with him. With no words, she was begging for mercy and reached out her arm. Kayden was reminded of something he'd seen before; many years ago. He took her hand and her skin felt like ice, melting through his fingers. Placing his other hand over Pandra's he tried to offer a silent reassurance.

'Very well,' he said, facing the ranger who had challenged him. 'Treat her.'

Kayden released his slave's hand and stepped away whilst the ranger dismounted. 'We don't have time to waste. You need to fix her quickly.'

The ranger snatched a pouch from the saddle of his orgo, then hurried over to Pandra. The moment when he clenched her hair, was when Kayden discovered an unexpected concern for his slave's wellbeing. Kayden felt in some way threatened like he was fearing his own life. He refused to watch when the ranger yanked mercilessly at Pandra's head, convincing her mouth to fall open. Then, when the ranger placed his other hand in his pouch, Kayden intervened.

'Stop! Let me do it.'

Taking the pouch from the ranger, Kayden was relieved when Pandra's head was released. He tipped a few of the granules into his hand, then offered them a few at a time from his fingers. The smell alone almost instantly brought a little life back into the slave. She opened her mouth for Kayden to feed her the orchid. The look in Pandra's eyes changed and she fought to show her gratitude.

'This isn't very dignified,' whispered Kayden. 'Perhaps you would like to take them?'

Pandra offered a shallow nod in agreement, then took hold of the pouch. She touched Kayden's hand tenderly. Still sprawled across the back of his steed, she made an admirable effort to salvage her own health. Her skin was still cold, but the orgo's body heat would protect her.

'Sir,' another ranger muttered to alert their leader.

Kayden lifted his head to be greeted by all five rangers gawping at him. There were rare moments, if any, where Kayden had ever engaged in such public displays of compassion. The tenderness he had offered Pandra had disturbed them. Saved from his shame, Kayden was thankful for a voice shouting in the distance. The noise distracted his rangers, and he listened attentively.

The calls were coming from one of Haylee's people. A female voice, shouting 'Ditto,' over and again.

Delighted at the breakthrough, Kayden took hold of his saddle ready to mount his orgo. 'Follow her!'

'Wait,' one of the rangers shouted, holding out his transmitter. 'There is a message from home. It's marked urgent, sir.'

Lights flashed, giving life to the small device lodged in the ranger's hand. Kayden needed to work fast; the message was obviously important, but he didn't want to lose his chance to find Ditto. Seizing the pebble-like transmitter, he inspected it closely. Whilst reading the message, Kayden found it impossible to suppress his fury.

With a prolonged, punishing scream, Kayden tossed the communicator aside and slapped the orchid pouch from Pandra's fists. 'You...You...You are working...for Rada.' He could feel how red his face was, and his rage made it difficult to find words.

Pandra held out her palms in front of her face, using them as protection in case Kayden struck her again. She was quivering but still didn't answer. When Kayden's fingers embedded in her hair, she whimpered and squirmed on his orgo. She looked pitiful.

'You thought you could trick me?' Kayden yelled. 'Spy on me? Inform Rada about me? I knew it…there was something not right. Well…your plot…whatever it was…is over!'

'I had no choice,' Pandra finally said. 'I'm a warden. It is my job to do Rada's bidding. You were stealing supplies. You're guilty of dissent…against The Union.'

'Why…*slave*…would I steal? We have plenty of supplies in Eklips.'

Pandra grimaced in pain. 'Only because you have stolen them. Your people are the Renegades.'

Tugging at his slave's hair, Kayden's wrath was overpowering. 'I have no idea what you're talking about. With your ridiculous delusions…it is little wonder that you are now a slave. And a slave you will remain. Your loyalty was misguided…Rada has abandoned you. The same way Rada abandons everyone who is loyal to her.'

'No! I'm a warden,' Pandra whined. 'She wouldn't.'

Kayden smiled. 'You *were* a warden…my dear Pandra. Devotion to Rada is foolish. And you have been the fool this time. I don't know what made you think I was stealing…you can fill me in when we return to Eklips. For now, we find Ditto. I will deal with you later.'

'Rada will send people for me,' Pandra said, her cheeks moistening with sorrow. 'I won't be going with you to Eklips.'

Brutally wrenching the hair in his grasp, Kayden began to enjoy hearing his slave's suffering. 'Trust me…you will be coming back with me,' he said. 'And Rada will pay dearly for deceiving me. This isn't the first time…but this time there will be a price for her actions.'

'What do you mean?' Pandra asked. 'Not the first time?'

'Not your concern. All you need to know is that she will not be rescuing you. Rada has already forgotten about you. The sooner you get used to that…the better for you. You are a slave now…that is all you will be. And I won't be stupid enough to show you mercy anymore.'

'Sir,' one of the rangers intruded.

Kayden growled. 'What?'

The ranger was signalling at something in the distance. 'There. Ditto. It's Ditto!'

Eyes wide, Kayden felt like he almost lost his head when he swung around to see for himself. His ranger was right; Ditto was there, at the end of the very street in which they were standing. What was disturbing, was the arrogant way she cantered by. The fact that she was staring at them, suggested that Ditto must know that Kayden was there. Even so, she didn't seem at all worried.

Mounting his orgo, Kayden was deliberate. 'After her. She cannot get away. Stop her!'

chapter fourteen

Dissent

Sage snorted loudly as he veered away from the track and entered a small crevice within the rock-face. *Maybe he doesn't trust me yet*, Evan thought. Inside was pitch black and little could be seen. The damp smell was uncomfortable, but with Ellie, he trekked further into the shadows regardless. As they followed the route into the caves, Evan caught sight of a hazy lamp up ahead.

'There. Follow the light.'

Ellie was silent, and it would be understandable if she was uneasy. Nevertheless, she must have had faith in Evan and she allowed Sage to continue their journey. Lamps lit the pathway gradually, as they ventured deeper within until Ellie forced a standstill by wrenching at her orgo's fleece. There were rustling noises beyond them.

'What's that?' Ellie asked, sounding nervy.

Evan held out his hand for her to join him, then dismounted. 'I need you to trust me.'

'I'm not goin' anywhere, precious. Until you tell me what that noise is.'

'Friends.'

Ellie gripped to Sage tightly, refusing to move. 'Inside a cave?'

'Trust me.'

It was possible to see how tense Ellie had become, as she untangled her fingers from the orgo and swung her leg round to dismount. 'That,' she howled sharply. 'What is that?'

Ahead, the face of a nine-year-old boy peered from behind a rock. Tufts of unkempt, red hair dangled around his grubby face. When he stepped out from his hiding place in his black, waxy body suit, he stared at them. In each hand, he held a short rod fashioned from stone, and he started tapping them together vigorously. Evan noticed the rhythm to the noise he created with the chunks of stone, like there was a purpose to his banging. From nowhere, more children appeared; two at first, followed by another, then another. In all, a group of eight youngsters gathered close to Ellie and Evan, and the small boy who had first arrived silenced the noise he was making.

It was like Evan's arm almost yanked out of place when Ellie pulled him toward her. 'Who are they?' she asked.

Evan beckoned at the first child. 'I've told you. They're friends.'

'They're children.'

'They are. An excellent observation.'

Ellie squatted next to Evan. She seemed wary but waved half-heartedly at the children. With one guarded step at a time, the red-haired boy wanted to meet the newcomer. As he started to beat the devices in his hands again, some of the other children reciprocated. This time was different, with no definable rhythm to the noises they made. They were using their pieces of stone to communicate instead, and the sounds they created were more irregular. After an exchange with members of the group behind him, the boy placed his stones on the ground. He stretched out his fingers to stroke Ellie's hand.

'What's his name?' she asked.

'Harrup. He's called Harrup,' Evan informed her.

Hesitantly, Ellie tried to take Harrup's hand, but he immediately tugged it away from her. Collecting his stone communicators from the floor, he scuttled back amongst the other children.

'Where are they from?' Ellie pressed. 'Why are they here? Where are their parents?'

'You ask a lot of questions girl.'

'So…I'm told.'

'This way…there's more. You'll get your answers.'

Leaving Sage behind them, Evan led the way down a brightened pathway. Behind them, the children followed, making occasional clicking sounds with their messaging tools. Only they understood what each other was saying. The jagged walls of rock shimmered, reflecting the lamps that marked the route. Clusters of orchids were crawling on each surface, feeding on the moisture that trickled down every crack. All down the passage, moths fluttered about the orchid's flowers, busying themselves chaotically.

'Always wondered where you found the orgo food,' Ellie said, stopping suddenly with a gasp, as they reached the end of the tunnel. 'What?' she blurted out, seeming unable to utter more words.

The view through the opening at the end of the passage had stunned Ellie. She gawped as the youngsters shoved passed them and darted into the large cavern ahead. It was an immense cavity that reached beyond sight, concealed deep inside Port Harmony's hillside. Abstract, stony structures cascaded from the roof, a little above where they were standing. Their surfaces were almost entirely coated with more orchids. Many feet beneath them, people bustled about, in a sort of courtyard area at the base of the unusual rock formations. The cavern was damp, but rather like an indoor replica of the street market where Evan worked. Inhabitants were trading items and busying themselves constantly. Walkways wound their way around the perimeter of the cavern. Each path climbed steadily from the courtyard and up the surrounding rocks.

'It's okay,' said Evan, trying to encourage Ellie to enter the over-sized grotto. 'This way.'

'No!' Ellie screamed, and her eyes widened. 'They're elrupe?'

Evan threw a smile to comfort her. 'Yes.'

Ellie looked threatened, as though she had just discovered something from a night-terror. She was focused intently on the children who had stopped at the cavern boundary. Uncurling a finger, she pointed at them, and her bottom lip twitched. For someone who usually had plenty to say, Ellie was beginning to unsettle Evan.

'Tails! They're elrupe,' she said. 'With tails!'

'You're being very rude,' Evan snapped, wishing she had stayed quiet. 'Yes…they're elrupe.'

Disappointed in Ellie's reaction, Evan walked further into the cave and joined the youngsters. They seemed excited, and their unique conversations were frantic. The noise they made with their pieces of stone had become rowdy. As he turned, Evan was pleased to see Ellie following him.

'They want to meet you,' he said, watching the children ignore him and group around Ellie.

Smiling indistinctly, Ellie didn't falter when the young elrupe took hold of her hands to welcome her. 'Have they always been here?'

'Not always,' Evan explained. 'Since The Union agreement was formed and they were forced to leave.'

'But they didn't leave? Wait…that's four years ago!'

'No, they didn't leave. And yes, it's a while ago now. Expelling them from The Union was Rada's will. But Port Harmony was founded by people…humans…who believed that our two species need each other.'

Together, Evan and Ellie followed a route toward the courtyard. The children were curious and hung around Ellie tightly, whilst Harrup gripped her hand. He treated her like she was some treasure he had unearthed. In contrast, Ellie glanced around, trying hard to digest her surroundings. Evan had to admit, the elrupe caves were an incredible sight. Along their way, they passed by gaps in the stone with every few steps; entrances to sleeping quarters, built within the main construct of the cavern. All the elrupe lived there as far as Evan knew.

'You went against Rada's will?' Ellie went on, sounding concerned.

'Well,' pondered Evan, continuing forwards. 'Not only me. But yes…I was part of it. Does that bother you?'

'It's dissent! You're a…a…dissenter. You have broken Scorr Tanta law and would be banished to Eklips as a slave if Rada found out.

Yeah, precious...that bothers me. And it should bother you too.'

'I remember it, Ellie,' said Evan, feeling as though he didn't recognise her. 'I remember Scorr Tanta. Living there when Rada came. She had no right to treat the elrupe how she did. We built that city together...us humans *and* the elrupe. What thanks did they get for that? Some of them already lived their lives as slaves, in Eklips, treated in horrific ways by people like Kayden. Then, when Rada came to Scorr Tanta...she banished them completely. I believed in our reasons for leaving that place...for building Port Harmony. I still do. We were right to stick by the elrupe.'

As they approached the courtyard, Ellie moaned. 'But building Port Harmony didn't work. When we formed The Union, it was decided that Rada was right. The elrupe had to go. For humans to survive...the elrupe had to go.'

Evan stopped and turned to face her. 'Who decided? Rada?' he asked, yelling and struggling to control his temper. 'Humans and elrupe...we are all the same. We have the same ancestors...evolved from the same species. Humans have changed too...they say our bodies adapted to the cold. Elrupe are no different to us...they just evolved differently. They have other qualities—'

'You're blinded by your sympathy for them,' Ellie cut in. 'They're a lot different.'

'Look at them Ellie,' Evan scolded, growing impatient. 'Look at them. We may appear a little different...but we are still the same. You sound like—'

'Like what?'

Evan breathed, taking in as much air as it took to calm his anger. 'Never mind! Listen...Haylee and the others...they risk their lives to make sure the elrupe don't go hungry. Perhaps you could at least try to understand.'

Someone tapped Evan on the shoulder. Turning away from Ellie, he was relieved to come across a friendly face. It was the one known as Chief. His thick suit formed from pygboar skins matched those that the children wore, whilst rays of light bounced off his hairless head. All elrupe lost their hair when they entered adulthood. Similarly, they all wore pygboar skins, as a sign of their worship for their companion cave-dwelling animals. Only when pygboars died naturally, were they then harvested, and their carcasses used by the elrupe for beneficial means. Pygboars didn't have a very long lifespan.

'Chief,' said Evan. 'Good to see you again.'

Muted, Chief lifted his hand and directed it toward Ellie. None of the elrupe had spoken a word since they had taken refuge in Port Harmony's hills. Only through instruments like the children used, would they communicate with each other.

Evan acknowledged Chief's concerns. 'It's okay. She's with me. She is a friend. Well…sort of.'

When he looked around, it was clear to Evan that things never improved for their species. Despite being a proud race, the elrupe had been reduced to what could only be described as scavengers. Many of them hurried around in the courtyard in front of him, stuffing any scraps of food they found into their mouths. Most of the elrupe were emaciated from hunger. Yet there was an odd dignity about them. No matter how desperate they became, every single member of their race treated each other with honour, trying to share out supplies evenly.

The youngsters dragged Ellie in front of their leader and she looked horrified. Shaking, Ellie stood silently. Her head dropped to avoid Chief. The uncomfortable scene lasted a few moments and Evan considered how to intervene. His disappointment in Ellie began to grow, until out of nowhere, her deliberate hesitation ended. Kneeling before Chief, she lifted her head to greet him. Her eyes had altered, exposing a vulnerability that crushed Evan's concern.

'Good to meet you,' she said, offering an unexpected gesture of friendship.

Evan's relief breathed from deep inside him.

Chief placed one hand on Ellie's shoulder and beckoned with the other. He wanted her to stand. When Ellie rose to her feet, he bowed his head as a sign of acceptance, and a noise erupted as the children banged their stones excitedly. Chief had welcomed Ellie without question. After everything his species had been through, it would be reasonable if he had doubts.

'We need a place to shelter,' Evan said. 'Just for tonight.'

Folding his arms, Chief bobbed his head, then turned and made his way back into the courtyard. Evan grabbed Ellie by the hand, knowing Chief intended for them to follow. What he also needed to know, was whether his companion might ever understand his beliefs. She didn't need to feel the same way he did about the elrupe, but Evan didn't want Ellie to offend them either.

'A minute ago,' Evan said, assessing the situation, 'you didn't seem to think very much of them. Or the fact we helped them. Or both.'

Ellie laughed shakily whilst Evan rambled. 'A few minutes ago, you dragged me in here with no explanation. It was unexpected…that's all. I was shocked. I never knew.'

As they reached the courtyard, a swarm of adult elrupe gathered around Ellie. They were offering her food, blankets and all manner of things to make her more comfortable. Evan spotted tears falling from the corners of Ellie's eyes. She was overwhelmed by the warm-hearted elrupe, and with her purity laid bare, she couldn't control her reaction. Watching, as each of the adults welcomed his companion, Evan could see the immediate change in Ellie's expression. Her doubts had been shattered by the generosity of their hosts.

'You need to accept their offerings,' Evan spoke quietly, to avoid attracting attention.

'But look at them,' Ellie said, choking on her sadness. 'They have nothing. They look starving. How can I take from them?'

'It's what they want,' Evan explained. 'They would be offended if you didn't.'

Ellie offered her hands, whilst some of the adults passed her indistinguishable scrapings and crumbs. Her charming smile appeared beneath her sorrow, as she tried to show strength. Evan watched her intently, impressed by how she was accepted.

Close to a pool in the middle of the courtyard, Evan stopped momentarily. 'May I?'

Chief nodded and held out his arm. As a mark of respect, Evan kneeled and cupped his hands to scoop some water. The pool was sacred to the elrupe, and when threatened they would gather around it. Drinking from it showed solidarity with their kind. Before he could take any water, however, Evan noticed Harrup approaching. He was heaving a sack along the ground that was almost as big as he was.

'For me?' Evan asked. 'My orchids?'

Harrup released the bag of orgo food, then knelt and slurped from the pool noisily.

Evan grinned, inspecting the gift. 'You've certainly been busy collecting these.'

Almost bouncing with excitement, Harrup jumped to his feet and scuttled toward Ellie. She turned courteously to greet him, which comforted Evan. There had been an almost instant change in her approach to the elrupe. Then again, any honest person would be charmed by them. Selfless and caring, every member of the elrupe oozed qualities that Evan admired.

Ellie offered her new friend a cheeky grin. 'Hi. Harrup isn't it?'

In response, Harrup dropped to one knee like he was in the company of royalty. He extended his arm toward Ellie and Evan could see that he was clutching something. Harrup's fingers uncoiled slowly, and Ellie had a look of confusion about her.

'What's this?' she asked in a whisper.

Grunting, Harrup shoved his arm further forward.

Taking the strange object from the boy, Ellie analysed it. 'Is this…This is…Is this…me? This is me.'

Evan saw it more clearly now. Harrup's gift to her was a small stone sculpture which apparently resembled Ellie, whose mystified expression deepened. Ellie's fingers stroked the figurine with interest, whilst she rotated it to view every surface. Focusing her attention on Harrup, Ellie crouched.

'How? How did you do that?'

Harrup wouldn't have responded even if he wanted to. Instead, he reached out and stroked Ellie's hand where she held his offering. Insistently, he pushed the object further toward her whilst she held it. In turn, she glanced at the statuette, then at Harrup. Evan found her naivety captivating.

'Ellie,' he bellowed from next to the pool, intruding on their moment. 'Your turn.'

As though snapping out of a trance, Ellie looked over at Evan. 'But…I don't understand how he did that.'

Whilst Ellie was distracted, Harrup hurried away, and when she turned to find him, he was nowhere to be seen. After checking this way and that, she wandered over to Evan seeming a little delirious. Mimicking Evan, Ellie sat by the pool in a daze.

'What are we doing?'

'It's a sign of peace and friendship,' Evan said, taking mouthfuls of the water as it trickled through his fingers. 'Have a few sips…it's just water.'

Ellie admired the gift she had received from Harrup. 'How did he do that?'

'Later,' Evan offered. 'I'll explain later. For now, take some water.'

Ellie's eyes seemed empty; she must have been lost in her thoughts. Eventually, she placed the statue inside one of her overall pockets and began to drink. Preoccupied with her encounter, Ellie's eyes brimmed with confusion. Needing clarity, Evan glanced at her.

'I have to ask. Do you really think it's dissent? Helping the elrupe. Do you still not approve?'

Instantly, Ellie touched the pocket where she had placed Harrup's gift. 'Of course, it's dissent,' she said so nobody could hear. 'This…it goes against The Union. Against Rada. And it's breaking the law.'

'But, after everything you've just—'

Ellie placed her hand on Evan's to cut him short. 'But after everything I've just seen…I think it's compassion, Evan. I had no idea what they were like…the elrupe. I don't blame you for helping them. They have nothing, but they're so generous with what little they have. Like I said…I had no idea.'

Evan placed his other hand over Ellie's grinning.

Adult elrupe began congregating by an opening in the courtyard wall. Around them, pygboar skulls littered the floor; distinguished by their large eye sockets and sharp snouts. Pygboars were all born blind yet had huge eyeballs despite that. Evan had no idea why nature still gave them this feature when they lived in complete darkness. Eyes were of little use in the deeper caves where pygboars could be found.

Inscriptions coloured the stone all around the hollow where the elrupe had started to mingle. Evan wasn't sure what they meant. To him, they were peculiar images that weren't easily understood, but he did know that they had been placed there for a reason. Larger items of food were hauled from the opening and a strong odour immediately filled the air.

Ellie watched them closely. 'Is that where they get their food?'

'You're observant too, as well as being good at asking questions.' Evan giggled like he was five years old.

While Evan poked fun at her, Ellie stared at the group of elrupe. They had begun to disperse, but her eyes were fixed on the crevice. A frown consumed her, and as her eyes screwed, her fingers scraped at the edge of the pool.

'Evan. We need to go.' It seemed like Ellie was having to make an effort to sound calm.

'Go? Where? We only just got here.'

Ellie was determined, but maybe desperate too. 'I won't say it again,' she mumbled, with an obvious distress. 'We have to go. Now!'

Without any hesitation, Ellie turned and hurried toward the walkway. Evan glanced inside the food store, puzzled about what had caused her sudden upset. Inside the fissure, all he could distinguish were battered metal containers. Several elrupe were removing the contents and there was nothing to explain Ellie's distress.

Evan knew that he had little choice but to run after her, even though her unpredictability was beginning to annoy him. What mattered most to him though, was to stop Ellie from leaving the caves by herself at night. Being beyond the outskirts of Port Harmony in the dark, wasn't safe.

'Ellie,' he shouted, over and again. 'Ellie…stop!'

There was no response. Ellie picked up speed on the walkway, whilst Evan trailed behind. Obviously, she had no intention of stopping.

chapter fifteen

Minus One

'Explain it to me again,' Haylee demanded. 'What do you mean she's missing?'

Haylee didn't take bad news well, and she couldn't stomach things deviating from how she planned them.

Morrigan stared at the floor, tugging at her dark hair nervously. 'She vanished Hay. I'm sorry.'

'Where did she vanish? When did you lose her?' Haylee paced around, trying not to trip on the fleece furnishings. Some of the candles had burnt out; the main room of her house had turned gloomy.

'She just went. We were on our way to Cedric's...I turned around and she was gone!'

Haylee had no idea what to do with her anger; it wasn't fair to take it out on Morrigan. Ditto had her own mind and wouldn't have given Morrigan the chance to stop her. Always the most impulsive of the group, Ditto was becoming a liability. Haylee was struggling to keep her in tow.

'I'm so sorry Hay,' Morrigan was all but whimpering, which wasn't like her. 'I looked everywhere.'

'You didn't check on Cedric's either?'

'No...I...When I noticed she was gone, I went to find her.'

A clattering noise in the back room tore through the tense atmosphere. Tik had been preparing their orgo for the night's work. He was being his usual heavy-handed self, whilst collecting their saddles. Haylee considered things carefully. It would be easy to go and search for Ditto, and with Tik and Morrigan by her side, it may not take long either. But if Ditto's intention was what Haylee thought, she could sacrifice everything they had worked so hard for.

Morrigan intruded on Haylee's thoughts. 'Hay! Kayden...he's still out there somewhere.'

'What about Blue?'

'Blue? Who's? Oh her,' Morrigan griped. 'Never saw her...she was never with me after we left here.'

'So...she's missing too?'

'Doubt it,' said Morrigan. 'She will be with Evan. But Hay...Kayden is still in Port Harmony.'

'Okay, stop...I'm thinking.'

'We need to—'

'Sssssh…I'm thinking!'

'But we need to find Ditto.'

'Stop!' yelled Haylee. Taking long slow breaths, she felt her grip on her friends slipping. They were all admirable and strong in their independence. But rash decisions made things difficult, and she was beginning to think it would be their undoing. Haylee needed to keep them on track. They all had to work towards the same goal. The goal they had given up everything for, and one very big part of that, was their pledge to always protect each other.

'What's with all the shouting?' Tik entered the house through the back room and Toze scuttled next to him.

Morrigan ran to them. 'Ditto. She's gone. We need to go look for her…but Haylee is doing nothing.'

Tik looked bewildered when he turned to look for a response off Haylee. 'Wait…what? Ditto has done what?'

Haylee was quiet and determined to gather her thoughts. She needed to make a calculated decision about what they should do next. They had to keep on track, but they also needed to find Ditto before she got herself killed. Toze's behaviour wasn't helping her to focus, and he jumped from fleece to fleece, rolling around on the floor.

'Haylee…what's she talking about?' Tik looked serious, standing there in only his black tunic. It wasn't like him.

'Sssssh…I'm thinking,' said Haylee.

'She keeps sayin' that,' Morrigan shrieked. 'Ditto is still out there. We need to go and get her. Tik, come with me…please.'

Circling round and moving closer to her friends, Haylee felt determined. 'Alright look...Tik, get the animals ready. Morrigan, tether your ride out back. Time to go to work.'

Morrigan looked flushed. 'What about Ditto?' Her shrill voice explained her frustration, and the moth image on her cheek looked almost alive.

Haylee was trying her hardest to keep calm. 'We will find her on the way.'

Tik rushed toward the back, closely tailed by Toze. The little balkutar's fur was standing on end through excitement. Morrigan stepped in their way and would not let them pass. Stubborn was something Morrigan excelled at.

'You always do whatever she tells you,' she screamed at Tik, repositioning her cloak. 'Always! You never question anything she says. Why?'

Tik looked dumbstruck. 'Well…because she's—'

'Whatever!' Morrigan said, not wanting to listen to Tik's answer. 'We need to find Ditto. Ditto is what matters.'

'Enough!' Haylee had no tolerance for defiance.

The room fell quiet whilst everyone seemed to try and compose themselves. They were faced with a dilemma, and nobody had any particularly strong suggestions. Haylee began pacing across the fleeces, kicking at them with her feet. She was determined to take her annoyance out on something. Collecting a taper from a hole in the stone wall, she found the nearest candle and held the flimsy stick inside the flame.

Before she could light any more candles as she intended, the front door flung open. Haylee span, hoping to see Ditto. The person who entered wasn't who she expected.

'Haylee...I...I...' Ellie looked as though she had discovered all her fears when she fell into the room.

Behind her, Evan rushed in through the doorway appearing equally flustered. For a minute he stood there, entirely speechless. Haylee waited for Ellie to continue, but something was holding her back. Then, Morrigan chose to intervene, marching towards Ellie with conviction.

'Where did you go?' she cried. 'Thought you were helping us.' It was fair to say, that the situation with Ditto had enraged Morrigan. When her arm extended toward Ellie, Evan moved between them protectively.

Haylee was frustrated. 'Out with it Blue! We're in the middle of something.' She wasn't finding it easy to get Morrigan and Tik organised, and Ellie turning up right at that point was not what she needed. Morrigan wasn't the apprentice's biggest fan either. Any anger she was feeling would surely be directed toward Ellie.

With eyes that swelled with some sort of sadness, Ellie didn't reply.

'She's been like this all the way back,' Evan said, still obstructing Morrigan.

'From where?' Haylee probed.

'What?'

Haylee breathed deeply. 'Back...from where. Where have you been?'

Morrigan faced Haylee with raised eyebrows and she tilted her head. Her face blended fury with a hint of sarcasm.

'Ne...ver...mind! I don't want to know,' Haylee quipped.

Evan shook his head. 'Later. What matters now is that I don't know what's wrong with her.'

Morrigan's arms became animated, and she transformed into a crazed animal right in front of Evan's face. 'What matters...is where *she* was,' she snarled, waggling her finger in Ellie's direction. 'What matters...is that *she* should have been with us. What matters...is that...if *she* had been with us...Ditto may not have disappeared. And Ditto is still missing. And what matters…is that we are all here now…doing nothing about it.'

'Haylee…I…I…you need…' Ellie fought to speak. She looked like she wanted to say something important, but nothing logical surfaced.

'Where's Ditto, Hay?' Evan asked.

'I just told you…we don't know,' hissed Morrigan. 'She's missing!'

The tension in the room was intolerable; like a horrendous deadlock in a game of Deception. Haylee was concerned that they were going around in circles. Decisiveness was needed. But she still didn't have an ideal solution to offer.

'Right…listen,' she ordered. 'Morri…enough with the blame. You and Tik need to go and get the orgo ready. Evan, you take Blue…find Ditto.'

Moving her focus in Tik's direction, Morrigan seemed ready to conform. Tik meanwhile, bobbed his head reassuringly. It was possible that Morrigan didn't feel like she had any choice. She pulled away from her confrontation, following Tik into the back room. Evan meanwhile, looked stunned.

Haylee tried to snap him out of his daydream. 'Evan! Why are you still here?'

Evan looked at his sister blankly; she assumed he was lost for words. Despair was not something Haylee welcomed. As awkward as everything was, she needed her people to fall in line promptly. They all needed to move faster.

Seeing something peculiar, Haylee's focus shifted to Ellie. 'Blue! What's that?'

Ellie's grimy overalls had taken on a life of their own. Movement in the pocket at her waist was unmistakable, and tiny lights seemed to flash inside. Ellie looked horrified and slapped her hand down to conceal the disturbance. By this point, she was visibly trembling. She looked up at Evan with tears bubbling around her eyes.

'I need to go,' she cried. 'I'm sorry.'

When Ellie turned for the door, Evan blocked her route. 'Go…where?'

Haylee studied Ellie's clothing, trying hard to define what was happening. The pocket almost bounced against the apprentice's middle, and it glimmered furiously. She had never seen anything like the mysterious bulge.

'Evan,' Ellie whimpered. 'Please…help your sister. But I have to go…Now!'

'Not without some sort of explanation. I'm worried about you.'

Ellie pushed passed him and ran out of the building, faster than an orgo. 'I'm sorry,' she sobbed as she left.

chapter sixteen

Hunting for Ditto

In many ways, Ditto was enjoying the chase. She had no idea if it would end well for her, but the buzz from galloping through Port Harmony's meandering streets was extraordinary. After many laps of the town, Kayden had still been unable to capture her. Although to be fair, she found his resolve inspiring. Each time that he had made attempts to surround Ditto, she had escaped with style. But despite his shortcomings, Kayden was ever determined.

Taking more risks, Ditto swerved into a narrow alley. It was pitch black, and every building appeared to be closing in on her. 'This was a mistake,' she said, mocking her own decision.

With Kayden's army closing in on her, Ditto realised that she needed to find a route where she could see better. The series of rounded homes seemed to go on for an eternity, and there was no visible way out. Trapped, Ditto pulled back on the reins of her steed and brought her journey to a halt. She had no choice other than to devise a new plan.

Kayden was closing in on her and began to snigger noisily. 'Looks like this is the end of the hunt. Time to surrender Ditto.'

Ditto wasn't ready to give up; not without a fight. Positioning her orgo to face the six adversaries, she waited with patience. Her hands quivered, but Ditto's need to survive kept her going. Seconds before Kayden's people were upon her, she flinched her wrists, and sped toward them.

'Stop her!' Kayden's voice was ear-piercing.

Hurtling into the pod of enemy orgo, Ditto pushed her own animal forward. 'Yah,' she screamed when she shoved between them.

Kayden steadied his slave with one hand, whilst clutching reins in the other. The girl lay still in front of his saddle, and it looked like there was little life in her. As all the orgo reared and snorted aggressively, Ditto glanced at the slave. *Blue is right*, she thought. *That girl needs saving*. Still pushing her orgo to drive them through the opposing group, Ditto stretched out. She was trying to pull the slave away from Kayden.

'That was stupid,' Kayden said when Ditto felt a burning across her arm.

One of Kayden's rangers was wielding a mace. The weapon had caused a deep wound in her flesh, making sure Ditto couldn't take hold of Kayden's prisoner. Squeezing on her reins, she continued her attempts to break free of the mob. Overhead, she could hear the awful calls of gliders, as if they were there as extra protection for Kayden.

'Hit her again,' Kayden called, but his orders were too late, and Ditto had prized her way through them.

Still in her saddle, Ditto grinned at her accomplishment. She could barely believe that she had managed to evade her attackers. But with a single cry from Kayden, her hopes were soon destroyed.

'Now!' Kayden's command was firm and methodical.

Ditto heard small snapping sounds from behind, and her orgo lurched. The noises continued, and before she could react, her animal collapsed, throwing her from the saddle. Sprawled across the rough cobbles, Ditto was stunned. Her face drooped into the slush coated ground. She had no idea what had happened, but somehow, Kayden's people had felled her orgo.

In seconds, the claws of Kayden's steed were beside Ditto. 'Nin are amazing little creatures. There's a beauty in it...the way they take down such large mammals so easily.'

Hurt, but not defeated, Ditto stood and pounced at him. Clenching his black cape, she yanked him from his orgo with a strength she didn't know she owned. Kayden fell to the floor screaming, whilst the assault rangers fenced them in. There was little chance of Ditto escaping, but she was ready for a fight.

'Surrender yourself now,' Kayden yapped, lifting to his feet. 'We will take you with us. As payment for your loss. This is your only chance to—'

When her fist reached Kayden's cheek it stung, but there was no way Ditto would consider submission. 'Never!'

Kayden rubbed his face. 'Very well. Rangers take her—'

Interrupted again, he screeched aloud when his slave staggered in Ditto's direction. Arms held high and wide, she was attempting to prevent the rangers' attack. Her actions were suicidal, and Ditto couldn't believe how such a spindly woman was able to make such a bold gesture. Nor could she understand why; the slave didn't even know Ditto. All she knew, was that in her cloak and tunic she still felt the bitter cold. How the slave—dressed only in rags—hadn't turned to an ice block, was beyond understanding.

Placing her hand on the slave's shoulder, Ditto whispered, 'Pandra isn't it? You're the one they call Pandra.'

The slave nodded feebly. 'Yes.'

Kayden took hold of Pandra's arms and tossed her aside. 'Not today slave. I haven't yet finished watching you suffer.'

Ditto flew at Kayden again, shoving him back into the side of his orgo. The animal snorted with the blow, stamping its claws ferociously. The gliders above joined in with the protest. With a sly grin, Kayden stepped forward, turning to face his rangers. In some way, he found immense pleasure in tormenting Ditto.

'Rangers,' he said. 'Take her down.'

Before Kayden's troops could react, an unforeseen hissing emerged in the alleyway. The sound disrupted their assault, and one of the rangers fell from his saddle. Instinctively, his steed bolted, charging passed Ditto, and away down the alley.

'What?' roared Kayden.

Ditto span round to witness lumps of metal heading toward them, glistening in the moonlight. As the machine drew closer, she recognised the person at the centre of it. Junkyard had made a timely entrance.

'Hello old friend,' he called out to Kayden. 'We need to talk.'

Encased in metal, Junkyard was like a walking appliance. His hands looked like they were his main armament, and the casing around them was moulded into barrels. These must have been the weapons that toppled the ranger.

Conscious that she shouldn't relax too soon, Ditto sighed.

'This is not your business,' Kayden returned. 'Leave now!'

Junkyard giggled. 'It's you who needs to leave Kayden. You are not welcome here.'

'I will happily go. But Ditto is coming with me.' Stepping toward the inventor, Kayden remained undeterred.

'Not gonna happen,' Junkyard said. 'Ditto asked for my help. And…well…your weapons are of little use against my new toy.'

If the weapons he referred to were the nin, he was right. Steel almost completely shielded Junkyard; the bugs wouldn't even touch him. He was like a shiny knight from stories that Ditto had heard as a child, and he was also armed. Gliders circled in the sky, and Junkyard pointed his hand in their direction. With a thud, the barrel at the end of his arm discharged, immediately followed by an ugly squawk. One of the gliders hit the ground hard, a few inches from Junkyard, its tail flinching wildly. Of anyone, Junkyard would be pleased the world had one less glider. Above, the other creatures swooped boisterously, after witnessing the death of one of their own.

Kayden turned to his rangers and snickered. The noise seemed to go on for some time. Encouraged to follow their leader, the rangers joined in with the howling. With a single step,

Kayden snatched Ditto and pulled her into him. He was brutal in his efficiency, locking Ditto in place with a single arm, and digging his other hand into her knotty hair.

'The nin may not be a threat to you,' he said. 'But…where our mutual friend Ditto is concerned, that is not the case.'

Junkyard lowered his arms, staring at Ditto and probably trying to concoct a new plan. 'We have a real problem here Kayden. You are threatening a friend of mine. That's not something I take well. Neither of us wants things to get out of hand.'

'She has a debt to repay,' Kayden said, in a raspy tone. 'It is only fair that I take her as recompense.'

Whilst the standoff played out, nobody other than Ditto appeared to notice Pandra. She had crawled amongst the rangers and was fiddling with something on their saddles. Whatever she was doing, it only took a few seconds for her to tamper with each one, and Ditto watched her curiously.

Clanking further toward them, Junkyard was not discouraged. 'Ditto isn't going anywhere.'

Ditto could feel the rage in Kayden. His heavy breathing rubbed her back, and his hand tightened in her mane of messy hair. He wasn't about to give her up now that he had caught her, but she was unsure what his next move may be.

The feel of his hands all over her, made Ditto feel like she needed to bathe.

'This is your last chance Junkyard,' Kayden said. 'Back away…forget about Ditto.'

Junkyard nodded, but Ditto realised that it wasn't in agreement when she noticed his grin. 'Not a chance!' Reacting swiftly, Junkyard raised his hand and shot another of the rangers with astonishing skill. Again, out of self-preservation, the victim's orgo galloped away in a haze of black fur.

Unexpectedly shoved in the direction of the enduring rangers, Ditto closed her eyes. She knew what was coming next. Her only choice was to make some sort of attempt to get to Junkyard. Thinking quickly, she thrust forward, wincing when she heard a crackling from behind. Yet Ditto felt nothing. She had presumed there would be pain or even a stinging. Opening her eyes and glancing across her tunic, there was nothing there. Not a nin to be seen; not one insect. She pulled her cloak to see if that had been contaminated, but there was nothing there either.

When Junkyard's merriment grew louder, she turned to establish what had happened. With dim fizzing sounds and bright sparks, the rangers' saddles were malfunctioning. Ditto also found it amusing, watching the small army dumfounded by the fiasco.

'No!' screeched Kayden, watching Ditto find safety alongside Junkyard. His head lowered, and he was glaring at Pandra. He had already determined that his slave was to blame for the sabotage.

Junkyard directed his weapon at their adversary. 'I've already made light work of two of your men,' he gloated. 'Don't make me take you down. Leave the girl alone.'

Ignoring Junkyard's warning, Kayden lifted Pandra and struck her face with the back of his hand. He showed no remorse and held onto her when she wilted. The slave would be lucky to escape her living nightmare, but proceeding toward them, Junkyard had not given up. His weapon remained fixed on Kayden.

'Hand…your slave…over.'

Kayden had a firm grip on Pandra. 'Her? Do you even know who she is? What she is?'

Junkyard tipped his head to Ditto. 'I think we've established that she's your slave. But you're not in Eklips, and you will let her go.'

'She's a spy! Worse…she is Rada's spy.'

'Whoever she is,' Junkyard said. 'She doesn't deserve to be treated that way.'

'Really?' Kayden looked crazy. 'I wouldn't have thought that you would care much for someone dedicated to Rada. We have a mutual interest in protecting ourselves from the power-hungry ruler of Scorr Tanta.'

'I only have your word...that she is who you say she is. From what I saw...she was trying to protect Ditto.'

Kayden shook his slave like he was deranged. 'Apparently, someone has been stealing supplies. Union supplies. This girl you seem so concerned about...was employed by Rada to confirm it was me. It seems Rada's forces have even been to Eklips in my absence. Injured many of my people. They were that sure it was me.'

'Am I supposed to care about all this?' The sarcasm is Junkyard's tone was undeniable. Ditto was sure that he didn't believe a word Kayden was saying.

'I'm innocent. I have suspected Rada has been watching me for some time,' Kayden went on. 'And I was very sceptical of receiving a slave...who had previously been a warden. But I honoured my agreement with The Union...played my part. Now it seems I have been deceived...by this...'

Pandra's state couldn't be defined, and Ditto watched in horror whilst Kayden jostled her around like she was a sack of dirt. Junkyard meanwhile, gave the impression that he was restless. He too must have found watching Kayden's brutality disturbing.

'Do you know how paranoid you sound?' he asked. 'Again...why should I care anyway? I just want you to hand over the girl...like a good little tyrant.'

'No! She will suffer for her deception—'

'Was she not suffering anyway?' Junkyard shook his arm to intimidate his opponent. 'Like all your other slaves? Last chance...hand her over. Enough with the nonsense! I'm not interested in all that.'

'You would be wise to take an interest,' Kayden said. 'If Rada is spying on Eklips...who knows what else she is up to.'

Junkyard stepped forward and readied his armaments. He had a clear and direct shot at Kayden.

'Rangers!' Kayden hollered.

The three remaining rangers found their mace weapons and prepared to dismount. But their efforts were worthless, and Junkyard efficiently blasted another one of them from his saddle. When only two of them remained, they knew their opponent had the upper hand, and they lowered their maces.

Kayden shrieked, in an ear-piercing way. 'Rangers!'

This time, his men ignored him, staying quiet in their saddles.

'Looks like you're out of options.' Junkyard was rightfully smug. 'Let her go.'

Kayden's head swung from one side to the other, assessing his dilemma. He had lost his cause. 'Very well,' he said, in an uncharacteristically soft tone. 'Take her.'

Pandra collapsed in the dirt when Kayden released his grip. She was in a bad way, and it was difficult to tell whether she was still conscious.

Junkyard glanced at Ditto. 'Go! Take the girl...and go.'

'What about you?' Ditto was concerned.

'Don't worry about me. She needs your help...not me. Me and Kayden...we will be fine. We have some catching up to do. Isn't that right old friend?'

Whilst Kayden seemed to growl, Ditto scurried over to Pandra. Examining the slave's condition, she could see that there was still some life in her. Ditto crouched and threw Pandra's arm across her own shoulder.

'It's all going to be okay now,' she said, lifting Pandra to her feet.

Pandra moaned whilst Ditto limped back down the passage clutching onto her. Without looking back, Ditto passed Junkyard. He raised his eyebrows and smiled, offering encouragement.

Ditto had no idea how to express the enormity of her gratitude. 'Thank you.'

'What are friends for?' Junkyard replied, his arm still directed at Kayden.

Ditto worked hard to keep her momentum, but Pandra was a fair bit taller, and her feet bounced floppily on the cobbles. Liberating the slave was gruelling, to say the least. Even so, all Ditto could think about was getting back home, and how she might be able to help the woman slumped in her arms. Haylee would know what to do, and if not, Evan would.

'Just keep going,' Junkyard called out, urging Ditto on.

A few seconds later, as she approached the end of the alleyway, Ditto could only just hear when Junkyard issued more instructions to Kayden.

'Well then. You have overstayed your welcome, don't you think? I came to inform you, that a mutual friend has asked for you to leave this place. I suggest you never come back.'

chapter seventeen

Back to Reality

Sprinting faster than she thought possible, Ellie realised it wasn't wise to be alone in Port Harmony after nightfall. That didn't matter, she had to get away — and fast. So fast, she had even left Sage still tethered outside Haylee's. With her feet sliding on the icy cobbles, she ran as far as she was able, refusing to stop until she began gasping for air. Beyond was a small alleyway, and checking behind her, Ellie snuck into it, convinced she hadn't been seen.

Hidden in the dark, her fingers fumbled with a button on one of her pockets. Shoving her hand inside, Ellie took hold of the rock-like object that she retrieved from Cedric's earlier. After lifting it out, she paused for composure, holding it in her palm. Wiping the remnants of tears from her cheeks, Ellie gazed down.

'I'm here,' she said.

The rock appeared to crumble in Ellie's hand, and instantly, two fragments twisted into place.

After the item stood on these new appendages, two more pieces splintered on either side of it. Beneath these sections, rusted metallic arms were exposed. Through hushed mechanical whirring sounds, the contraption wobbled on its stone-clad legs. At that moment, a telescopic neck punched its way out of the highest point of the rock. At the end of the neck, a spherical head revealed two large eyes, which turned green as it faced Ellie. Metal eyelids blinked whilst it focused. In Ellie's hand, a tiny robot had emerged from the pebble which encased it.

'Nice to see you again, Widget,' Ellie remarked. 'Although you nearly got me caught back there.'

The robot's gears made sharp grinding noises as he moved. 'Well…I'm sorry Miss Ellie, but Rada is waiting to speak with you,' he said. Lights flickered where his mouth should have been. 'Perhaps if you hadn't kept me hidden away all this time, you wouldn't have missed me so much. It's not easy Miss Ellie, spending every day trapped inside a rock. I mean…you should try it some time. Trust me, you wouldn't like it. I mean—'

'Widget,' Ellie interrupted, trying to end the ramblings of her motorised companion. 'Did you say Rada is waiting?'

Widget jostled an arm. 'Well yes, Miss Ellie. Indeed, she is.'

'Then put her through please, precious,' Ellie said, wanting to hurry things along.

Widget rotated his head. 'Very well.'

From his eyes, a blurry grey image of Rada projected onto the stony surface of the closest building. Ellie had no idea how long Rada had been waiting to talk to her, but her mood would be impossible to establish under that mask.

'My Lady,' Ellie said. She noticed how frightened she suddenly felt. Ellie's tummy was rumbling loudly. The day's events were catching up with her and taking their toll. She didn't know what scared her more; Rada, the dark, or being discovered talking to the ruler of Scorr Tanta.

'Aah…Warden Dee Twelve,' Rada answered, sternly. 'How nice to finally see you. It has been a long time since your last update.'

'Yes, My Lady,' Ellie said, trying to sound confident. 'There has been nothing to report really.'

'You haven't yet found the Renegades?'

'No, My Lady.' Ellie shivered. The air was getting worse, and Ellie's nerves weren't helping her to withstand the temperature.

'I'm confused. Tell me…are you certain that you don't know their identity?'

Ellie considered her response for a moment. She felt conflicted, and this conversation had come too soon for her to reflect. Rada wanted answers, but Ellie wasn't sure if she had them. She wasn't sure of much anymore.

'My Lady, if the description we have of the Renegades is true. Then…haven't they been found in Eklips by now?'

Rada shoved her staff forwards. If she had been there in person, it would have certainly struck Ellie. Her actions illustrated her wrath.

'You think they are Kayden's people?' she asked.

'Aren't they? They wear the same.'

'It seems…Dee Twelve…that you are very much behind the rest of us,' Rada bellowed. 'I stationed you there to bring me information, and to uncover who these outlaws are. Instead…it is me who needs to update you.'

Ellie was desperate to find a way out of her dilemma. 'I don't understand My Lady.'

'Pandra came to the same conclusion,' said Rada, in a much calmer manner. 'That Kayden and his people were behind these crimes. That is not the case, and I assumed that because of that, you would have some more information. If these Renegades aren't from Eklips…which I assure you, they aren't…then they come from Port Harmony. They are there…with you.'

Ellie wanted the conversation with Rada to end, and fumbled around, trying to find a switch to turn off Widget. 'Pandra is here…My Lady…she is in Port Harmony. She is with Kayden. And his army…they're…well—'

'It is not them!' Screaming, Rada expected more from her spy.

Ellie understood she had been in Port Harmony for a long time, and that her ruler would want results. Her head drooped. 'Then...I haven't discovered anything. I assumed the Renegades weren't from Port Harmony in the end. I was convinced it was Kayden's rangers.'

'So...you are you saying, that you have learned nothing in your time there?'

'No, My Lady. No...it appears not. Nothing.' Ellie was struggling. Lying to Rada went against all her principles. Growing up in Scorr Tanta, she was encouraged to respect and serve their ruler by her parents. But then, Ellie didn't even know if she was lying. To say she was muddled, would be an understatement.

'Yet, you seem uncertain Dee Twelve,' Rada cautioned. 'It would be wise to tell me what you know.'

'I need more time, My Lady. Unless you have any useful information for me?'

'No!' Rada's voice was scarier than Ellie had ever heard. 'Your time has run out. If I don't bring these Renegades to justice...give the people something...then there will be riots in our streets.'

Ellie hugged her body tightly with one arm, keeping Widget balanced in her other. Her breaths were short and irregular from the wintry weather. She felt Harrup's sculpture of her, in the pocket where she had placed it.

'Weren't you supposed to be watching Haylee?' Rada went on. 'She is responsible. Haylee and her people…they must be the Renegades. Whilst you have done nothing…we have already prepared to capture them. I have set a trap. Tonight…the Renegades…Haylee…they're finished. We will not fail this time.'

'My Lady, with respect...What…What if it isn't…Haylee and her people? What makes you think it is them?'

Nonetheless, she knew Rada was right. Ellie had seen the Scorr Tanta insignia on the shabby food containers in the caves. Evan had told her that Haylee helped the elrupe; it all made sense. Ellie had a sort of hollow feeling like someone had stolen her thoughts. At odds with her own principles, she realised that she had become forced her to question everything she had ever believed. Her chance meeting with the elrupe had changed it all, and she blamed Rada for their suffering. The world she lived in had twisted, and she had no idea who, or what, to trust.

'You said you have seen Pandra? In Port Harmony?' Rada's own question ignored Ellie's concerns.

'Yes, My Lady.'

'Am I to assume she has endured much suffering at the hands of Kayden?'

'I don't think she will survive much longer.'

Rada took time to contemplate. 'Pandra's sacrifice will not go in vain. We know now that the Renegades are not coming from Eklips. Haylee and her people…they are the only others that we know of who have the appropriate skills.'

'Yes, My Lady.' Ellie lifted Harrup's figurine from her pocket. Taking another look, she still couldn't believe how well the object resembled her.

'On this very night…we will end this,' Rada insisted. 'For good! Your job now is to attempt to retrieve Pandra. You are to do anything necessary to bring her home. Kayden will know by now, that she is working for me. For that, she will pay a heavy price. Find her, and after that…at daybreak…you will report to Dee Squad. I am sending blastguards to Port Harmony. They will escort you all home and bring the Renegades to justice.'

'Will my father be coming?' Ellie asked. 'To Port Harmony.'

'Reuniting with your father, Dee Twelve, is none of my concern.'

'I see.'

Rada grunted. 'Is there anything else? Do you understand your orders?'

Discreetly gazing down at the statue in her hand, Ellie found her resolve. 'My Lady, just one other thing. This trap you have set...for the Renegades. What is it? I'm curious how you plan on capturing them?'

Without any parting words, Rada cut off their transmission. Ellie was left with an overwhelming need to warn Haylee. She had heard talk about the work they had to do. Now, Haylee would likely be walking—or riding—straight into Rada's trap. Still unable to determine a sensible course of action, Ellie trusted her instincts.

Widget rotated back to face Ellie, then tilted his head near her other hand. 'Miss Ellie, if you don't mind me asking...What is that? Where did you get it? It looks very much like you.'

'I got it from an...well...a friend.'

Making a sudden whirr, Widget retracted his neck. 'Oh...I see. You've made new friends here.'

'None as special as you. Don't worry. But I do need you to shut down now. I must hurry.'

'But Miss Ellie. Won't you be needing me? I can locate Miss Pandra and help you. Then, when we have her—'

'That won't be necessary,' said Ellie. She was finding the little robot somewhat annoying, and she felt tense enough already. 'Shut down! Now please Widget.

As Widget clunked back into his secret form, Ellie tried to relax. If she was to be of any use, she needed to calm down. Sliding her companion back into the pocket of her overalls, she backtracked down the dim alley, still admiring Harrup's mini-tribute. But after only a couple of steps, she halted in her tracks.

Evan was standing in the shadows, only a few feet away from where Ellie had communicated with Rada. His face held an expression that she had never seen before. When she looked at him, Ellie's stomach felt like something crushed it from inside. She couldn't move; he must have seen everything.

chapter eighteen

The Truth Hurts

Crazed, Ellie found herself thumping at Haylee's door for a second time that day. When Evan had dashed away from the alleyway, she hadn't been fast enough to catch him. She knew he was inside, but she couldn't blame him for ignoring her. Nevertheless, Ellie had to speak to him—and quickly. Realising that her efforts at the front door were futile, she remembered there was a way in at the rear of the building.

Still bound to the wooden post behind her, Sage snorted obnoxiously. He was trying to get Ellie's attention when she ventured into the gap between Haylee's and the next building. The space was only just wide enough for an orgo to fit through. In the dark, Ellie could make out some of the markings etched into the side of Haylee's home. The engravings depicted the elrupe and orgo, amongst other things she couldn't decipher; she hadn't noticed them earlier. Regardless of the cold, Ellie's palms felt sweaty; she had no idea what she would say to Evan once she found him.

Ellie flinched when a gugubat materialised on the wall of Haylee's home. Equally startled, the fluffy, grey rodent turned and glowered at her. Through almost indistinguishable eyes, set within its small skull, it studied Ellie as she approached. With a plump, rounded body and lengthy hind legs, its shape resembled that of a miniature orgo; only without the long neck. In fact, the creature had a complete absence of anything resembling a neck and was no bigger than Ellie's foot. Tiny paws at the end of short arms rubbed at its nose when it sniffled, and its shady fur blended into the darkness well. Despite that, a well-defined white stripe ran centrally from the tip of its blunt snout and across the top of its head, making it more distinguishable. Ellie noticed it had large wings, especially when considering its body size. She had never seen a gugubat up close before; they were mostly nocturnal. As Ellie passed the creature, it darted away as fast as it had appeared.

Once behind the building, Ellie spotted the rear entrance. Opposite, four orgo were fastened beneath a timber canopy — three of them white, and the other black. They were becoming agitated with the noise Sage was creating; pulling hard on their reins that secured them to a shelter. The black orgo, being the purest wild-type, were also the fiercest. Ellie wondered how long that one may take to yank itself free.

As fast as she could, Ellie slipped into Haylee's home. 'Evan,' she called out. 'Evan…I know you're here. We need to—'

Ellie's entire body numbed from shock when fingers lodged in her hair. Dragged into the main room, she squealed whilst her feet floundered beneath her. In a blink, her back was against the wall and a sturdy palm pressed against her chest. Although her hair was released, Ellie's relief was stolen in an instant. Within the sparse room, discovering Evan's expression seemed to make her legs wilt.

'Traitor,' Evan roared. His free hand clutched a timber baton.

Moaning was all Ellie mustered at first, unable to move. 'Please,' she pleaded, managing to focus. 'Please…let me explain.'

Evan's hand tightened against Ellie's overalls, making her wince. The discomfort was bearable, but she was more concerned about the chunk of wood in his other hand. Instinctively, she had always known that Evan wouldn't hurt her. Nevertheless, he would now feel betrayed. Ellie had no idea how that may make him react.

Lifting her own hand, Ellie rested it on the one that held her in place. 'Evan…please. Please.'

Evan looked full of sadness more than anything. 'You need to leave. You need to leave Port Harmony…tonight. Never come back. You shouldn't have come here.'

'I can't leave,' Ellie said. 'Not right now.'

Refusing to look at her, Evan groaned. 'Why?'

'We need to warn Haylee.' Ellie brushed her fingers across Evan's hand. She wanted his eyes to meet hers. More than anything, she needed to regain his trust. But that might prove impossible.

The wooden baton bounced over and again against Evan's shoulder. 'Warn her? About what?'

'Did you not hear Rada?'

'I heard nothing. But I saw plenty.'

Evan pulled his hand back, releasing his hold on Ellie. To her surprise, he tossed his timber weapon to one side. She stepped toward him and reached her hand forward. Touching his cheek, she nudged his gaze in her direction. His grief was hard for her to take in.

'Thought you might hit me!' Ellie said, unexpectedly giggling. She wasn't sure why she found the thought funny; maybe it was because she didn't feel as threatened.

'I shouldn't have grabbed you like that. I didn't know what to expect. Seeing you...with Rada. Just leave Ellie. Go!'

'No, precious. I need you to listen.'

'Listen,' Evan thundered, now facing her. 'Listen! To who? Who are you, Ellie? I mean...other than a traitor. You're working for Rada!'

'We're all on the same side,' Ellie said, striding over a fleece to get closer to him.

Evan laughed in a hysterical way. 'Same side?'

'We are all members of The Union. I'm not a traitor. But you need to let me explain.'

'What I need…is for you to leave. I don't want to hear it.'

Ellie saw the loathing in Evan and blamed herself. 'I'm a warden, and I work for Scorr Tanta. That doesn't make me a traitor.'

'A warden?' Evan's turmoil was obvious. 'That's what you are? And you haven't told anyone that…not as far as I can tell. Why are you hiding, if you're not a traitor?'

'A traitor? Really? Traitors go against the very people they are supposed to be loyal to. They dissent…break the law…undermine it. Treachery is what the Renegades are guilty of. Not me…I was asked to bring them to justice.'

'Justice?' Evan said. 'That's why you're here? To enforce justice?'

Pausing to find better ways to explain her position, Ellie wondered if Evan may pick up the baton again. She had hurt him; it was plain to see. With his fists clenching, and a scrunched face, it seemed unlikely that Evan would be convinced of Ellie's intentions.

'As a warden,' Ellie said, trying again. 'It is my job to ensure the safety and wellbeing of people living wherever I am posted. Right now, that is here…in Port Harmony.'

'By hiding amongst us?' Evan was rightfully sceptical.

Ellie sighed. 'None of that matters now. Where's Haylee?'

'Of course, it matters. It matters because Haylee let you in. She let you get close to us…she never does that. Then today she did do that. And now it appears you were working against us all along.'

'Working against you. Why? Because of you…Haylee…the others…you're working against The Union. I was doing my job.'

'And we are trying to support the elrupe. We are making sure they survive.'

Ellie gazed at Evan, unsure of how to say what she wanted to. 'You are the Renegades.'

'We are the people doing what is right.' Tears had formed around Evan's eyes.

'But the elrupe…it was decided they had to go,' Ellie said softly, hoping to show at least some compassion. 'We couldn't sustain ourselves and them…they were a burden. The elrupe had to go. Don't you understand that it is you that is wrong?'

Evan approached Ellie, pushing her back against the wall. 'Wrong? We've been through this already. You think helping the elrupe is wrong?'

'Rada would…and that's what matters.'

Evan's hands clamped Ellie by her shoulders. The cold stone wall rubbed against her from behind. Whilst they stared at each other for a while, Ellie started to tremble. She felt like she'd been deceived throughout her life and could no longer justify being a warden.

'Do you…think it's wrong?' Evan eventually asked, determined to force Ellie's answer. 'Even after meeting them. What about Harrup? Is it wrong to want more for him?'

Ellie's head drooped. An immediate shame prevented her from looking at Evan. Reaching into her pocket, she lifted out the figurine that Harrup had given her. Words escaped her, and she rubbed the object, still fascinated. After what she had seen, Ellie understood Evan's principles and saw value in his cause. But admitting that, went against everything that she had ever relied on. That included the reasons for the mission she had undertaken. Throughout her childhood, Ellie's parents had always educated her about the problems that the elrupe had caused. She had been led to believe that their existence threatened human survival. Yet today, meeting the elrupe had contradicted anything Ellie had faith in. It wasn't fair to blame such a gentile species for the struggles of people.

'Well?' Evan pressed for a reply. 'Look at me, Ellie. I need an answer.'

'Enough Evan. You need to tell me where Haylee is.'

One of Evan's hands slid across to her jaw. 'Why?'

Feeling her head forced upward, Ellie closed her eyes. Confusion had taken over. She no longer knew what Evan was feeling; other than an obvious anger. Wriggling her shoulder free, she reached out.

'Because your sister is in trouble Evan. What matters now is that we help her. You care about the elrupe...about your sister. You must do, or you wouldn't have thought about hitting me. That's what is important, and I need you to let me help them. You're Haylee's only hope now.'

'You want me to help, but you won't answer my questions.' Evan leaned even closer when Ellie touched the back of his neck. She could feel his breath running across her face.

'Rada. She's set a trap,' Ellie said. 'Tonight. For the Renegades. For Haylee. Evan...where is Haylee. We need to warn her.'

'I'm not telling you anything,' Evan sounded croaky. 'I can't trust you with anything. Haylee can look after herself.'

'Not against the full force of Scorr Tanta. Rada knows that it's Haylee Evan.' Ellie nudged him nearer and opened her eyes.

'It's too late anyway. You're too late. Haylee...she's already gone.'

Ellie's hand slipped into Evan's tufts of hair and she edged forward. 'Tell me where she is,' she said softly; her lips almost touching Evan's cheek. His whiskers brushed against her skin. Tossing away her pride, Ellie needed Evan to reconnect with her. All the same, the moment didn't last as long as Ellie hoped it would.

'No!' Evan said, pulling away. 'How do I know you're not going to help Rada capture her? Besides…I don't even know where she is. You can't charm it out of me.'

Ellie slid Harrup's statue back inside her pocket. 'I'm not trying to. Forget that I'm a warden, I want you to remember who I am to you. I want to help Haylee, but I need to show you something. Please Evan…trust me. I know I haven't earned it…but your sister is in trouble. I can find her…if you truly don't know where she is. Let me show you.'

Evan mumbled, 'Go on.'

Fumbling around inside her other pocket, Ellie pulled out Widget. 'I'm here,' she said.

With grinding gears, Widget transformed from a chunk of rock, back into his mechanical form. Evan's lip dropped a little. He mustn't have seen anything like the little machine before and shifted for a closer look.

'What…is…that?' he asked, shakily.

'Excuse me, sir,' Widget rattled, twisting his head to focus on Evan. 'They call me Widget…I am not a what…but a who. You may call me Widget if you don't mind.'

Gobsmacked, Evan didn't even comment.

'Widget,' Ellie said. 'This is my friend Evan.'

'Nice to meet you,' Widget cheeped, his little rusted arm gesturing at Evan.

Ellie kept her resolve. 'I need you to find out where Dee Squad is please, Widget.'

'Not Pandra, Miss Ellie?' was the reply.

Holding her associate up to her face, Ellie frowned. 'I don't have time to waste. Where is Dee Squad?'

'Certainly. One moment.' Sharp, high-pitched sounds buzzed from Widget, followed by some sort of fuzzy noise. As the din subsided, it was then possible to establish voices. Widget was managing to tune into the wardens' communications. Their conversation was difficult to decode at first, but gradually, it got clearer.

'…lose them,' a voice said, as the sound became sharper.

A warped noise followed, whilst nobody else communicated. Ellie moved Widget closer to her ear. She was determined to prove to Evan that she could be trusted. After a short crackling sound, a different voice emerged.

'I think I see something,'

'I repeat…do not lose them,' came the reply. The voice must have been that of the warden in charge of their operation.

'Yes sir,' a woman's voice said. 'They're approaching the wharf now sir.'

'Are we prepared?' asked another of the squad. This one was a man.

'They seem to be moving toward the supply shed as planned sir,' the female warden answered.

Ellie faced Evan. 'The supply shed…on the wharf. That's where they are? We need to go. Now! That will be all Widget.'

With his head turning toward Evan, then back to Ellie and so on, Widget seemed bemused. 'That's it? You need me to go again? I haven't even had a chance to make your friend's acquaintance. It's not easy you know—'

'Widget,' Ellie said, jumping in. 'As you were.'

After tutting, a little disgruntled, Widget complied and folded back into his rock casing. Ellie gave Evan another look, but he still appeared stunned. Placing Widget back in her pocket, she stepped closer to him. She understood why he was finding it hard to have faith in her. It was no surprise that he had been rough either; she would have done the same thing. Attempting to snap him out of his trance, Ellie placed her hand on Evan's shoulder.

'Evan…if it helps…I don't believe the elrupe are a burden. Not anymore. I know now…that what you're doing is right. Rada is wrong to treat them the way she has. I just don't know where that leaves me. I need you to believe that I thought I was doing the right thing. I was doing my job. As far as I know, Rada has no idea that the elrupe are still here, and I will do everything I can to help protect them...if you will let me. But for now, we need to stop Haylee.'

Life flooded back into Evan, and he glared at Ellie smiling. 'Wait here.'

Without delay, Evan marched into the back room. Ellie didn't dare question him, things were fragile enough as it was. She needed to respect his right to process what she had told him, and what he had seen. Rustling away, out of sight, it was as though Evan was searching for something. Ellie still thought it was wiser not to ask.

'Here,' yelled Evan, returning quickly. 'You will need this.'

A skull landed at Ellie's feet; she recognised it immediately from her time in the caves. Next, Evan tossed a deep red cloak in the same direction. Together, the items made up the costume of a Renegade. Rada had described it to her before and it instantly made Ellie want to run in the other direction. Evan held another skull and cloak set in his own hands.

'Put them on,' Evan said. 'If we're going after Haylee...we aren't going to just hand them our identity. Besides...if you really want to help her…that definitely makes you a traitor now. You don't want Rada coming after you too.'

Ellie wasn't sure what caused the wriggling feeling inside of her. It could have been the sight of Evan disguising himself, or the thought of doing it herself. Aware that she had completely switched her allegiance felt like someone had thumped her with a rock. Ellie noticed that her hands had become clammy again. Doing what was right was tough to reconcile. After spending a lifetime following Rada's will, Ellie found herself conflicted.

'Ellie,' Evan said, about to cover his head with the skull. 'I thought we needed to hurry.'

With a thud, the main door to Haylee's flung open, startling Evan. Ditto limped inside, with Pandra drooped across her shoulder. Refusing to stop until she reached the fleeces, Ditto finally collapsed, taking the slave down with her.

Ellie rushed over to them. 'What happened?'

Ditto shoved Ellie aside. 'Leave her.'

'Ditto…what's goin' on?' Evan intervened.

'Need orgo food.' Ditto said, rising to her feet. 'Orchids…need orchids. She ain't got long.'

When Evan dashed away, Ellie crouched down beside Pandra. She was unconscious, but still breathing, and cold to touch when Ellie placed her hand on her arm. Ditto was right, Pandra needed help in a hurry. A muffled whimper oozing from her signalled how sick she was.

'Here,' Evan called, tossing a pouch to Ditto. 'Little and often. If it works, she should recover quickly.'

Ellie gawped when Ditto sat back on the fleece, resting Pandra's head on her lap tenderly. 'Can you help her?'

'Evan,' Ditto said, choosing not to reply to Ellie. 'Why is she here again? And why are you dressed like that?'

'I'll explain later. How did you wind up with her? Where's Kayden?'

Ditto grunted, lifting an arm. 'Gone. Junkyard took care of him. Not before he left me this souvenir though.'

'You saw him leave?' Ellie asked, inspecting the huge gash on Ditto's arm, and trying to engage with her.

As she started to rub orchids across Pandra's lips, Ditto glanced at Ellie. 'I saw Junkyard dressed to the chin in armour, with weapons aimed at him. He told him to leave.'

'We're running out of time,' Evan said, putting an end to the conversation. 'Dit, I'll explain everything later. For now, look after her. C'mon El, we need to go…now!'

As Evan darted for the exit, Ditto gifted Ellie with a casual smile. 'Look after him. Don't know what you're doin' but take care of him. He's not one to get involved normally.'

Ellie formed a friendly grin whilst fastening the Renegade cloak across her shoulders. 'I will…I promise.'

'You'd better,' Ditto replied.

chapter nineteen

Ambushed

'Don't think I've ever seen the wharf this quiet at night,' Morrigan said. A pygboar skull concealed her face.

Haylee held her reins firmly, steadying her orgo. 'Too quiet. Something's wrong.'

Like Tik and Morrigan, Haylee waited cautiously in her saddle. Each of their animals was snorting, eager to move in from the edge of the wharf. It was possible that they loved the heist as much as Tik did. The claws of all three orgo scraped on the solid ground, as they prepared for the next move.

'What do we do?' asked Morrigan.

'We've come this far, and people are depending on us,' Haylee suggested. 'I say we take our chances.'

'I will do whatever you want to do,' Tik chirped in. 'Whatever that is, can we get on with it please?'

'Eyes on me,' Haylee ordered. 'Let's not get too cocky.'

Haylee trotted into the wharf heading for the supply store, whilst Morrigan, then Tik dutifully trailed behind. Disguised by their *Renegade* attire, nobody would be able to identify them. But the wharf was eerie; shadowed by darkness and more silent than Haylee had ever known. Fishing vessels creaked next to the harbour wall and Haylee's instincts were drumming around her ears. Even so, she was glad of the extra cloak to keep warm.

As they closed in on the entrance to the shelter, Haylee heard a distant rasping sound. She stopped momentarily, raising her hand to halt the others.

'Did anyone hear that?'

'Wasn't it one of them?' Tik laughed, pointing at their orgo, one by one. 'Not long since they ate.'

Haylee's eyes rolled, but Tik wouldn't have seen through her skull-mask. 'This your work?' she asked, pointing at the reddish scrawled lettering on the gates.

'Er…well,' stammered Tik, when they began to enter the building. 'That is a fantastic piece of art…if I ever saw one. Don't ya think so Morri? Fabulous.'

When a scatty gugubat darted across the timber right in front of her, Haylee assumed that it was the source of the noise she had heard.

Their orgo pushed through the heavy shelter gates almost effortlessly. Yet Haylee was stunned when she scanned the open space inside. The supply store was empty — completely bare. No land transport, no food crates, and no wardens.

Morrigan gasped, sounding as horrified as Haylee. 'What the — '

There was no time to think when someone shouted behind them. 'We have you surrounded. I suggest you surrender now…In Rada's name. Renegades…you won't find anything here today.'

Wardens!

'Okay…now what?' asked Tik.

'Eyes on me!' yelled Haylee, galloping toward the back of the supply store.

'Don't need to keep saying that,' chuckled Tik, before chasing after her. 'Never taken my eyes off you!'

With Morrigan tailing, the three Renegades gathered at the rear of the building. Haylee had no idea how many wardens were beyond the gates. Neither did she know how to escape. If they were surrounded, it appeared Rada's troops had the upper hand for the first time. And that wasn't something Haylee was familiar with.

'If you don't come out,' called the warden, 'then we will come in. Trust me…that will be worse for you. Surrender is your best option now.'

'Let them come,' Haylee said quietly, so only her friends could hear.

Morrigan tugged hard at her reins when her orgo became nervous. 'I ain't lettin' them take me. I've seen the state of Kayden's slaves.'

'What do we do?' Tik probed.

Haylee looked at him. 'For now, we wait! They won't take long. Wardens are impatient. When they come…follow me.'

For a few seconds, all that could be heard were the frantic snorts of their black orgo. They were confused, and probably frightened — the same as Haylee and her friends. Keeping their animals under control was a challenge for all of them.

'How did we get so stupid?' Morrigan asked.

'Not stupid,' Haylee said. 'But perhaps desperate.'

A fizz could be heard from behind the shelter gates. The wardens were charging their lances and preparing their assault. Haylee calmed her breathing and held fast.

'Be ready,' she called. 'They're coming.'

Morrigan and Tik faced front, whilst Haylee edged forward, keeping her eyes fixed on the gates. The fizzing was getting louder, and it sounded like there were more wardens than she had ever seen in one place. Her orgo reared in anticipation.

When the gates fell open, Haylee issued the order. 'Now!'

Charging forwards, Haylee's group headed directly for the gateway, but Haylee still couldn't see any wardens. They weren't entering as she had expected, and she couldn't see anything outside the shelter; it was too dark. At the opening, Haylee swerved when a flash of light caught her attention. Whatever the light was, it cut deep into the surface of the supply shed's wall.

'They're firing at us,' screeched Morrigan, making a swift turn away from the gates. 'What are they armed with?'

Tik copied Morrigan, turning back inside the building. Haylee, on the other hand, halted her orgo at the gateway. More flashes came, but they weren't necessarily aimed in their direction.

'Warning shots!' shouted Haylee. 'They're trying not to hit us.'

'Warning shots! From what?' Morrigan was frantic.

Positioning his steed, Tik looked confident. 'Morri...we can do this!'

'Wait!' Haylee said. 'Morrigan, get as far over there as you can.'

Whilst Haylee wafted her hand toward the side wall, Morrigan delayed. 'Now Morri...hurry. Tik...you take the other side.'

As always, Tik reacted without question, but Morrigan didn't seem as decisive. Further bolts struck the walls inside the shelter, and still, Haylee couldn't make out where they were coming from. She and her friends needed to take care with their next actions. Their lives could depend on it.

'Listen,' Haylee went on. 'If this goes badly, get to safety. You know what to do…Where to go!'

'Home?' Tik asked.

'Not home,' Haylee commanded. 'Safety!'

Morrigan nodded several times, and when Haylee turned to Tik, his head offered a similar bob in agreement. Haylee faced the opening, but still, the wardens remained out of view. She had no choice but to try and mount an escape for her friends.

'Count to ten, then go. Don't stop until you're safe.' Haylee yanked on her reins and galloped forward. She could hear Tik as she made her exit.

'Wait…why?' he questioned.

Outside, Haylee pressed on, but wardens enclosed the area around the shelter efficiently. Blazes of light burst from their lances; new improved versions that Haylee had never encountered before. Careering in the direction of her attackers, Haylee knew evading them was unlikely. Morrigan and Tik's safety was her priority.

'Yah!' she screamed, flinching on her reins when they turned their lances in her direction.

Light obscured Haylee's vision; she couldn't see anything. Nonetheless, the unmistakable squawk from her orgo, made it apparent when it was struck. Haylee lurched from her saddle when her steed's legs gave way. At that exact time, Morrigan and Tik exploded through the gateway. As Haylee had expected, whilst distracted by her, the wardens were unable to stop her friends. Deliriously, they discharged energy bolts from their lances. But their efforts were futile. Caught unawares, each warden was unsuccessful in stopping the other two Renegades.

Haylee scrambled, trying to flee, but the glowing point of a lance swung in front of her.

'On your feet!' someone barked.

The order came from a squadron leader; he went by the name of Ermine. Haylee could identify his rank from the band worn on his arm, and she knew his face. For some time, she had familiarised herself with many of the higher-ranking wardens. Mostly, so she knew exactly who she was working against.

Haylee stood before him, holding out her arms. Inspecting the wharf, all she could see was land transports and members of the warden patrol. Almost twenty wardens were posted around the supply store; she had never seen so many in one place. When another warden approached, also pointing her lance, Haylee raised her hands high. There was no chance of escape. Yet, at the expense of her own freedom, her friends had gotten away. She was confident that they would continue her work.

'Now, I'm not sure,' Haylee said to the oncoming warden, 'but I don't think Rada would appreciate you killing me. I'm the only Renegade that you've ever managed to catch.'

'Haylee, I presume,' snarled Ermine, tugging the pygboar skull from her head.

Red hair spilt across her face and Haylee eyeballed Ermine. He seemed pleased with himself, and she recognised the contraption he held in his hand. Haylee started to tremble unexpectedly. Nothing much intimidated her, but the thought of being fitted with a Limiter was terrifying. Any chance of regaining her freedom would be lost once she wore the cruel device.

chapter twenty

Return to The Wharf

'You could have picked a faster animal,' bawled Evan. He kept a tight hold of Ellie as they raced through the twisting streets.

Ellie looked behind; directly at him. 'Been a long day grumpy, give him chance.'

Sage was galloping well, despite less than ideal conditions. The street-lining lamps were fading, and snow crunched between his toes. Yet it was as though Sage instinctively understood Ellie's urgency. Tiny snorts surfaced, every time he navigated harder bends, yet still, he pushed forward refusing to slow down.

'So, assuming we find Haylee,' Evan said, from over Ellie's shoulder, 'what then?'

'What then?' Ellie wasn't sure what he was asking.

Evan's long, hard breath drifted over her. 'What happens to you?'

Ellie hadn't even considered what happened next. She had her orders from Rada, and if she didn't follow them, she would be found guilty of dissent. Rada expected complete obedience from her wardens and wouldn't accept anything else. Suddenly, reality struck Ellie; her time in Port Harmony was ending. Whatever happened next, everything was about to change, and there was little she could do to stop it.

'Let's worry about Haylee for now,' said Ellie, blocking out her own concerns. 'We can deal with the rest after.'

'You could seek refuge with the elrupe. Nobody will find you there.'

Evan wouldn't have seen the grin on Ellie's face. 'Not sure that will go down well. Now you know who I am…what I am…I don't think they would welcome me. Neither would Haylee either.'

'We don't need to tell them. They don't need to know.'

'They will know. Once this is all over…they will know.'

'Leave Haylee to me,' Evan said softly. 'By the way, do you have a plan to help Hay?'

Ellie's shoulders twitched. 'Take it as it comes.'

'Well…I hope you have something in mind. We're here.'

The gathering of wardens was plain to see as they cantered between the last series of dwellings. Huddled on the wharf around the biggest supply store, every member of the squad was armed with a lance. From close to the harbour wall, a gleaming red transport made its way toward the group. Ellie couldn't see any signs of Haylee or the others.

'There's too many of them,' Evan grumbled whilst his arms became restless.

Sage came to a standstill when Ellie pulled at the deeper fur around the base of his neck. He growled when he caught sight of the wardens and scratched at the cobbles through agitation.

'Hush boy,' Ellie said. 'Don't want them to see us.'

'Now what?' asked Evan.

Ellie pulled her crimson cloak to one side, reaching into the pocket of her overalls. 'Widget,' she whispered. 'We need help.'

Popping into shape, Widget jiggled in her hand. 'Oh! Do you Miss Ellie? You need me now. That means I have to jump to it…ready for action…prepare to do your bidding. All because you need help now. No-one cares about what I need. I get stuffed in your pocket…in a dirty old chest…for as long as—'

'Widget,' Ellie intruded. 'Please be quiet.'

'You need me to be quiet as well,' Widget rambled. 'Don't ask much—'

'Shush,' Ellie said.

Her small companion finally stopped talking.

'Lot to say for a machine,' Evan added.

'Widget, we need to disarm Dee Squad,' Ellie said. 'Can you help us?'

'You, yes Miss Ellie,' Widget snapped. He glared at Ellie but lifted his metal finger toward Evan. 'But I can't help him. I don't take orders from him.'

'He's with me. Widget…he is my friend, and he is a good man. I just need to know if you can disarm them?'

Widget's head whirred round to study the wharf. 'That's a lot of wardens Miss Ellie.'

'We know that,' Evan jumped in. 'Can you help or not?'

'I can disarm the lances, yes,' Widget said. 'If you can get me closer to them.'

'That's still a huge group of wardens,' Evan offered. 'Even without their charge, those lances will be plenty to stop us.'

'Would you like them to put their weapons down sir?' Widget asked, turning his attention to Evan.

'How are you goin' to get them to do that?' Evan's voice had a hint of doubt.

With his head rotating this way and that, the miniature robot seemed to giggle. 'Leave it to me. Just get me closer. Although I must ask, Miss Ellie…if you don't mind. Why would you want to disarm the wardens? From the signals I'm receiving, it appears that they've finally apprehended a Renegade. Is that not what you wanted?'

Evan's shuffling worsened with the news. 'Apprehended! Who? Who have they apprehended?'

'The one called Haylee. That's what I'm led to believe sir.'

Ellie raised her associate to within an inch of her face. 'Widget, I need you to trust me. There has been a change in our mission. We need to help the Renegades.'

'Help them, Miss Ellie?'

'Please Widget,' Ellie begged. 'You take orders from me. We are to help the Renegades. Your job…is to disarm Dee Squad.'

'Certainly, Miss Ellie. Then what are we waiting for?'

Glancing at Evan, Ellie bobbed her head. 'Let's do this!'

Evan tightened his hold on her waist and would have been able to feel how afraid she was. Against that many wardens, Ellie wasn't particularly confident of their chances. Nonetheless, they had to try, and she made sure she had a firm grip on Sage.

A flinch on the scruff of his neck was all the powerful orgo required, and he bolted headlong onto the wharf. At first, the group of wardens didn't seem to notice, and something else held their attention. But as Sage charged toward them, all their heads lifted at once. Their lances sparkled with the energy surging through them.

Widget made weird sounds, jolting in Ellie's hand. She clutched him tightly, waiting for the right moment. They only had one opportunity to help Haylee, and they had to get it right.

'You ready?' Ellie checked, seconds away from their adversaries.

'Yes, Miss. When…you…are.' Widget's response was wobbly from the ride.

'Now!' Ellie tossed Widget forward when every lance pointed toward them.

Assuming his rock shape, Widget clunked on the slushy ground and rolled close to the squad. A deafening hum that he released, instantly caused each weapon to flare. The wardens yelped aloud all at once. Clanging on the floor, the backfiring lances dropped simultaneously.

'Impressive,' remarked Evan.

Haylee was moved into view by Ermine. He wouldn't have been able to identify Ellie through her mask. Nevertheless, Ellie still felt nervous about attacking her superior, even though his rank now seemed irrelevant. Noticing the Limiter that Haylee had been fitted with, Ellie had faith in her conviction. The devotion to helping Haylee overpowered any of her past allegiances. Ermine was now Ellie's enemy, and that was clear in her thoughts.

The wardens were disordered as Sage barged between them. Muddled, they hadn't expected an ambush. One of them reached down, attempting to reclaim his lance, but screeched in pain when it zapped his fingers. In the meantime, Ermine held Haylee in place for protection. Ellie spotted the control device for Haylee's Limiter in his grip.

'Eyes on me!' Ellie called, to alert Haylee by mimicking her.

Stamping on Ermine's boot and pulling herself free, Haylee stumbled over to Sage. The wardens ran in her direction, but one of the lances began discharging energy bolts at anyone trying to block her path. Somehow, Widget was controlling it. From the looks of things, he had many talents Ellie hadn't been aware of.

Widget called out from somewhere nearby. 'I have to say,' he declared, 'this is a lot of fun.'

Haylee had just reached for Evan when Ermine moved forward. 'Not today,' he sneered, fumbling with the Limiter controls.

Dropping beside Sage, the blow numbed Haylee through the chains around her and she fell out of Evan's reach. Sage began stamping to intimidate the aggressors, but the wardens continued to gather around. Ellie panicked when she saw Haylee's chest heaving in defeat. It was impossible to see Haylee's face through the reddish hair that concealed it, so Ellie prepared to dismount.

Miraculously, with the wardens almost upon them, Haylee found strength. Despite the agony that she must have endured, she clutched onto Sage's fur and began to climb. Then, once she was close enough, Evan grabbed onto her and tugged.

Whilst Sage reared and growled, Ellie inspected the floor for her small robot companion. 'Widget!' she called.

From Ermine's direction, a dim voice replied, 'One moment Miss.' Widget was forcing another lance to blast at the Squadron Leader's boot.

Ermine span and fled, whilst his other wardens scattered across the wharf. The lack of conviction they displayed made Ellie wonder why she had ever respected them. Once Haylee was secured between Evan and Ellie, Sage grunted. The steadfast orgo appeared to think that it was the right time to leave.

'Widget,' Ellie called.

'Right here, Miss Ellie.'

Ellie glanced down to see Widget clinging onto Sage's fleece. His big green eyes blinked to focus. She had no idea how he had gotten there, but with everyone gathered on Sage, she steered him away from the wharf. Once out of view, Ellie took hold of her skull-mask and slid it from her head. It was much easier to see without it, so she placed it in front of her lap.

'Well Blue, you seem to be makin' a habit out of this,' Haylee said. 'Second time in one day. Love the outfit by the way.'

Ellie waited whilst Haylee got comfortable. Squished between her back and Evan, and still wearing a Limiter, it couldn't have been easy.

Widget clambered up the side of Sage, making sure he had a safe hold of the orgo's furry coat.

'I can help you with that, Miss...er...well...' Next to Ellie's leg, Widget pointed behind her. He was offering to assist with Haylee's restraints.

'What! Is that?' Haylee sounded somewhat disgusted.

Evan laughed. 'It's okay Hay. He's done a fantastic job so far.'

Widget crawled forward unsteadily. Ellie couldn't see what he was doing but heard a muffled whirring from behind. Mere seconds later, the jangling chain clattered on the ground. Somehow, he had removed the Limiter, with very little effort.

'I'm impressed, little guy,' said Haylee. 'Even though I don't know what you are. Does anyone want to tell me what just happened?'

'Later,' Evan said. 'Where's Morri and Tik?'

'Safe!' answered Haylee. 'But I still want answers.'

'Be patient,' Evan insisted. 'Please Hay.'

'It's okay,' Ellie jumped in, without really wanting to. 'She deserves to know.'

'No! It can wait.'

Haylee moaned and squirmed against Ellie. 'Let her speak Evan. Besides, I'd love to hear how you ended up at the wharf and took on more wardens than I've ever seen in one place.

Not to mention, how Blue wound up here…with you.'

'I'm a warden,' Ellie spoke quickly before she changed her mind. 'I was employed to find out who the Renegades are.'

Ellie could feel the skirmish when Evan gripped his sister to stop her attack. 'Haylee, no!' he yelled. 'Let her explain.'

Haylee murmured and wriggled but didn't reply. The fuss carried on for a few minutes, and Ellie tried hard to concentrate on the cobbled streets ahead. She was attempting to disappear into Port Harmony. With the conflict behind her, it was difficult to navigate. On top of that, the deep snow burying Sage's toes, also made the journey even more of a challenge.

Eventually, Haylee seemed to give up her efforts to attack Ellie. 'She's a warden! Why…or how…or what? What is that?'

'My name's Widget,' said Widget. Haylee must have drawn attention to him again.

'And what exactly are you?' Haylee growled.

'He's what we call a drudge,' Ellie explained. 'But he prefers the name Widget.'

When Ellie tensed in anticipation, Haylee heaved a sigh. 'We? Rada's wardens you mean? Scorr Tanta people?'

'Let her have her say, Haylee,' Evan said.

'I'm listening.'

Ellie gulped down her worries. 'You have managed to outwit the wardens with every heist. Some time ago, I was asked to live amongst you. My assignment was to find the Renegades...to find you. Haylee...you and the others were the only real suspects in Port Harmony. But even watching you, I wasn't certain until today. The only other place we thought that the Renegades could come from was Eklips. I was convinced it was them.'

Haylee sniggered. 'At least that worked. You were supposed to think we were assault rangers. That we came from Eklips.'

'Go on Ellie,' Evan prompted. His voice remained gentle and full of compassion.

'That deception worked,' Ellie said. 'For some time, Rada has tried to prove it was Kayden, and she had someone watching him too.'

'Pandra!' cheered Haylee, celebrating her own intuition. 'So Pandra was spying on Kayden, and you were spying on me. Wait...where is Kayden? And Dit? Have we found her yet?'

'Ditto is safe,' Evan said. 'She says Junkyard got rid of Kayden, and somehow she also freed Pandra.'

'At least there is some good news,' Haylee said. 'Anyway, let's carry on with why we are here now. Riding on the back of an orgo, with a warden who has been trying to hunt me down.'

'She's with us now!'

Haylee stirred. 'Is she? How do we know that? Where is she taking us? Actually…why can't I just—'

'Because without her help, you would've been taken by the wardens,' Evan said.

Haylee prodded Ellie. 'Where are you taking us?'

'Blastguards are coming,' Ellie replied.

'Blast…what?' screeched Haylee.

For a second, Ellie thought it best to face her interrogator, but Haylee's eyes were tight with fury. 'The blastguards are Rada's army,' she clarified.

'Thought the wardens were her army?' Haylee queried.

Ellie sniffed; the cold was irritating her nostrils. 'Trust me…the wardens are pups compared to blastguards. We need to get you to Ditto and Pandra, then find somewhere for you to hide. Make sure neither Kayden or Rada find any of you.'

'Where is Dit anyway?' asked Haylee.

'Home,' Evan filled in.

'What?' Haylee twitched, bumping against Ellie's back. 'We need to get there. Like quickly. She's not safe there.'

'Kayden won't find her there,' Evan said. 'You've said that yourself. Besides…he's gone.'

'Maybe. But now the wardens know who I am, we're not safe at home.'

'That's why we need to get you all somewhere else,' Ellie said. 'You need to hide. Find...safety.'

'Unlikely,' Haylee moaned. 'Not too many places to hide. Besides...we still have work to do.'

'Looking after the elrupe?' Ellie had no doubt that the elrupe would perish without Haylee.

'Yeah!' Haylee murmured, sounding like someone had winded her. 'You told her about them too big brother?'

'I took her,' said Evan. 'Think that's what changed her...er...perspective. It wasn't her fault Hay, she's a victim of that dictator's propaganda. What are people from Scorr Tanta supposed to believe?'

Roaring, Haylee twisted behind Ellie. 'People from Scorr Tanta need to grow some—'

'They don't know any better,' Evan intruded.

'Then they're stupid. Following Rada is stupid.'

Ellie felt herself droop. 'She's right. But how we convince everyone else...I don't know. Well not yet.'

'Had our chance to do that years ago,' said Haylee. 'We blew it...which is why we're in this mess now. Anyway, once we have Dit and the slave, what then? What are you gonna do, little miss warden?'

'I can look after myself.'

Haylee snuffled. 'What…against Rada? It won't take her long to find out what you did.'

'How?' Ellie wondered if she had missed something.

Stretching across the top of Ellie's leg, Haylee took hold of some of Sage's fur. 'You may have been dressed like a Renegade, but you weren't riding like one. Two of you, on a brown orgo…and there was no way Renegades could have known about the wardens. Oh, and then there's this little thing.'

When Haylee prodded Widget, he hummed loudly. 'Widget, if you please.'

In their hurry, Ellie hadn't thought things through. She had done everything she could to rescue Haylee, but without considering her own disguise. Rada would soon know that she had been betrayed — if she didn't already.

'Won't Rada go easy on you?' Evan asked.

Haylee's laughter grew louder.

Considering her options, Ellie concocted a solution. 'My father…he's a blastguard—'

'Wow!' Haylee blasted. 'Gets better all the time! Is Rada your uncle too?'

'Widget was stolen,' Ellie went on. 'And Sage! I had nothing to do with it. Whoever jumped me stole them both. To save you.'

'I was stolen?' Widget chirped. 'Excuse me. When was I stolen? I'm a little confused.'

'Doesn't sound very believable to me,' Haylee said. 'How's Rada goin' to believe it?'

'When I received a message from her,' Ellie muttered, still working out a plan, 'that's when I was assaulted. If I'm returned injured, my father will protect me. He will believe me...stand by my story.'

'You don't have any injuries. Well not really. Other than, that cut on your belly. Where did you get that anyway?'

Ellie could see the entrance to Haylee's street beyond them. 'I'm sure you won't mind helping. Make it look like I was attacked.'

'Sounds like fun,' Haylee said, relishing the thought. 'There's just one other thing first though.'

'What's that?'

'Thought you told me Kayden was gone! So, why are they still here?'

Ellie tracked Haylee's finger when it pointed ahead. Above some of the buildings, vague silhouettes swooped randomly. There were several of them, bouncing around the skyline and causing the street lamps to flicker. Gliders; they hadn't yet left Port Harmony.

chapter twenty-one

Rada's Torment

'I trust that you are bringing me stories of success,' Rada said.

When the image of Ermine projected against the glossy, grey wall of her bedchamber, it was perfectly clear. Behind him, Rada could see the other wardens gathering, yet there was no sign of prisoners.

'My Lady,' Ermine mumbled. 'The Renegades were unsuccessful in their attempts to steal supplies tonight.'

Rada carried on removing her cloak, then tossed it across the bed. 'Excellent…and about time. How many of them do you have in custody?'

'Well…there was a problem. Something that—'

'How many?' Rada screamed, slamming the end of her staff into the wall. A spiralled metal lantern dislodged next to Ermine's impression, dangling loosely and fading. With only one other lamp in the entire room, it darkened further.

'None yet, My Lady,' Ermine said. 'We were close. We had the one called Haylee. She is most definitely their leader. But she had help that we couldn't have foreseen.'

Wandering around the chamber in her taut, grey tunic, Rada found it demanding to mould her thoughts into language. Her hand took hold of her mask and wrenched it from her face to help her breathing. She approached Ermine, resting her hand on the cold stone wall, next to the image of his head.

'Everything, I gave you everything I had Ermine. The plan was foolproof. How can you still fail me?'

Ermine's head dropped. 'My Lady, forgive me. We are still searching for them now. I will bring you these Renegades. You have my word.'

'No!' said Rada, gliding backwards. 'Your word is worth nothing. The blastguards will relieve your squad when they arrive.'

'Yes, My Lady,' whimpered Ermine. Rada's staff struck the wall again, crumbling the stone beneath where his face was.

'You will answer for your pathetic shortcomings when you return,' Rada wailed. She felt like a crazed demon had possessed her; one that she couldn't control.

To quieten her rage, Rada glanced around. She had only just retired, but the thought of resting was now distant. The silky white sheets that covered her bed looked inviting, and perhaps a good place to hide from her own temper. Oversized, the bed took up most of the space in the room, as she preferred. Rada's bedchamber was perfect in its simplicity, and usually her private space. Yet tonight, eager to hear of the Renegades capture, she had allowed her drudge to put Ermine through. *Being ignorant to the wardens' incompetence may have been better,* she thought.

'My Lady,' Ermine said, shattering Rada's drifting thoughts. 'The others, they can see your face.'

Rada stormed toward him. 'Let them see!'

Ermine didn't reply, and could only watch when his ruler stepped back and tossed her staff onto the floor. Deliberately, Rada's hands clenched the fabric at the base of her tunic. She glared at Ermine, tasting hatred on her tongue. Her fingers stiffened. Then, without further hesitation, she rolled her tunic upward and slipped it over her head. As the clump of material left her grasp, Rada felt liberated. The wrath that was influencing her of its own accord, had become empowering. Fragile cloth undergarments were all that hugged Rada's upper body and hips, and she meandered closer to Ermine. Each of her footsteps was slow and pronounced.

'Pick up your drudge,' she said, shifting her arms behind her back. 'Show the others, make sure they can see. Let them see.'

'My Lady,' cried Ermine, 'it's not right.'

'Pick it up!'

Rada watched as Ermine's hand came into view. The other wardens appeared blurry when he moved his drudge around with a shaky hand. The entire squad was staring, perplexed, but otherwise their faces were hard to make out.

'Ermine,' Rada said, making sure he recognised her composure. 'You are a fool. All of you are fools. Do you think I care what you see? It doesn't matter. The blastguards will bring you home in disgrace, and others will replace you. But even Kayden wouldn't appreciate such wretched specimens as slaves. You will be removed from The Union. I will personally see to it that you never return.'

Ermine came back into focus. 'I see My Lady…'

The transmission ended. Rada knew Ermine would try to flee; he was too stupid to realise that he had nowhere to go. Backing away from the wall to retrieve her tunic, Rada caught a glimpse of what she had displayed to Ermine's squad. Instantly, her feelings of supremacy were stripped away, when her eyes discovered the scars that littered her body. The marks brought back traumatic memories and made her gag. Each one, a reminder of a past she wanted to erase from her memory.

Like something drained all her energy at once, Rada stooped. Her fingers trembled as they delicately explored some of the larger blemishes in her skin. Heaving, she withered onto the solid flooring. Lying on her side, Rada shivered, and violent spasms engulfed her. She had no choice but to concede. Her eyes rolled, and her saliva dripped onto the tiles beneath her throughout the attack. Then, once the episode faded, she felt deathly cold; as though someone had pushed open a window. Nonetheless, there weren't any openings in her room.

Whirring, the drudge behind her came back to life. 'Are you ok, Miss Rada?'

'You weren't invited to speak,' Rada murmured, feeling numb. It was standing directly behind her, where she had placed it to receive Ermine's message.

The drudge looked up and down at its mistress. 'Yes….cer…certainly. My apologies, but you looked unwell.'

'Leave me,' Rada said, twisting to place her hand on her staff. She watched, as the gadget folded back into its rock form.

Rada reached for her mask and placed it back over her head. Desperate to control her panting, she focused on her heavy chest, almost meditating for a glimpse of time. In some sort of trance, she gazed around. Then, she found her tunic, close to the drudge which had concealed itself on the tiled floor. Then, still shuddering as she planned to replace her clothing, something disturbed her.

With a soft creak, the door to Rada's quarters started to open. Recovering, she clenched her drudge and hurled it toward the uninvited visitor. As the robot crunched into the wall beside the hefty timber door, someone entered.

'My lady,' called a voice, concealed by darkness. He would have been able to see her, but Rada couldn't identify him, no matter how much her eyes squinted.

Frantically tugging her tunic back over her body, Rada stood and peered harder through her mask. 'Speak.'

'My Lady,' the stranger garbled. 'You asked to be informed once the blastguards were entering Port Harmony.'

'They are there already?' she asked, noticing sparks dancing across her deceased drudge.

The messenger—a sentry—moved further into view. 'They are, My Lady, and they wait for further instructions. Oh…and they have eyes on the Renegades.'

Rada grinned, although the man in her room couldn't have seen. 'Then tell them to move in. Ermine has failed. If nothing else…the blastguards must take Haylee. It doesn't matter about her friends, they will be nothing without her. I want Haylee arrested, but will accept her body if killing becomes their only option.'

'Yes, My Lady,' nodded the sentry, already making his exit. 'I will return the orders immediately.'

chapter twenty-two

Out of Time

With gentle tugs, Ellie slowed Sage when they approached Haylee's building. At first, the street seemed quiet; even the gliders above had hushed. The dark was interspersed with patches of light from lanterns, and two large silhouettes confronted them. Ellie knew exactly what they were. She had hoped Haylee was wrong.

'He's not gone then,' said Haylee. 'What is with this day? It doesn't like me much.'

Evan removed his skull mask. 'Ssssh.'

'Forget shushing,' Haylee snapped, keeping her voice as quiet as she could. 'Kayden's here. How did he find us?'

'Dunno,' whispered Ellie. 'But what about the rangers? Their orgo are there, but I don't see the rangers.'

Haylee wriggled. 'If Ditto is in there, then she needs our help.'

'There's something really great...' Evan mumbled, 'about having a sister...who always wants to get herself killed.'

'Well we can't leave her in there,' Haylee said.

Ellie dismounted. Peering at the orgo ahead, she tried to make out where Kayden was, but couldn't even see his rangers. With each careful step, she crept closer, not wanting to disturb their orgo. There was no sign of life in any of the nearby buildings, and Ellie could hear Haylee mumbling behind her.

'Where does she think she's goin'?'

Evan sniggered. 'Must like the thought of getting herself killed too. Maybe you two aren't that different after all, Hay.'

Sage snorted. It sounded like he was in distress. Ellie swung round to see Haylee dismounting behind her. Obviously reluctant to follow, Evan stayed put whilst Widget squirmed in front of him. As she stepped toward Ellie, Haylee pointed at her home. Listening carefully, Ellie heard a muffled commotion from inside.

'We need to get in there,' Ellie said, turning back toward the noise.

Haylee placed her hand on Ellie's shoulder. 'This is none of your business.'

Ellie shrugged away the comment.

Together, they glared at the building; waiting for an opportunity to intervene. Then, the sounds they had heard silenced. Ellie felt uncomfortable. Her fingers fiddled with the clasps of the red cloak she wore. There was no way she could stand by and do nothing.

'What are you doing?' Haylee asked when Ellie removed her cape.

'Trust me,' Ellie said, holding the material out at her side. 'Hey…over here.'

'Stop it,' Haylee shrieked. 'You'll disturb them…' She paused for a moment. 'Oh…I see!'

The two black orgo turned at the sound of Ellie's voice. Their eyes followed the bright red cloak that she wafted beside her. Snorting wildly, they began yanking at the ropes that tethered them.'

'That's it,' Ellie garbled, mostly thinking aloud. 'Keep pullin'. Keep pullin'.'

The aggression from the animals became louder, whilst they tore at their bonds. They were desperate to charge at Ellie's cloak, but couldn't break free. It didn't take long for the rangers to notice their animal's behaviour either, and they emerged from the building. In their hands, they held their mace weapons. Ellie wasn't sure what to do next.

'Hey fellas,' Haylee called out. 'Remember me?'

Stunned, Ellie could only watch whilst Haylee marched toward them. Before she could even think to act, Evan trotted by her on Sage. All Ellie could do was continue agitating the rangers' orgo. At least that way they couldn't ride.

Haylee continued her approach. 'Where's Kayden?'

The rangers didn't respond.

'Answer my sister,' Evan said.

Still nothing.

Haylee stopped in front of the rangers. 'Where is he? I want to speak to—'

Before she could finish, the door to her home flung open. Pandra stumbled outside, followed closely by Kayden. In his hand, he clutched a rope. As he moved further into view, Ellie spotted Ditto being towed behind him. The other end of the rope was tied around her neck, and her wrists were bound behind her back.

'Haylee,' Kayden snickered. 'How great you could join us. And you brought friends too.'

Evan steadied Sage next to his sister. 'Let Ditto go Kayden. Take the slave and leave.'

'No!' Ellie squeaked. 'She stays too.'

Haylee's stared at Ellie. Her eyes seemed angered, but the moment only lasted only a second. Then, she turned back to face Kayden. All along, Pandra stepped closer to the rangers. Unlike Ditto, she wore no restraints and didn't seem to resist her fate. If Ellie wasn't wrong, Pandra was surrendering willfully.

'Fine,' Haylee said. 'I need you to let both of them go Kayden. Before this gets ugly.'

Kayden cackled, mocking Haylee.

'Ignore her,' Evan said, carrying on with the negotiation. 'Hand over Ditto. The slave is nothing to do with us.'

'Will you be quiet!' Haylee's frustration was clear. 'You're not taking them. Ditto isn't yours to take…and the other one belongs to Rada I believe.'

Kayden yanked Ditto out onto the street. 'So…you know who Pandra is?'

'I know everything,' replied Haylee. 'And I know that we don't need to be enemies. Rada has sent more of her army. From what I hear, they are best avoided. Let's put our differences aside…for all our sakes.'

'Ditto has a debt to pay,' said Kayden. 'As for Pandra…her fate will be that of someone who has betrayed me.'

Evan nudged Sage further toward their adversaries. 'I will repay Ditto's debt. You have my word. Just do as Haylee asks. Let them go.'

Ellie caught sight of Pandra. Locking her arm around one of the rangers, she seemed to be offering affection. Gazing at her, Ellie couldn't understand why she would be so submissive. Before being a slave, Pandra had been a warden; it didn't make sense. Nevertheless, her hands ran up and down one of the ranger's arms. Her tenderness was astonishing.

'She wants to go with them,' Ellie shouted to Haylee, draping her cloak back across her shoulders. 'Forget Pandra.'

'What?' Haylee asked.

Ellie stepped nearer when the rangers' orgo began to calm. 'Pandra. She wants to go. Look.'

As Pandra's hands explored the ranger, Ellie's eyes narrowed. She still couldn't believe what she was seeing. Kayden moved closer to his allies, still guiding Ditto. He was determined to leave with his prize. Equally, Ellie was committed to helping free Ditto.

'We are going to leave now,' Kayden said. 'I suggest that you do the same. If you have anywhere to go that is. You did say more troops were on their way after all.'

Still caressing the ranger, Pandra moved in front of him. Her hands ran across his face and through his bedraggled hair. Then, to Ellie's surprise, she changed tact. Taking a handful of the ranger's locks, Pandra wrenched his head back and snatched the mace from his grasp. With one brutal swing, she felled him and made it look easy. Unrelenting, she turned her attention to the other ranger and ferociously jabbed. He too was knocked from his feet. With no remorse, Pandra continued. Blow by blow, she struck the rangers with ferocity.

'No!' Kayden screamed. 'Stop her!'

Seeing an opportunity, Ditto ran at Kayden. Shoulder first, she collided with her captor and he lost balance. Haylee headed into the brawl, with Evan behind her on Sage. Meanwhile, Ellie's eyes were fixed on Pandra. In her unrelenting attack, she was hysterical; like a beast.

Haylee confronted Kayden. 'You won't be taking anyone. Not today.'

'You will all pay for this,' Kayden retorted. His arm quivered and he handed Haylee the piece of rope from his hand.

'I think I could be of help in this situation,' Widget said, hopping off Sage. He rolled across the ground to Ditto and clambered up her leg. His small metal fingers clenched at her tunic as he climbed. Then, whilst he worked at cutting the cord that bound Ditto's wrists, Kayden could be seen stepping away. Like a coward, he retreated until he had disappeared. With no more rangers, he had abandoned his cause.

'Come on,' Evan shouted; his urgency was clear. 'Time to leave.'

Haylee lifted the rope from Ditto's neck when Widget released her wrists. 'Go with Evan. I'll get the slave.'

A distant booming noise started. Ellie immediately knew what it meant. Darting toward Pandra, she realised that it was time they were somewhere safer. With one glance at the rangers, it was apparent that they wouldn't be fighting back. In the centre of the street, dappled in shadows from some of the dwellings, Pandra was bent over the rangers appearing deranged. Ellie crouched down and placed her hand on the ex-warden's back.

Pandra circled with the mace. 'Leave me!'

'We need to go,' Ellie said, softening her voice. 'I know they hurt you. They can't anymore. But we need to get you somewhere safe now.'

Pandra seemed to freeze, and her breathing was hectic. Her eyes were glazed, and she held the mace firmly in her hands. Unsure whether she was even making eye contact, Ellie rested her hand on the weapon. She hoped that she wouldn't regret the gesture.

'Blastguards are coming,' Ellie said, tightening her hold on the mace's handle. 'It's not safe here. I need you to come with me.'

'I want to go home.'

'We will, I promise. But for now, it isn't safe for us in Scorr Tanta. Rada will see us as traitors.'

Pandra's pupils engaged with Ellie. 'I don't know who to trust. What to believe.'

'Ditto helped you,' Ellie said when Pandra's grip loosened on the mace. 'Didn't she?'

'Yes. She saved my life.'

'Then go with her. Go with her and her friend Haylee. They will keep you safe. I promise you.'

Pandra's hand weakened and Ellie lifted the weapon away, placing it on the ground beside them. Listening hard, she gauged how imminent the danger was. The noise from the oncoming troops was intensifying. Ellie glanced at Evan who was fighting to steady Sage.

'Ellie!' he said, sounding panicky. 'Now! We need to go now!'

Together, Ellie and Pandra got to their feet. Inspecting the area, Ellie still couldn't see any signs of the threat they faced. But the noise from their transports was thunderous. They wouldn't be long.

Ellie directed Pandra toward Evan. 'Take her.'

Holding her hand forward, Pandra clutched Evan's arm, allowing herself to be lifted onto Sage. Still frail, she struggled into position behind him, placing her arms around him.

'You next Dit,' Haylee suggested. 'Take one of the ranger's animals. Time to go.'

Ditto did exactly as she was told. In awe, Ellie studied how well she took control of the orgo's reins and mounted him with skill. She made it look easy. Yet it had always taken Ellie time to bond with any of Cedric's orgo, before deciding to ride them. To master a black orgo the first time, was unknown. Even so, once in the saddle, Ditto cantered over to Evan and made it look easy.

'Hay,' Evan called. 'C'mon.'

Haylee focused on Ellie. 'You go. I'll be right behind you.'

'No! We don't have time. Ellie comes with us.'

'I can't,' Ellie butted in. 'I need to go back. If they have me, they may leave you alone.'

Widget scurried over. 'Excuse me, Miss Ellie. But actually…the blastguards appear to have orders to take her.' His finger pointed at Haylee. 'Then again,' he went on, 'they won't take kindly to your actions either Miss. So, it's probable that they will arrest you too. Well…that is…if they don't kill you first of course.'

'That settles it then,' Evan said. 'You're both—'

A series of sharp sounds surged around them. The noises carried on constantly, but Ellie couldn't determine where they were coming from. Tipping her head one way, then the other, she attempted to work out what was happening. Then, from beside Haylee's building, she saw flashes of light emerge. She had wrongly assumed that the noise was created by the incoming blastguards.

'Dit,' Haylee screeched. 'Move!'

Out of his hiding place, Kayden reappeared. He was on the back of his orgo, and the ear-splitting sounds were originating from him. With a disgusting arrogance, he rode toward Ditto; his saddle flickering along the way. Kayden closed in on his target unchallenged.

Ditto jerked in her seat. Her twitching was relentless. Taken by surprise, there was no way she could avoid Kayden's assault. She extended an arm, then slumped in her saddle. Whatever Kayden was firing at her, subdued Ditto almost instantly. Her legs shuddered, and her arms wilted beside her.

'Noooooooooooooooooo!' Haylee seemed to howl forever.

Ellie ran toward Ditto, but Evan steered Sage in her path. She stopped in her tracks, feeling completely helpless. Kayden was almost upon Ditto, and his saddle still targeted her. He was unforgiving. After only a few moments, Ditto's steed fell, taking her with it. The smile on Kayden's face was easy to see when the bright lights around his saddle faded.

'Now…our score is settled.' The sound of Kayden's voice was more like a cackle. Pulling on the reins of his orgo, he turned and galloped away. There wasn't time for anyone to stop him.

A thud shattered one of the buildings behind them.

'I suggest that now is an appropriate time to leave,' Widget piped up. His mechanical fingers grabbed onto Sage, and he tugged himself close to Pandra.

Ellie shoved passed, only reaching Ditto when life escaped the orgo she'd been riding. Ditto was trapped beneath. Her eyes were wide, and she gasped for breath. Attempting to move her arms, she failed. A weak groan was all she could manage.

When Ellie bent down to assist, she was immediately wrenched away by the back of her overalls.

'Get away from her,' Haylee cried.

Ellie floundered but remained standing. 'Let me help.'

'You've done enough,' Haylee countered. 'Go!'

Another boulder smashed an even closer building. Sage was pounding his claws hard, ready to make an exit. The blastguards were upon them.

'It's you who needs to go,' said Ellie. 'I will do everything I can for her.'

Evan jumped from Sage to intervene. 'Hay, we need to leave.' When he grabbed her arm, Haylee tugged it away.

'You go. I'm not leaving her.'

The surrounding buildings continued to fall. Rada's army was decisive and deliberate. They didn't seem to care how much damage they caused. In pursuit of someone guilty of dissent, they were unlikely to stop until they succeeded.

Haylee stayed with Ditto. She grabbed her friend's lifeless arms, making attempts to move her. Yet her efforts were futile; Ditto's eyes were dwindling. On and on, Haylee hauled at her refusing to give up. Then, wheezing, Ditto jolted. Haylee fell into Evan's arms.

'C'mon Hay,' Evan whispered. 'She's gone. Ditto wouldn't want you to be taken. She wouldn't want this.'

'No!' Haylee screamed aloud. 'Not Dit. No!'

Guiding his sister, Evan worked his way back to Sage. Haylee didn't resist. Her distress destroyed her resolve, giving Evan enough time to shove her onto the orgo. When Haylee fell into position, Pandra wrapped her arms around her.

'Ellie,' Evan said. 'There's no time left.'

Looking behind, Ellie could see the devastation. Along with the boulders colliding into buildings, she could see several large rocks rolling toward them. Large, the spherical chunks of granite were deliberate in their movements. Blastguards! When one of the rounded rocks split, she could see the soldier within. Dressed in a simple black bodysuit; a globular helmet protected her head. The blastguards' granite casing worked on a similar principle to Widget's. Sheathed by a stony armour, they were shielded from any opposing weapons. At the same time, the guards could tuck themselves into a ball fashioned from the granite. Their offensive looked something like a rockfall. Without concern, the blastguards were trundling through Port Harmony with an appalling agenda.

Whilst Evan mounted Sage, Ellie approached. She reached for Sage's head and petted him gently when his neck swung to face her. As though he knew what she was thinking, Sage offered a soft snort when Ellie ran her fingers through his fleecy neck. Evan looked down at her and his concern was obvious. Ellie worked to hide her anguish. Moving her hand to touch Evan's, she managed a smile, then gazed around the group sitting on Sage.

'I will miss you,' she said, tightening her hold on Evan's fingers for only a second.

'You're coming with us. Don't be—'

Evan didn't have time to finish when Ellie's free hand struck Sage. Her orgo had been anxious to leave. The blow from Ellie was all it took to get him moving. Sage galloped away, seconds before more boulders came into view. This time, Haylee's home took the beating. Ellie dropped to her knees and could only watch as chunks of stone fell around her.

'There's one,' a voice bellowed from behind. 'Take her!'

chapter twenty-three

Rendezvous

'Keep to the side streets,' Haylee called, managing to suck in her anguish. 'We need to stay low.'

They had travelled a small distance from the onslaught, but the crashing sounds were still ear-splitting. Rada's army was shifting across Port Harmony. Whoever these blastguards were, they appeared determined to dismantle the town. Haylee found herself squashed between two people on the back of Sage again. This time, she felt a strange comfort from the arms holding her.

Evan broke the silence that he had invoked for the last few minutes. 'We need to go back for her.'

'Now who wants to get killed?' asked Haylee.

'She saved you. More than once.'

'She's gone, Evan. They'll have taken her by now. Well on her way to Scorr Tanta. Which is where she belongs by the way. Or had you forgotten that?'

Steering Sage down a tight track, Evan sighed. 'You're happy that she's gone?'

Haylee refused to answer and glanced behind when she heard another explosion. Rada's need for control was beyond her. The lengths she was going to, to apprehend Haylee, was astounding. At the rate they were going, the blastguards would leave nothing left of Port Harmony. For the time being, they appeared to be sheltered from the attack, tucked between two rows of stumpy buildings.

'Where are we going?' Pandra enquired. Her tone was slight.

'Safety,' Haylee said. 'We need to get somewhere safe.'

'Doesn't feel very safe.'

'You always this grateful?'

Squeezing tighter at Haylee's waist, Pandra moved her head closer. 'I am thankful,' she muttered into Haylee's ear. 'For getting me away from Kayden. I'm sorry about your friend. She was good to me. She didn't deserve…well…'

'To die?' Haylee said, completing Pandra's thoughts. 'No! She didn't.'

Evan's head span and he glared at his sister. 'Try to be nice Hay. She's not had it that easy.'

'She's still one of Rada's spies,' Haylee growled. 'Or are you forgetting her sins too?'

Haylee noticed daylight breaking through the gloomy sky. In some way, it felt soothing. Pandra's soft fingers started brushing at her arm. She wasn't sure what it meant, but either way, the gesture sent tingles right through her. It was a feeling that Haylee had never encountered before.

'If I might,' whirred Widget. 'I too would like to know where this safe place is.' His eyes shone a brighter green.

'Who asked that to speak?' When Widget spoke, Haylee found his blinking lights annoying.

'He might be of some use to us,' Evan said. 'Let him have his say.'

'Thank you, Mister…erm...Oh yes, Evan is your name,' Widget spluttered. 'Thank you, Mister Evan. As I was saying…it appears that the patrol is heading for the wharf. From what I can tell, they have orders to capture the entire Dee Squadron. The ones that we tormented earlier. Oh, and Haylee of course. Miss Ellie is also to be retrieved. But I don't know what they plan to do with her. Anyway, it does appear that the wharf would not be a very safe place.'

The urge to flick Widget off their steed was unbearable for Haylee. 'Not going to the wharf genius. We are meeting our friends. They are in the best place.'

'Oh…' answered Widget. 'Well if you're sure.'

'Of course, I'm sure.'

Pandra wriggled. 'Aah be gentle with the little guy. For a drudge, he's kinda cute.'

Haylee paused, then giggled unexpectedly. 'Cute isn't how I'd describe him. I'll take your word for it.'

Somehow, Pandra's aura eased Haylee's sorrow. It was becoming harder to be her usual grumpy self too. Everything had been replaced by an unexpected calm; one that numbed her entire body. Pandra's touch appeared to be supercharged.

'Almost there,' Evan said, as they reached a turn in their route.

'Wait,' Haylee responded. Alert, she shrugged off her — Pandra-sized — distraction.

Kayden was in sight, and he was talking to two wardens. They were members of the squad that almost imprisoned Haylee earlier. Still saddled, another orgo was tethered alongside Kayden's. Wrapped in sheets, someone was roped on top of the second animal. Haylee listened hard, but she couldn't hear what any of them were saying.

Evan turned to face Haylee again. 'Thought he'd be long gone. Now is not the time for crusades though.'

'I'm not stupid,' Haylee said, feeling restless. 'He does seem quite chummy with these wardens though. For someone who despises Rada.'

Pandra shivered against Haylee. 'Is there another way we can go?'

'No need,' Evan said. 'He's leaving. Look.'

Leading the other orgo, Kayden trotted away from their route with his prize. In no time, the wardens had scattered too. Haylee wondered who Kayden had taken. If it wasn't for the presence of heavily armed blastguards, she might have intervened.

'Can we go?' asked Pandra.

With caution, Evan nudged Sage to canter on. 'Steady boy,' he commanded. The larger streets were coated in a frozen slush.

'How long is it since you spoke with the old guy anyway?' Haylee probed, focusing on their pending arrival.

Evan shrugged. 'Long enough. Listen…they've stopped firing.'

Preoccupied with Kayden's activities, Haylee hadn't noticed that the noise had ended. In many ways, that was more daunting. There was nothing to suggest why they had stopped the blitz on Port Harmony. The blastguards didn't have everything that they had come for. If Widget was right, they still had orders to arrest Haylee. Up ahead, Cedric's barn faced them. Haylee tensed.

'You ready sis?' Evan twittered when they approached the doorway. It was likely he was nervous too.

'Right now,' Haylee said. 'We have no choice.'

As they entered the barn, Cedric hobbled over. His walking was worse than Haylee remembered, and he appeared much older. Wasting no time, she dismounted and surveyed the barn. The mess that the rangers had caused was apparent. Even the carcass of an orgo still lay in one of the pens. With none of the burners lit, the room was icy.

'Where are the others?' she called. 'Did they make it.'

Cedric hesitated before answering. 'Yes, girl. They did.'

'Where are they?'

'In the bunker,' he replied. His hand rubbed at his head. 'Well, Morrigan is. The other went looking for you.'

Haylee felt like her stomach had a life of its own. 'Tik,' she whimpered. 'When did he leave?'

'Not too long ago.'

'That was who Kayden had,' Haylee said, facing Evan. 'The wardens got him. Handed him over.'

Evan's head shook, without much conviction. 'You don't know that for sure. Could have been anyone.'

'I beg to differ,' Widget twittered, scrambling from Sage. 'Miss Haylee is most likely to be right in this situation. That Kayden…he wasn't going to stay here for long without a reason. I'd say taking one of your friends, might be a good enough reason to hang about.' Once his clunky feet found the floor, his ramblings ended.

With her head drooped, Haylee fought for self-control. 'Yeah. It could have been anyone Evan. But it wasn't. It was him.'

'We will wait for trouble to pass,' Evan said. 'Then we will know what is what.'

Cedric stepped closer to Haylee. 'This trouble,' he groaned. 'You have brought it here to Port Harmony. Lots of it too.'

Haylee held out her arm to assist Pandra. 'Think you'll find you brought some of that trouble. That apprentice of yours…she was working for Rada. This little lump of metal is hers too. I presume it's also been living here under your nose.'

'Well…actually, yes,' Widget agreed. 'Sort of anyway. She kept me locked in a box somewhere. Safekeeping she told me.'

Squinting, Cedric studied the tiny robot. 'Long time since I've seen a drudge.'

'Long time since you did anything of much use,' Haylee barked.

Refusing to respond to her taunts, Cedric eyed Evan. 'How have you been?'

'No time for that now,' Evan said, fiddling with Sage's fleece. 'I trust they will be safe here?'

Cedric offered him a simple grin. 'You're leaving? Rada's people are here.'

'Don't you dare,' Haylee yelped, balancing Pandra across her arm. 'You're going after her, aren't you?' With Pandra resting against her, Haylee had to concentrate on how to place her hands. Pandra was only wearing tattered pieces of cloth, which made things tricky. Now Haylee had to focus on stopping Evan from leaving too.

'Who are you going after?' Cedric queried.

'Your apprentice, that's who,' Haylee said. 'You know…that warden you housed here.'

'She's not like them,' Evan moaned. 'Not like Rada. She knows what's right. She doesn't deserve what she has coming.'

'Your opinion!' Haylee teetered further inside the barn, trying not to say something she may regret.

Pandra formed a sort of gurgling sound before speech developed. 'He's right. We don't…know… what Rada…may do to her.'

Haylee was glued to the compassion in Pandra's eyes. She wanted to make things better for her; to help her heal. However, where Ellie was concerned, she still felt betrayed. Deception had eclipsed her loyalty. Even though Pandra was one of Rada's spies too, it didn't seem to matter. Ellie had specifically hoodwinked Haylee.

Transfixed, Haylee worked hard to stand her ground. 'Do what you want Evan. Just don't expect me to come after you when it all goes wrong. I'm certainly not coming to your rescue.'

When Evan steered Sage in the direction of the door, Cedric intervened. 'Wait!' he cried, shuffling across the barn.

Finding it hard to stay upright, Haylee could hear Cedric rustling somewhere beyond sight. The clunking and banging became quite loud, but it only lasted a few seconds. Meanwhile, Evan did as he was asked and steadied his steed whilst he waited.

'Here,' called Cedric, waddling back over holding a wooden trunk by its rope handles. 'Take this. When you find Ellie, give it to her.'

'What is it?' asked Evan, retrieving the battered chest from Cedric.

'Make sure she gets it.' Cedric gave no real explanation.

With a great deal of effort, Evan placed the chest in front of him. Then, he glanced at Haylee and nodded. Deliberately tugging at Sage, he charged through the doorway without delay. Haylee couldn't deny how much she admired him; even if his actions seemed crazy. It wasn't her place to understand the feelings he still had for Ellie. Whatever his reasons, it was clear how important she was to him.

Cedric collected the pebble, known as Widget, from the floor. 'Well little guy, I bet *you* can tell us a thing or two.' All the time, he acted like he hadn't just watched someone he should care about, setting off on a suicide quest.

Suddenly, Haylee felt completely alone. She scowled at Cedric whilst struggling to manoeuvre Pandra. Haylee held tightly whilst trudging across the barn, but she was certain that Pandra had begun to reject her help. Judging from Pandra's wiggling, it was as if she needed to do something she couldn't. Carrying on, Haylee dismissed the resistance.

'That's how I know you,' Pandra uttered from nowhere. 'Seen your face before. You…you…you're Aldora.' Her eyes had firmed on Cedric.

That name sent chills through Haylee and she halted. Her head skewed, and she stared at Cedric. He looked disturbed and tapped his walking stick with one finger. Then, after a brief pause, he wobbled over as though nothing had happened, carrying Widget with him.

'What you standin' around for?' he asked. 'Stood here long enough, don't you think? Time to take shelter.'

Haylee sighed and started hauling Pandra again. 'Yes father,' she said, hiding a smirk. 'As you wish.'

chapter twenty-four

Ellie's fate

In her haste, the woman who fitted Ellie's Limiter had been cruel. She had tightened the device until it dug into Ellie's skin. It was impossible to move. Each time Ellie tried, the chain links bit at her waist, where a section of her overalls had been cut away. The guard had removed her sleeves too, exposing her arms. A simple rope, knotted below the Limiter, acted as a belt; to support the material covering her legs. Ellie had been prepped efficiently so that the full potential of the restraints could be used if required.

'You pleased with your catch?' Ellie enquired, trying to get the attention of her captor. She lifted her arms as much as the shackles on her wrists allowed.

The blastguard didn't appear too chatty.

Blackness consumed the rear of the Land Transport where Ellie had been stowed. She sat on the hard floor, with her back pressed against the inside wall of the load area. Opposite, the blastguard responsible for seizing her, stared at her prize. The whites of her eyes were about all Ellie could make out. Her refusal to talk was possibly more intimidating than the Limiter.

Ellie glanced down. A sharp pain in her back had been irritating throughout their journey. There was no way she could see what was causing it. Not without her chaperone getting fidgety with her controller at least. Nonetheless, the ache was worsening. Wriggling a little, Ellie was desperate for relief.

Finally speaking, the guard had a stern look about her. 'Sit still!'

Her discomfort was overbearing, and Ellie twisted. 'What's digging in me? It's not just a Limiter. What is it?' she asked. Ellie rubbed into the metal plate behind her.

'Stop moving,' the blastguard ordered. She grabbed a rope handle that was fitted in the roof of the transport. Standing, she loomed over Ellie. Her fist held the red cape that she had confiscated from her catch.

'I can't,' cried Ellie. 'What is it?'

The guard sniggered. 'When Rada discovered that her star infiltrator was guilty of dissent, she wasn't pleased. Not only did you fail to apprehend the Renegades, but it appears that you sympathise with them too. Once we had reported that, Rada wanted to ensure you arrived home…er…safely. Took precautions.'

'What are you talking about?' Ellie noticed the sensation near her spine altering. Rather than a stabbing, it had turned into a dull throb; and it was spreading.

The blastguard leaned closer, thrusting the tattered crimson cloak toward Ellie. 'We were ordered to take no chances. You seem to have become top of Rada's wanted list. Almost more so than the Renegades themselves.'

'But why?' Ellie noticed that the blastguard also held a gadget that she'd never seen before. It looked like a Limiter controller, but more complex. Either way, her new keeper had her finger pressed against one of the buttons.

With the throb strengthening, and travelling through her core, Ellie cringed. She couldn't take much more. Her fingernails stabbed into the rusted floor where she was seated, and she worked hard not to move. If she shifted any further, her Limiter might activate. To her horror, Ellie realised that she could no longer move her legs, even if she wanted to. They had numbed from whatever was injuring her. Next to go were her fingers, then her arms started to tingle.

'Wha…is…happ…to…meh?' Ellie slurred, feeling weak. 'Plee…stop.'

Her vision began to blur, and Ellie attempted to keep focused on her aggressor. All the same, she was deteriorating fast. As Ellie's eyes faltered, she noticed a flickering of lights on the blastguard's rock-clad arm.

'My Lady,' the guard said, severely. 'I have Dee Twelve in custody. We are bringing her to you now.'

Rada's image burst onto the vehicle's corroded insides, across from Ellie. 'That is good news. And what about the one called Haylee?'

The projection lit the entire inside of the Land Transport. To Ellie, it was an obscure brightness, but enough that she could get a better, yet gloomy view of the guard. There was nothing else with them in the cargo area of the vehicle; only Ellie and her jailor. Within her stony suit, the guard looked delicate. Her slender frame and tidy reddish-brown hair were not what Ellie had expected. Young and eager, the guard confronted her faceless superior obediently.

'Patrols are still hunting for her, My Lady,' she said. 'But we are confident that we shall find where she is hiding.'

'We will maintain our presence in Port Harmony. Eventually she will surface, but for now, there is no rush. She can do no further harm at this time.'

'Yes, My Lady.'

'Tell me,' Rada said, with her voice muffled beneath her mask. 'Dee Twelve is looking somewhat subdued. I assume that you've invoked The Sleep.'

'I have, My Lady.' The blastguard seemed to quaver.

Rada's face became larger in the projection whilst she studied Ellie. 'Seems to work well. That is good to know. But for now, I need to speak with your prisoner. Release her please.'

Without the blastguard replying, Ellie knew instantly that she had complied. Moments before her eyes became too heavy to keep open, the deadening sensation subsided. It took only seconds for the ache to withdraw. Ellie could feel her limbs gaining life, but the stinging in her back remained. She could endure that now that she had experienced much worse.

'Dee Twelve,' Rada said, seeming to peer at Ellie, 'it seems that you have been busy. Only not in ways that you were assigned for.'

Ellie looked away. Once, she would have felt honoured to speak with Rada. Yet now, she tasted disgust. In only a few hours, she had discovered the terror caused by Rada's leadership. Not to mention, that she had just witnessed the brutal destruction of much of Port Harmony. Innocent people had likely been killed, and many would be wounded. All in the hunt for the Renegades, who were only trying to protect a forgotten species. The last person Ellie wanted to speak with was Rada.

'It would be wise,' Rada scolded, 'to not ignore me.'

Sticking to her convictions, Ellie refused to respond. Instead, her eyes drifted across the skin peeping above the legs of her overalls. There, beneath the Limiter, lay the wound Haylee had given her in the market. So much had happened since then. Despite how sore the gash looked, Ellie found a bizarre comfort in it. Until the injury healed, she knew it would serve as a reminder of the truths she had discovered. The mark was a souvenir, which in many ways she cherished. Whilst Ellie was lost in her thoughts, the blastguard shuffled about in anticipation. Ellie's deadlock with Rada didn't last long before Rada changed her approach.

'Guard. Please motivate Dee Twelve to speak with me.'

Unable to prevent the convulsions, Ellie reeled when the guard activated her Limiter. The device was merciless. Working as a warden, Ellie had used them every so often in the past. But she had never worn one or even recognised how much they punished the people that had.

'Are you ready to speak to me now Dee Twelve?'

Ellie couldn't bear the assault. She slammed her hand down onto the metal surface beneath her. Writhing, she flopped against the floor of the transport.

'Enough,' Rada boomed. 'Place her where she was.'

The pain ceased, and Ellie gasped. 'Get off me,' she shrieked when the blastguard began dragging her into position.

Giggling, Rada went on. 'At least we know that you can speak. I will keep this simple Dee Twelve. You know what I want. Where is your friend Haylee?'

Sore, Ellie lifted her head to face her tormentor. 'She's not my friend.'

'Where is she?' Rada screamed.

'No idea. How would I know?' Ellie grunted when the blastguard stamped on her fingers.

Rada's voice altered, and she sounded more composed. 'Things will be much worse for you if you do not cooperate Dee Twelve.'

'Worse? Think they're already much worse.'

'Fine. We will talk again when you arrive. I shall look forward to it, and I'm sure you will too.'

'Not like I'll know anything more,' Ellie said.

'Guard, your prisoner needs to be more compliant when you get back to Scorr Tanta,' Rada went on. 'Fix her for me please.'

'Yes, My Lady,' the blastguard replied as Rada's image dissipated. 'Of course.'

Ellie turned her head when the guard knelt before her. The girl's breath rushed across her cheek, and the controls for whatever was attached to Ellie were in her hand. Rada had referred to something as The Sleep, but she wasn't sure what that was. Ellie had never heard of it before. Although it was certain that she had experienced it before Rada's transmission.

'You could tell me where this Haylee is,' the guard said. 'That way, things may get better for us both.'

'I don't know where she is, precious. And I don't know why you think I would.'

A dense throbbing flooded through Ellie almost immediately. She could see the blastguard fiddling with the controller again. This time, Ellie's decline was much quicker. Already, her limbs were disabled, and the pounding in her neck was intolerable.

'Give me an answer,' demanded the blastguard, tossing Ellie's cloak aside. 'Then this can stop.'

Trying to reply, Ellie's mouth fell open. She couldn't mould words, and an involuntary moan escaped her. Her body succumbed without her consent, and Ellie's eyelids weighed down. Even so, she didn't lose consciousness as she'd expected. Instead, she could still sense the blastguard. To her surprise, Ellie was fully awake but completely paralysed. She couldn't feel any part of her body or utter a sound, yet she could hear everything.

'Stay like that for a while,' the guard cackled. 'Perhaps you will feel a little more cooperative when I deliver you to Rada.'

Ellie's body had deadened, but from within she was screaming. It was a cry for help that not a soul could hear. There was no way for Ellie to prevent the terror that consumed her.

chapter twenty-five

The Bunker

'They came here,' said the one they called Cedric. 'Looking for you…and your menace friends.'

Pandra was certain that his name wasn't Cedric. But as the newcomer, she thought it was wise to not poke where she wasn't that welcome.

Haylee stomped around the limited floorspace. 'We came to you for refuge,' she bawled, 'not a lecture. Anyway…you brought Blue here. Gave her a job. You led them right to us.'

'I wasn't to know,' said Cedric. 'Ellie has been a good apprentice. It isn't like you keep me informed of your schemes.'

'Schemes?' screamed Haylee. 'You're the one guilty of schemes. You agreed to that thing we call The Union. You let us all down and allowed Rada to send away the elrupe. If it wasn't for me, they would all be dead. Genocide, of an entire species that we all owe our lives to.'

'We would have all perished if I hadn't.'

'So, you made a choice for us to live instead of them? Hope that helps you sleep at night.'

Cedric's face revealed his anger. 'I made the only choice that I could. Then...all the time...you wander around upsetting these dictators. When it goes wrong...you come to me. Not only that, but you have brought another of Rada's employees along with you. And you lecture me about Ellie?'

A series of spiralled brackets on the chalky walls held candles. They were the only source of light. Pandra still felt like she was squinting whilst she gazed around. Although she was unable to see much, the pungent smell that engulfed the room was unavoidable. She assumed that it came from the penned orgo in the barn above. Beside her, was a girl that she had heard Cedric refer to as Morrigan. Along with Pandra, she was perched on a rotting wooden bench. It was the only seat within the small room. Morrigan's face was inked with the image of a strange bug, which was hard for Pandra to avoid when she glanced over. Apart from anything, Morrigan stayed quiet; perhaps stunned. In only a few minutes she had received terrible news about her friends. If Morrigan was in shock, it was no surprise.

Haylee carried on tramping about and looked like she was ready to implode.

Cedric hobbled toward his daughter, helped by his stick. 'I'm saying that I warned you about crossing Rada. What do you plan to do now? You cannot stay here forever.'

'Don't you think I know that?' said Haylee. Despite her hostility, she was entrancing to watch.

Pandra looked down at the floor. Close by was the drudge they had acquired from the other warden spy. The one known as Ellie that they'd left behind. On Cedric's instruction, the drudge had resumed its rock shape when they had descended into the bunker beneath his barn. Leaning down, Pandra retrieved it.

'May I interrupt?' she asked, inspecting the robot more closely. 'I might be able to help.'

Haylee span on her heels, locking her eyes on Pandra. 'I'm listening.'

'I'm here,' Pandra said, moving the item closer to her lips. 'I need your help please drudge.'

On her hand, the tiny pebble unfolded. 'I prefer Widget, Miss Pandra. If that's not too much trouble.' His tiny arms flipped about.

'Widget then,' agreed Pandra. 'Could you do something for me?'

'Well, that all depends on what you want me to do. I mean, there are lots of things that I can do. Then again, there are many things that I can't. My mistress, Miss Ellie...she often asked me to do things that—'

'Oh...my...word,' yelled Morrigan, still staring at nothing specific. 'Shut it up.'

'Morri,' said Haylee. 'Let's see if they can help.'

'But she's a spy! Like the other one you trusted.'

Haylee heaved a sigh. 'Please Morri.'

Morrigan was right. In fairness, the drudge did seem to speak a lot — for a drudge. She also had no reason to trust Pandra. Nonetheless, Pandra placed Widget in her lap and glimpsed at Haylee.

'Okay…Widget, can you tell me where the blastguards are located?'

Widget whirred, and his emerald eyes turned to Pandra. 'Um…Port Harmony, Miss Ellie.'

'I know that,' Pandra said. 'But where? Exactly where.'

Creaking, Widget's head turned from side to side. He was analysing each person in the bunker. First, he looked Haylee up and down. Next, he spent a while observing Cedric. Then, he followed that with an inspection of Morrigan. In the end, he turned his attention back to Pandra.

'Everywhere,' he muttered. 'There isn't anywhere in Port Harmony that the blastguards cannot be detected.'

'Great,' cried Haylee. 'How do we get rid of them?'

Haylee's face was partly concealed by her own reddened hair. She looked like she had lived through better days. Nevertheless, every time Pandra watched her, she felt something squeeze inside her stomach. Pandra's own thoughts were beginning to become hard to organise. She was consumed by something that she had never known.

Morrigan moved from the bench and hovered in Cedric's direction. 'Surely *you* must have an idea what we do.'

'I don't,' Cedric replied. His head lowered.

Taking time to listen, Pandra could tell that Widget was right. 'Explosions. They've started again.'

'Apparently,' Widget cheeped, 'they have taken Miss Ellie. She is on the way back to Scorr Tanta. The guards escorting her have orders to take her directly to Rada.'

'Good riddance!' Morrigan retorted.

'Is there any word on Tik?' Haylee asked.

Focusing on Haylee, then turning back to Pandra, Widget squeaked. 'I know only about Miss Ellie. Oh…and that the rest of the blastguards have orders to remain here until you are found.'

Haylee's head dropped when Widget's metal finger clanked in her direction. 'Then I need to hand myself in.'

'No!' screeched Morrigan. 'That is not what you need to do Hay. I've already lost Ditto…and Tik. Even your brother is missing now. Why is nobody asking about him anyway?'

'Because Morrigan, despite everything, he is still better at this than we are. Evan will be fine.'

'On that,' said Cedric, 'we agree.'

Haylee edged closer to Pandra. 'Can this little thing not disarm the blastguards? He managed it with the wardens earlier.'

With Haylee's hand resting on hers, Pandra was unable to make eye contact. 'Drudges are a warden's tool. Although he can tune into communications from Scorr Tanta, and he can hear the guards, he can't do much more. He certainly can't control their weapons. That's only for emergencies if the wardens get disarmed. Their drudges can assist.'

'That's a no?' Haylee sniffed.

'Yes,' Pandra said, noticing her own voice falter. 'It's a no.'

Removing her hand, Haylee turned her attention to Morrigan. 'Then we don't have a choice. I have to give myself up.'

Morrigan slumped back onto the bench.

'There may be a way,' said Cedric. 'But it is still a risk.'

'I'm listening, father.'

'As long as Ellie doesn't tell Rada about the elrupe,' Cedric went on, 'you would be safe there. In the caves…with them.'

'I don't mean to be argumentative sir,' Widget cut in. 'But if she leaves here, she won't get far until she is found.'

'The caves are too far,' added Morrigan. 'You'll die tryin' to get there.'

Cedric buffed his head with his sleeve. 'That they are. But Haylee can get most of the way there without being seen.'

'I don't think I'm the only one who's confused,' said Pandra, wincing as the bursts of noise seemed to get closer to them.

Stretching, Cedric placed his hand on the stone wall. 'Through here, you can get beyond the town limits. Closer to the hills. They shouldn't see you there.'

The back wall of the bunker groaned loudly as if the ground was quaking. With a thud, a panel emerged and began shifting. Behind the sheet of rock, Pandra could only see blackness. She wondered how Haylee would find her way down the passage that Cedric suggested.

'So, *she* is running...and hiding...or whatever,' grumbled Morrigan. 'What do the rest of us do?'

'We go out there,' Cedric said, smiling. 'Make them believe that Haylee has been killed during their siege. He can help!'

Confused, Widget's head span from side to side again when Cedric pointed at him. 'I'm not entirely sure that I understand.'

'May I?' Pandra asked, realising what Cedric had planned.

'You may,' Cedric nodded.

Pandra lifted Widget and made her way to Haylee. 'Can I have your hand?'

'Not until you explain what you're both on about.'

Feeling a frown develop, Pandra stepped up to Haylee. 'I trusted you, Haylee. Please...do the same for me.'

Haylee reached forward, ending her protest silently and allowing Pandra to take hold of her hand. 'Don't seem to have much choice.'

'Widget...register Haylee as deceased,' Pandra said, noticing her own fingers trembling. She nudged the robot onto Haylee's arm.

'As what?' Haylee protested.

Suddenly, Widget understood the plan. 'Oh, I see!' With that, he jabbed his arm into Haylee's wrist. 'Very clever plan, I have to say.'

Flinching, Haylee let out a blunt groan when Widget took a sample of her blood. Once he'd finished, she turned toward the tunnel that had now extended from their hideaway. The rock that had concealed her route had taken a few moments to shift. Pandra felt queasy just looking at what confronted Haylee.

'Go on then,' said Morrigan. 'Why are you still here? Leave! If you're going...leave!'

Glancing at Pandra, Haylee nodded. 'You need each other. Morri won't admit it, but you can help keep each other safe. You know stuff...about Scorr Tanta...about Rada. I don't know what the future holds for Blue, but your place is here now Pandra. And, so you know...I wouldn't have handed *her* in either. Blue...er...Ellie. She knew right from wrong.'

'I'm fine by myself,' snapped Morrigan. 'Don't need her.'

Haylee leant closer to her friend. 'Find Tik...and Evan. Pandra can help. Once they think I've gone, they will leave you alone. Work together and bring the others home.'

Swinging her head in Pandra's direction, Morrigan's nose crinkled. 'Fine. But I don't have to like it. When we have the others...we're finding a way to bring you back.'

Deliberately, Haylee chose not to respond. Marching forward, she entered the dark tunnel and circled for a farewell glimpse. In only minutes, Pandra found herself filled with an adoration for Haylee that she had never known possible. It looked like Haylee would do anything to protect her friends.

'Take this,' said Cedric, handing Haylee a stump of a candle. 'You must move quickly. Once your light has gone, you will have to feel the rest of your way. There is much distance to cover. Go now...'

When Cedric's hand met the wall again, Haylee bowed her head. 'Look after each other,' she said, in a way which felt more like an order. 'I'll see you soon.'

With that, Haylee disappeared, and the sheet of rock crunched into place. It had reformed the wall in an almost perfect way.

chapter twenty-six

Kayden's Plan

Tik withered. He had exhausted too much energy trying to escape. Cocooned in sheets, with his ankles and wrists bound, there was no way out. Waiting was his only option and he wondered what had happened to Toze when he had been taken. It was unlikely that the little balkutar could look after himself.

'Make sure you are prepared.' Kayden's creaky voice originated somewhere nearby.

They were in Eklips. It was obvious from the stench. Most people who lived there were slaves, and they lived in far from ideal conditions. Having competed in The Dispute there, Tik had seen some horrific sights. Now it was his turn. If Kayden got his way, he would likely spend the rest of his life as a slave. That was, if he ever managed to escape the fabric that encased him.

A man's voice spoke close to his head. 'Ready sir.'

Tugged in all directions, Tik felt nauseous when they began unwrapping him. He sealed his eyes to protect them. Daylight was crackling through the sheets as they were removed. Tik had spent hours without light. Once the final sheet was pulled away, he rolled into the mud. With care, he began opening his eyes; struggling to adjust at first.

He caught Kayden's hooting. The sound was unique to the rogue, and Tik had heard it many times. Shuffling, he tried to stand, but a nearby assault ranger had other ideas. With the blunt end of a mace rammed into Tik's chest, the ranger held him in place. There was no chance of Tik breaking free.

'I have to admit that I didn't expect such a prize today,' Kayden said. 'Ditto was who I expected to bring home. You're an incredible improvement.'

Grunting, Tik tried to shift from beneath the mace. 'You didn't find her,' he laughed. 'Knew she wouldn't get caught.'

'Far from it.' Kayden moved closer. He hovered over Tik like a fly, seeming self-assured.

Tik stared. 'Far from what?'

'Your friend has been extinguished,' Kayden said, smiling when he did. 'Killed her myself.'

In an effort to break loose, Tik fought the mace handle that held him. Each time he twisted, the ranger pressed harder. There was no relief.

'There's no way,' Tik moaned, continuing his tussle. 'You can't have.'

Kayden knelt. 'But I did,' he crowed. 'Today, Haylee lost two of her friends. I was the one to take them from her. Maybe now, she will learn not to cross me. Maybe you all will.'

With his arms hurting, Tik submitted. He glanced up. The ranger pinning him to the ground looked starved of emotion. Hair filled with grease dangled down around his grey tinted face. Tik considered the prospect of life in Eklips. Then, a hand fondled his face.

'Don't touch me!'

Resolved, Kayden continued with purpose. 'Wouldn't you like to know how I killed your friend.'

'Do us all a favour ol' man. Set me free. You'll regret this.'

'Far from it. You are going to be of much use to me.'

When the ranger's weapon began tearing his tunic, Tik clenched. 'How do you work that out?'

'Haylee will come for you…probably with her friends. I have plans for them.'

'You want to murder them too?' Tik growled, flexing to break away from his bonds. 'If you did kill Ditto…which I still don't believe.'

Kayden snickered. 'Not at all. Give it time, things are about to change. Trust me…you will like what I have in mind.'

'Doubt that,' Tik said from beneath the mace.

'From what I heard, you and your friends have been busy,' Kayden retorted, taking to his feet. 'Defying the will of Rada. Guilty of dissent. Stealing from The Union.' He wafted his hand at the ranger. 'Stand!'

Coated in sludge, Tik welcomed the ranger removing the mace. As the man bent to cut the rope on his ankles, he watched for any chance of freedom. The restraint severed, and Tik complied. Straining at first, he managed to manoeuvre upright.

'Good,' said Kayden. 'Think we will get along just fine.'

Tik glanced about. They weren't far from Kayden's palace, standing between some of the bordering slave dwellings. The timber on every structure looked like it had seen better days, and the ground was pure slime. It was clear that Kayden didn't give any consideration to the conditions in which people lived. Yet his palace somehow gleamed near the coastline. Behind it, the arena where The Dispute was held, was hidden from view. Tik had been there many times.

Leaving one of the buildings closest to the palace, and heading toward them, were two more assault rangers. Between them, they held a woman whose legs dragged on the floor. Tik wasn't sure if she was wearing the remnants of a warden's uniform. That was certainly what it looked like. Either way, her head sagged as she was carried.

'What next?' Tik asked, glancing back at Kayden.

Shoving his hand inside his hefty black cloak, Kayden smiled. 'That depends. On whether you're planning on being a good boy.'

'That depends on whether you are.' Tik fixed his eyes on the small glass capsule that Kayden pulled from his cloak.

With a large stride, Kayden budged closer to his prisoner. 'Stay still.'

'What in Eklips is that?' Tik yelled. When Kayden placed the object against Tik's chest he grimaced. Something bit into him.

Wild with anger, Tik barged forward, knocking Kayden to the floor. 'What was that?'

Without hesitation, the ranger swung with his weapon. The spikes slashed Tik's back and threw him forward. Losing his footing, Tik span to confront the assailant who was moving toward him. When the second swipe came, he narrowly managed to dodge it.

'Enough!' yelped Kayden, standing between Tik and the ranger. 'I want him in one piece.'

At that point, Tik stooped, dropping to the ground. 'What…'

'Nin venom!' Kayden said, by way of an explanation. 'It will keep you in line.'

Focused on the item still clutched in Kayden's hand, Tik felt dizzy. Inside the small container, he could see the tiny bug that had nipped him. His heart was racing, and there seemed no way to control it. He had underestimated Kayden. With his arms still secured behind him, he had no choice. There was no way to fight. For now, at least, he had to accept that he was beaten.

'Oh look,' Kayden shrilled. 'The formidable commander of the wardens has come to join us.'

Tik's eyes were stinging, but he watched as the other two rangers gathered next to Kayden. As they released the woman they carried, she sank into the muck at their feet. Her lengthy dark hair fell all around her face. Unable to see much of her, Tik wasn't sure if he knew who she was. Either way, the uniform she wore had been that of a warden. Kayden's people must have removed her boots and torn away the sleeves. Wrapped around her middle, there was also a chain, that didn't seem too sturdy. Regardless, it resembled a restraint and extended to both her wrists.

'I wasn't quite sure whether to believe it,' said Kayden, sounding even more upbeat. 'The mighty Nolan...in my custody. How easily you all fall!'

The prisoner — Nolan he called her — groaned, face down in the mud. She was in bad shape. Kayden meanwhile was enjoying his victory; whatever it was. Tik hadn't even heard of this Nolan, but Kayden had referred to her as the warden commander. *Surely not* Tik thought, watching Kayden bend down and place his hand into his victim's hair.

'I have to say,' Kayden said, lifting Nolan's head. 'You're not looking yourself, dear. Still, we are all going to get along fine...once you know what I have in mind.'

Nolan's eyes gazed at her new owner. Although she was conscious, she made no attempt to resist. The bare skin on her legs was blackened with grimy slush. Her limbs didn't give the impression that they'd support her either. The urge to defend Kayden's prize rushed through Tik, and he budged forward. As he stumbled in Nolan's direction, all the assault rangers began to cackle.

'Leave her alone,' Tik mumbled, realising he wasn't moving as he'd expected. He was barely moving at all. Disorientated, Tik was suffering the nin venom's influence.

Kayden released Nolan's head, joining in with the guffaw. 'Try if you like...but you won't be saving anyone today!' He approached Tik without concern.

'Let her go!' Tik said. Struggling to catch his breath, his words were limited. He floundered, with his legs twinging and a head that felt like it may roll off his neck at any second. In an attempt to lift an arm, he grunted. There was no doubt why the bullies were in hysterics; Tik knew he must look absurd.

Two of the rangers approached. 'This is for the last time we met,' one of them barked.

Glancing up, Tik recognised him as the ranger who cheated to beat Ditto. In the last Dispute he attended, Tik had to intervene to help her make a speedy exit. For a while after, his knuckles had been sore. The punch he had landed on the ranger was the only way he could get Ditto away. However, that man that he hit, now knelt beside him with an awkward expression.

'You never...did...like...a fair fight,' Tik gasped.

When the ranger dropped his mace, he smiled. There was a hint of scorn in his look. Without warning, his fist crunched into Tik's cheek. The ranger paused for a second to admire his handiwork, then clouted Tik again; this time in the centre of his belly.

Tik had no idea if the blows even hurt. His body tingled from the poison running through it, yet he knew the pain would present itself later. As a thump hit his cheek for the second time, Tik grunted. There was nothing he could do to stop the savage.

'This...how...it...works...now?' asked Tik. The fight for breath was getting ever harder.

Kayden moved in. 'He's been waiting for payback. It's only fair to let him have some fun.'

'You need...to let me...go.' Tik realised how cold he felt. Usually, the temperature didn't bother him. Yet with his tunic in tatters, and subdued by the nin venom, it was as though his insides had turned to ice.

'But we're only just getting to know each other,' Kayden said. 'Neither of you are going anywhere. You specifically Tik. I wanted you here. With the warden commander though, it seems I got lucky. But you will both be very useful to me. In time, you will understand. For now, have it your way. Rangers...stand down. We need him in decent shape after all. Leave him be and take them both away!'

Tik looked toward Nolan before receiving a blow from the handle of a mace. With that, he lost consciousness.

chapter twenty-seven

Downfall

Evading the blastguards had lengthened Haylee's journey. Drained, she continued up the hillside, her mind fixed on her destination. Snow on the ground had turned to ice, and the conditions were difficult. Around her, everything was coated white, from the ground up to occasional treetops. Yet Haylee had no choice; she had to keep moving.

Glancing back, the lumpy structure of Port Harmony appeared decimated. Many of the buildings were now in ruins. On closer inspection, she could make out a colossal machine. Clad in chunks of granite, the same as the blastguards, it was like a moving crag flattening anything in its path. The vehicle was almost twice the size of any of the surrounding dwellings, and much bigger than the wardens' Land Transports. Carved clearly into its topmost stony shell was the Scorr Tanta insignia.

Around it, individual members of Rada's army were beginning to board their mobile fortress.

Haylee paused, hopeful that the troops may leave. Her tummy growled, probably because it had been a while since she had eaten. In the distance, she could see another of the transports; then another travelling toward the wharf. Smoke enveloped much of the wreckage. Haylee wondered how many they had killed in their pursuit for her. Either way, the blastguards didn't seem to be planning an exit.

'My fault,' Haylee said, her voice hushed by exhaustion. Beyond what was left of her home, she could see icebergs bobbing in the ocean. They glistened under the sun; somehow peaceful in contrast to the barrage of destruction.

It was time to move on. With a moan, Haylee restarted her trek, lumbering along the jagged hill path. Away from the town, it wouldn't take long to reach her sanctuary. Although, the prospect of how long she would need to stay there wasn't easy to consider. Rada's forces could remain in Port Harmony for as long as their leader determined. Hiding away was Haylee's only hope for survival. Not to mention, that it was the only way she could guarantee the safety of those close to her.

The thought of revenge haunted Haylee. Kayden had murdered Ditto and taken Tik. For that, she wanted him to pay. Where Rada was concerned, the destruction of Port Harmony and the persecution of the elrupe was unforgivable. Even so, where either of her adversaries was concerned, Haylee had no clue how to settle the score.

Clumps of ice tumbled from the branches of a single pine tree as she passed. This tree was etched with designs that offered a short gush of hope. They reminded Haylee of her own strength. She grinned and leaned toward the tree's trunk. Refusing to allow tears, she caressed the knot-shaped impression. After a moment's reflection, Haylee bent down and lifted one of the pinecones that the tree had discarded. With care, she placed it in the small pocket of her tunic and stepped forward. Her determination was building.

Ahead, overgrown orchids concealed the entrance to the cave. They offered a splattering of jade amongst the crisp frost. Sliding on sheets of ice, Haylee pressed on until she was inside. The caves were gloomy, but in front, she saw the hazy lamps that lit the deeper chambers. Beside her, Haylee heard a clunking sound.

'Hey, little man. What you doin' here?'

Harrup stepped further into view. His face was mostly expressionless at first, but Haylee always found his red clumps of hair endearing. Placing his stony rods down beside him, Harrup grasped a vial of water from his body suit. There was a subtle smile on his face when he unscrewed the lid of the capsule.

'Looks like I'm one of you now,' Haylee sighed. 'Might be staying in this place for a while. Anyway, why are you here? You didn't tell me. You should be with the others.'

The elrupe boy didn't speak, and Haylee knew that he wouldn't. But something about him suggested that he was expecting her. It was like he knew that Haylee was approaching. Harrup certainly didn't seem surprised to see her. Instead, his free hand wafted above the vial that he held. Inside, the water bubbled. For a few seconds, Haylee watched in awe, as something formed in Harrup's empty palm.

Treading forward, Haylee scrutinised Harrup's hand, paying close attention to his fingers. 'You've got good at that.'

A grunt was all Harrup offered in response, and he formed a fist. The water in the vial settled and the bubbles dissipated. He then returned it to his suit.

'What is it?' Haylee asked, still glaring toward the young boy's hand.

Harrup reached forward, spreading his fingers. Within them, lay a small figurine in the shape of an orgo. His arm twitched; he wanted Haylee to take his gift.

'Wow! You really have got good at that,' Haylee remarked. 'Is it for me?' She took the offering and studied it, astonished at the detail. The elrupe's ability to manipulate water had always amazed her.

Harrup gazed at Haylee with an apparent empathy. 'A reminder,' he said. 'Of home.'

author acknowledgements

This book could never have been written without my most wonderful supporters. My deepest love and heartfelt gratitude go out to them…

To begin with, my gorgeous wife Emma. If it wasn't for your encouragement, patience and overwhelming love, I simply couldn't have done this. You are the most awesome person that I know. My heart belongs to you…forever.

Our stunning children, Lauren, Jordan, Olivia, Ian, and Lewis; live your dreams and blow people's minds. You are all so amazing! Greatness lies within each and every one of you.

Then, there is Dawn Beever; my remarkable sister in law. You brought life to the orgo. Not to mention the map, without which, people would find it much harder to navigate the world I created. What a true talent you are.

Amy Leslie. There are no limits to your imagination and flair, and your skill is astonishing. Your unrelenting friendship, devotion, and passion for these books blows my mind every day. I will never stop telling you how grateful I am to work alongside you.

Tegan Hufton, who is recording the 'dissent: RENEGADES' audiobook, as I write this. You are the perfect narrator for these books, a great friend, and so much more now. I can't thank you enough for your trust and faith in my stories.

Huge thanks also go to Natalie Hamer and Julie Leddy. The ideas and input that flowed from both of you, was invaluable. Despite your own schedules, you worked tirelessly to keep my chin propped up.

Everyone who has taken the time to read and review this book over the last few months. Your support has been incredible. Shannon A. Hiner, Meggan (Between The Pages), Heidi (The Meddlesome Scholar), Danielle (The Introverted Book Nerd), April (The Vagaries Of Us), Rachel's Rambling Reviews, Charlotte Burns (Charlotte, Somewhere), Sarah Campbell (Book Hooked Nook), Zoe Collins (No Safer Place) and Jenny (Turn Another Page). Phew! I hope I haven't missed anyone. You are all so awesome.

My new 'Twitter' and 'Facebook' friends. I cannot express how much your individual and collective reinforcement has kept me going.

Finally, I want to thank YOU, the person reading this book. If not for you, the world of Dissent could not come to life. You are all fully fledged 'Dissentians' now!

Much love — Eyes on me!

This is only the beginning…

R.J.

about the author

R. J. Furness has been passionate about great stories since he was able to read. At an early age, he would frequently create new characters, worlds, and creatures, then write crazy tales all about them. However, until now, he has always kept those ideas completely secret. As well as his love for reading (and writing), R.J. also developed a huge passion for things like Star Wars, Transformers, and as a teenager, Jurassic Park. After having a lifelong interest in animals, music, and anything spawned from pure imagination, R.J.'s first love is now his wife and children. Over time, he has also developed an overwhelming desire for mugs of tea, and good biscuits to dunk. He lives in Southport, England, with his family, a dog and lots of fish, chickens, and quails.

You can find out more about R.J. Furness, and the world of dissent, here…

www.rjfurness.com

or please come and say hello on social media…

Twitter: @rjfurness
Facebook: furnesswrites

watch out for

dissent
VENGEANCE

R.J. Furness

-2-

also available

Morrigan
a 'dissent' story

R.J. Furness

Printed in Poland
by Amazon Fulfillment
Poland Sp. z o.o., Wrocław